# THE CONSEQUENCE
# OF LOVING COLTON

ALSO BY RACHEL VAN DYKEN

### The Bet Series

*The Bet*
*The Wager*
*The Dare*

### The Ruin Series

*Ruin*
*Toxic*
*Fearless*
*Shame*

### The Elite Series

*Elite*
*Elect*
*Entice*
*Elicit*
*Bang Bang*
*Enforce*
*Ember*

### The Seaside Series

*Tear*
*Pull*
*Shatter*
*Forever*
*Fall*
*Eternal*

## Renwick House

*The Ugly Duckling Debutante*
*The Seduction of Sebastian St. James*
*The Redemption of Lord Rawlings*
*An Unlikely Alliance*
*The Devil Duke Takes a Bride*

## London Fairy Tales

*Upon A Midnight Dream*
*Whispered Music*
*The Wolf's Pursuit*
*When Ash Falls*

## Seasons of Paleo

*Savage Winter*

## Wallflower Series

*Waltzing with the Wallflower*
*Beguiling Bridget*
*Taming Wilde*

## Stand Alones:

*Every Girl Does It*
*The Parting Gift*
*Compromising Kessen*
*Divine Uprising*

# THE CONSEQUENCE OF LOVING COLTON

*RACHEL VAN DYKEN*

**SKYSCAPE**

**SKYSCAPE**

Text copyright © 2015 Rachel Van Dyken

Published by Skyscape, New York

www.apub.com

Amazon, the Amazon logo, and Skyscape are trademarks of Amazon.com, Inc., or its affiliates.

ISBN-13: 9781477829110

ISBN-10: 1477829113

Cover design by Kerrie Robertson

Library of Congress Control Number: 2014956180

Printed in the United States of America

*To the Rachel's Rockin Readers group on Facebook: This book would not be possible without you guys! I appreciate your encouragement and hilarious input. Who knew that with a little help from my friends (aka readers) we'd knock out what should have been a year-long process in a month :) Love you guys HARD!*

# PROLOGUE

*Summer 2009*

"I can't believe you're really going to college, Milo." Colton's teasing smile flashed right in front of me, rendering me temporarily blind. Man, he was beautiful. His normally dark-brown hair had shots of gold from the summer sun. Dimples peeked out from his mega-white smile and I was pretty confident that I saw a twinkle in his green eyes meant just for me. He'd been home for two months since graduation and was already off saving the world one fire at a time. I watched his full lips curve around the mouth of his Corona. He and my brother Jason had organized a going-away party for me. Apparently me getting accepted into NYU was a big deal: they'd even gone so far as to get a *Star Wars*–themed cake from Dairy Queen and a princess tiara that said "Pretty" across it. It was always their joke with me. I was a complete and total tomboy—I loved picking fights and getting muddy—yet still demanded they treat me like a princess.

With a sigh I leaned back on the picnic blanket and looked up at the stars. My crown fell to the side of my head, causing my hair to fall all over my face. The party had been over for a few hours, leaving me, Colt, and Jason. I should have been happy: after all, who does that for his little sister? What brother would even care? Furthermore, the fact that it had all been Colt's idea, someone who wasn't even family, was huge. But . . . maybe that's the part that left me feeling empty. I might as well be family to Colton. I was the little sister he'd never had—and secretly, I'd always wanted to be so much more.

"Aw, you messed up your hair," Colton teased, lifting the crown with the tip of his finger and giving me a sexy wink.

"Whatever shall I do?" I huffed.

"I'll save you." His voice was just above a whisper. "I've always wanted to save a princess."

"You did." My grin was huge. "You saved me a least a hundred times when we were little—slew the dragon at the top of the stairs and did it all without getting a scratch."

"Messy job." He let out a long, exaggerated sigh. "I don't know how I made it to my nineteenth birthday without getting singed."

"Donald didn't breathe fire. He was a fire*less* dragon, remember?"

"Oh, right." His eyes twinkled. "How is the old dragon anyway?"

I shrugged and chewed on my lower lip. "Haven't been in the attic since you guys left for school. I've been busy."

"Too busy to play?"

I rolled my eyes. "Too busy graduating to play, yeah."

"Where's the fun in that?"

"Fun." I snorted. "The last time I had fun was when we snuck into your parents' pool and—" I clamped my mouth shut before the words could tumble out on their own. *Crap. Crap. Crap.*

"Skinny-dipped." He finished my thought. "Yeah, that was a blast."

"Hey, guys!" Jason called as he ran out of the house. "Dad needs me to grab Mom from work so I'll be right back! Don't do anything fun without me! I mean it!"

The loud roar from his truck filled the night air for a brief second and then slowly dissipated as the vehicle barreled down the driveway.

"You thinking what I'm thinking?" Colton asked.

If his thoughts were along the line of finally getting him alone, away from my brother? "Absolutely." I grinned as he grabbed my hand and helped me off the blanket.

"Come on. Let's go have fun."

Curious, I followed Colt as we ran through a few backyards and finally ended up at his house.

"What are we doing?" I asked in a hushed voice.

"Having fun." I swear his grin made my heart almost stop. "Now strip, Milo, we don't have all night and Jason's going to be pissed he isn't with us."

Laughing, I took off my shirt and shorts—I'd spent years swimming with the guys in my sports bra and underwear, though as we got older it became weird, but only on my end. It felt strange to strip down to nothing, knowing that my feelings for Colton were very real whereas his were nonexistent. I mean, it was *Colton*. Sure, I had a crush on him, but he never, ever thought of me that way. Ever.

"Last one in's a rotten—"

I didn't hear him finish—but I did beat him into the water. His mom and stepdad's pool was always my favorite place to swim. It had a little waterfall in the deep end that you could swim under that always made me think of fairy tales and the movies. Then again, that could be because every time I broke through the water it was Colton's face I saw, and his smile that drew me. He was my own personal Prince Charming.

Laughing, Colton splashed around, then hauled himself out of the pool and did a cannonball right by my face. I was glad that it was dark—I must have been beet-red. Man, the guy was ripped.

"Wanna race?" he asked, out of breath.

"Wanna lose?" I countered.

"Never."

"Um, it's an everyday occurrence." I swam over to the edge. "Ready, set—"

"—go!" He ran instead of swam and then dove under water.

*Bastard!* Arms burning, I tried to make it to the other end of the pool. I usually didn't open my eyes under water, but this time I did to see where I was going.

His body was a blur in front of me. All I saw was hard-lined muscle.

I stopped right in front of him and jumped to the surface. "You cheated."

"I like to call it winning." He beamed triumphantly.

"Cheating." My teeth ground together as I pushed against his chest. Laughing, he fell backward, pulling me with him. Our bodies ground together, heat against heat, skin against skin.

And suddenly sneaking away from Jason wasn't funny anymore.

Neither of us was laughing.

His hands moved from my waist slowly up my body until they rested on my face. With a curse he pulled my head toward his. "We should . . ."

"Yeah," I whispered.

Neither of us pulled away.

His lips brushed mine, just enough to make me strain toward him—I needed him like I needed air.

"Kids!" His stepdad's voice rang through the night air. "You out here making noise?"

Colton pushed me away and I nearly hit my head on the water-fall rocks.

"Yeah, just . . . hanging out!" Colton called. "I'm with Jason's sister."

I froze. He'd never called me that before. He even said it in such a final way, as if that was all I would ever be. Period. My heart didn't just sink . . . it shuddered, then combusted, as all the hopes I'd harbored since I was thirteen came to a crushing world-altering halt. My suspicions were finally confirmed. Out loud. On the day the boy I liked had thought enough to throw me a party.

The line had been drawn. And I might as well be on the other side of the universe.

That was the day I lost Colton Mathews—forever.

# CHAPTER ONE
## MILO

*Four years later*

I gripped the steering wheel with both hands. Actually, I would have gripped it with my teeth, toes, and ankles had my brain actually fired fast enough to send the message: *Red alert! Red alert!*

Instead, mouth dry, I just sat there like an idiot.

I couldn't think of anything to say to make it better—anything. I couldn't even give the guy a smile, which really was a shame considering it was my best asset.

"Milo!" Colton tapped the door of my light-blue Mercedes. "You look good."

I blinked. Well, I thought I blinked, I wasn't really sure. The car was still running, you'd think I would at least have enough sense to take my foot off the pedal and put it into park, but all I could do was stare. Fantastic. Twenty-one years old and still dealing with sweaty palms because Colton Mathews had said my name.

One thing I was sure of—my mouth was still hanging slightly ajar. Drool would soon follow and then Colton would have just one more reason to make fun of me—Jason's little sister.

"You all right?" He leaned his muscled forearms against the open window and stuck his head in. Merciful God in heaven, he still smelled the same. His spicy cologne blending with his perfect tan skin would have made any girl pause, or swallow her tongue, or sweat; really, take your pick. "You do realize at some point you need to turn off the car and go inside the house, right, little girl?"

And there it was, I wasn't any girl. To Colt, I was Jason's little sister. Nothing more.

It didn't matter that my boobs cheerfully filled out a C cup or that I'd had my braces off for over seven years. I still wasn't a woman to him.

God must have taken pity on me, because for some reason, in that instant, when the smell of Acqua Di Gio floated into my car, I snapped out of my insane moment and smiled.

"Fine. Great. Awesome. Perfect. You?" *Too many answers, Milo. Too many answers.*

Colton chuckled. It was a deep chuckle. The type that makes girls sigh while simultaneously trying to figure out how to get out of their clothes and trap the man into marriage. Seriously. His smile was one that made girls *want* the condom to break.

Great, now I was thinking about condoms.

Condoms and Colton.

A barking dog interrupted my sexual daydreams. It was Max's ringtone. "Um, one second." I put up my finger and shooed Colton away from the window as I pressed "Answer" and let the window close. He smiled, seemingly amused, and leaned against the car.

"How goes the first day of childhood hell, my friend?"

"That depends," I whispered into the phone, not taking my eyes off Colton as he stood facing the window. He was tall enough that I was basically staring at his lower abs and lower . . . body. Heat flooded my face, informing me without a doubt that crimson decorated my cheeks.

"Why are we whispering?" asked Max, my best friend from college.

"Because we are in the car."

"*You* are in the car. I'm at Starbucks."

"Whatever," I conceded with a snort, waving my hand in the air flippantly. "And it's not going well. In fact, I'm pretty sure Colton thinks I have a learning disability."

"Why would he think that?"

I sighed into the phone and tried to concentrate on anything but the fact that Colton was standing a few inches away from me. So freaking close. "I kind of, sort of . . . blacked out when he was talking to me."

"So where are you now?"

"We've established this. I'm in the car."

Max sighed. "Then where's Colton?"

"Outside the car."

"I'm confused."

"I'm an idiot." I groaned and smacked my hand against my forehead. "When the phone rang I closed the window to answer it but now he's not moving."

"Well . . ." Max cleared his throat. "I guess there are worse things in life than a hot guy standing outside your window, right?"

"Right." My voice wavered. "But he's like facing the door. All of him."

"All of him?"

"His parts," I clarified. Swear I felt my entire body go up in flames. Great, so now I was going to hell for looking at his parts. His very nice parts. His yummy, tight, straining—I needed to stop before I gave myself a stroke. "He's facing the window and leaning against the car and I swear, Max, the whole front of his body is pressed up against . . . my car."

"Naked?"

"What?" I yelled.

"Well, you said his parts."

"Not his *parts*-parts," I clarified. Shoot me now. Could this conversation get any more awkward? "Never mind, I mean—oh, crap."

"What? What's happening?"

I could see Max now, coffee thrust in the air, pacing the Starbucks floor like a crazy person.

"He's stretching across the car and—" I stopped mid-sentence. "Shit, my brother's on the other side."

"Let me get this straight." Max chuckled. "You have your lifelong crush, who just so happens to be your brother's best friend, on one side, his parts pressed firmly against your hot little Mercedes, and your brother, who has no idea of this sad infatuation, on the other side, making it possible for you to ogle his best friend's goodies?"

"Yup." My breathing picked up as I heard Colton laugh and then his front pressed against my door. "Good Lord, I'm sweating. He's—"

"Please don't finish that sentence. It makes me want to puke, and as much as you make fun of me for not having a girlfriend, it's not because I prefer men, so please . . . spare me the details."

"Fine."

"Milo?"

"What?" My eyes were glued to Colton's hot body as his stomach stretched across an eight-pack straight off a glossy magazine cover.

"Seduce him."

"With what?" I whisper-yelled. "I have nothing to offer him!"

"It's not like I want you to plant a chocolate trail from the ground to your lips, Milo."

"I know that!" I snapped. "Besides, he's allergic to chocolate."

"Please tell me you don't have his medical history memorized."

"I don't," I lied, suddenly finding great interest in the black leather steering wheel while my shame increased. "Besides, it doesn't matter. His Facebook profile says he likes blondes. I have dark hair."

"I'm going to ignore the fact that you stalk him on Facebook and just help you fix the problem. So dye your hair."

"Yeah, let me just get the hair dye from the backseat, Max!"

"Sheesh, touchy. You, my friend, *need* to get laid."

"Tell me about it," I muttered. "I'm the one stuck in the damn car with nothing but my Kindle and a prayer to keep me occupied."

"Your life makes me sad."

"Shut up."

"Seduce him."

"Again, with what?"

"Your body."

"I have no body." I slumped against the seat in a pout. "Besides, I don't know the first thing about seduction. And he hates me."

"He doesn't hate you."

"I tried kissing him when I was sixteen and he laughed in my face."

"To be fair, your skirt was tucked into your underwear."

"Not the point!" I yelled for real this time. Why the heck had I drunk that entire bottle of wine and confessed all my embarrassing moments to Max? The terrible two outside my car began banging loudly on the windows. Great, I'd probably captured their attention when I raised my voice. And fantastic, the car began to move. I'd officially awakened the beasts.

"I'm in hell."

"Well . . ." Max laughed. "Don't let the flames give you a sunburn. I gotta run, just saw my Starbucks barista . . . I will get a date if it kills me! Oh, and good luck. You'll need it."

"Right." I clicked "End" and shut off the car.

Nothing was going as planned—that was for sure.

# CHAPTER TWO
## MILO

I opened the car door and faced the guys.

"Hey, Milo! You made it!" Jason, my older, sweeter brother joined Colton on the other side of the car and smacked him on the back. "You gonna stay in your car all night or come congratulate me?"

I shrugged and unbuckled my seat belt. "Sure, Jason, congrats. You grew a pair of balls and settled down. I'm so proud." I jumped into his arms for a hug before he could put me into a headlock.

"Very funny," he murmured against my hair. "By the way, Colt's date bailed on him so I kinda sacrificed you on the family favor altar. You guys are stuck with one another. That okay?"

*Is that okay?* I tried to keep my face from falling. How the heck was I supposed to get over my childhood crush if he was going to be around me every second of every day that weekend? Ever since Colton took my heart and drowned it in the bottom of his parents' pool, I'd been strategic about my visits home. It kinda pissed me off how easy it had been for us to grow apart. We went from spending every week together to barely seeing one another on Christmas. This last year he'd gone with his parents to Europe for Christmas so I was going on eighteen months of no Colton exposure . . . I imagined him kind of like the plague, only the good kind, the kind that I had to keep away from my girl parts at all costs. In theory I'd known he would be here for the wedding, I just hadn't realized I'd be forced into his presence or that just by smelling him I would be transported back to freshman year of high school when I used to trace his name with a glitter pen.

The point was, the eighteen months had been good. I'd done some casual dating and I'd stopped comparing every guy to him. Well, sort of. Okay, let's just say I was doing better, loads better. I was actually looking forward to the future, to graduation, to starting my life, and I couldn't do that if I was still stuck in the past. And Colton needed to stay in the past. I refused to keep hoping that he saw me as anything other than what I was . . . a friend.

"Sure," I heard myself croak. "No problem."

"I didn't think it would be." Jason gave me a lazy smile. "Besides, didn't you and that one guy break up like a few weeks ago?"

"Max?" I squeaked in full-on panic mode.

"Yeah."

"Who's Max?" asked Colton.

"Her boyfriend, they were pretty serious for a while." Jason elbowed me and waggled his eyebrows. "Right?"

"Uhh." Great. I was officially without words. Max was a friend—my best friend. He'd been a friend since my freshman year of college. He'd hit on me, my insecure self had thought he was gay, and, well, it was a match made in heaven. Max was gorgeous, and I was pretty sure the guy had a revolving door into his bedroom, not that I paid much attention. Guys like Max were never friends with girls—ever. But somehow it worked for us even though people always assumed there was more going on.

Until now.

"Why haven't I heard of Max?" Colton's gaze narrowed. "Is he a good guy? Does he still call you? Say the word and I'll kill him if he touches you, Milo."

"Whoa, dude." Jason put his hands on Colton's shoulders and massaged. "Back off, she has a brother."

"Yeah," I repeated. "I have a brother. Last time I checked you weren't family." I hadn't meant for it to sound like a barb, but it was still hard not to feel upset over his rejection from four years ago. Even now I still felt rejected, and he hadn't even done anything except remind me that I was the little sister. It was like a bad movie on replay.

"Believe me . . ." Colton's green eyes held mine. "I know."

"You're here!" my mom shouted from the door, waving the spatula in her hand. Her black hair was piled high on her head in a bun. Pearls adorned her ears and she wore a trendy apron that had a picture of a red stiletto heel.

"That I am." I smiled and walked into her embrace. She smelled of Oscar de La Renta perfume, my favorite scent next to Colton's. Which was just sad when I thought about it.

"How was the drive?" She draped her arm around my shoulder. "Boys, get Milo's stuff, will ya?"

"Sure, Mom!" Jason and Colton disappeared as Mom led me into the house.

"The drive was good." The smell of turkey dinner filled the room, and my stomach growled in anticipation. "I made it in record time."

Mom released me and walked over to the stove. "I still don't know why you don't just take the train, it's so much easier."

Shrugging, I answered, "I like to drive." And I did, but I also liked to have my own car and freedom whenever I came back to New Haven. Especially this time. Being stuck with Colton all weekend was sure to make me crazy. I couldn't even speak complete sentences around the guy, let alone be his date for the weekend wedding.

"Everything ready?" Dad bounded into the room and kissed my mom on the cheek before smacking her butt. "Oh, Milo, didn't see ya." He winked.

"Rogue, yes you did." I jumped into his arms and kissed his cheek. "I missed you."

"Missed you too, squirt."

My eyes narrowed into slits.

"Oh, come on," Jason said from the door. "You still think if you eat enough spinach you'll gain another few inches."

I ignored him and grabbed a stick of celery. "Couldn't hurt."

"You're not short." Colton snagged the celery out of my hand and stuck it between his teeth and wiggled it up and down like a fat green stick.

I reached across and snatched it back, taking a huge bite. So attractive, I know.

"You're just . . ." He tilted his head and eyed me up and down. The celery went dry in my mouth. "Perfect."

"Suck-up," Jason cough-spoke. "You're just saying that because you don't want her to stab you in your sleep this weekend."

Colton chuckled. "Got me there. No way am I going to escape this wedding unscathed, not with that one on the loose." He pointed at me, and my stomach sank.

I liked being one of them. Loved being included, which I always was. But I was grown. I was finally twenty-one and graduating college. I didn't want to be the kid sister who played basketball with the boys and refused to wear dresses.

I wanted to be a girl, and Colton had never seen me that way.

I swear he cried the day I hit puberty.

It was like he was more affected than I was that I was turning into a girl instead of a boy.

So started the first day of the rest of my life. Colton and Jason were two years older than me. In high school the girls wanted to date either Jason or Colton, which meant everyone wanted to be my friend.

My locker had more love notes in it than homework and books. I was always a good sport, passing on the notes and laughing when the guys read them.

I would have never lived it down had they known that every night in my diary I wrote my own love note to Colton. Though mine didn't suck; mine were awesome. Not that he would ever see them. Ever. *Crap. I need to go burn that book.* In the unlikely case that I died this weekend, the last thing I wanted was for them to read it at my funeral.

"Be right back." I ran up the stairs and opened the door to my childhood bedroom. Pictures of Justin Timberlake and Harry Potter littered my wall. Ah, memories.

I rummaged through my drawers and located the diary, stuffing it as far underneath my mattress as I could. Tomorrow I would burn it. Tonight I would read it, and then I would forget Colton for good. But before all that . . . before I gave up . . .

I was going to wear a dress.

And he was going to kiss me, damn it! I'd done nothing but try to forget him for the past four years and all it took was ten minutes in his presence and I was ready to jump back on the Colton bandwagon. Suddenly this weekend was about more than my brother getting married, it was also about me finally getting the thing I'd wanted since I knew I liked boys. One kiss and I'd be able to bury my diary along with the rest of my desires for Colton. I just wanted one instance where he saw me as something other than his little sister. I deserved it and I was going to take it.

# CHAPTER THREE
## MILO

"Milo! Dinner!" Mom called from downstairs. I quickly brushed out my hair and put on some clear lip gloss. I checked myself in the mirror. My long, golden-brown hair hung past my shoulders in loose waves. I had on a pair of ripped jeans topped by a white t-shirt that fell off my shoulder, revealing the tan I'd been trying to perfect for the past month in hopes of looking hot for my brother's wedding. My brown, almond-shaped eyes stared back at me with too much hope in them. Yes, I wanted to say aloud, we're doing this. Operation Get Kissed is officially a go. I ran my hands down my torso and took two soothing breaths. The outfit looked good, it showed off my athletic build. Plus I was showing skin, not a lot, but enough to make him wonder . . . at least I hoped.

"Coming." With one final glance in the mirror, I ran down the stairs and collided directly with a firm chest.

"Hungry?" Colton looked down at me; his hands moved to my shoulders to steady me. Instinctively, I looked at his lips and licked my own.

He pulled away and laughed. "Watch where you're going, squirt."

I stuck out my tongue and went to my usual chair at the table.

"So, Milo." Dad folded his hands behind his head and leaned back in his chair. "How's your senior year?"

"Yeah . . ." Colton smirked in my direction. "You still majoring in . . . what was that again? Cartoons?"

I rolled my eyes. "Art, with a minor in graphic design." I had to force myself to keep from sticking out my tongue again in self-defense. After all, he knew exactly what I did.

When he'd asked me to do a tattoo in honor of his father—I'd cried. I was so embarrassed. I mean, his dad had died saving people's lives on 9/11, and instead of crying, he was comforting me.

*"What do you want?" I whispered through my tears.*

*"Something that represents strength, honor, love . . ." His voice trailed off as he reached up and wiped the stray tears from my cheeks. "I trust you, Milo. I'll love whatever you come up with."*

*My breath caught in my throat. We were so close, I wanted to lean in; I wanted to feel his lips—just once—against mine.*

*"Anyway." He chuckled and looked away from me. "I'll pay you or whatever."*

*"No." I shook my head. "You won't pay me. I'm your friend." Crap, that word felt bitter. "It's what friends do."*

*"Right." He sighed, and repeated, "Friends."*

*"A favor from a friend," I said, trying to make it sound better.*

*"Thanks, Milo." He let out a sigh. "Thanks a lot."*

He had left. And that day I'd cried some more, not because of the refreshed grief but because I felt like I was constantly in limbo with him, so close but so far away, and I hated that it always seemed like if anything was going to happen, I would have to be the one to take the first step.

"Milo? You hear anything I just said?" Jason threw a dinner roll at my face.

I felt my cheeks heat. "Uh, sorry, just tired from the drive."

"It's an hour and a half," Colton teased. "Then again, you drive slower than my grandma, so—"

I aimed the roll at his wide grin and launched. *Take that!* The golden bun arched through the air on the perfect track to annihilation, but instead of its impacting my target, Colt intervened, snatching it out of the air and taking a huge bite, his perfect mouth taunting me with each chew. Yeah, good luck getting that particular image out of my mind for the next ten years. Perfect teeth, biting into a soft roll. I shivered and looked away. Great, so rolls did it for me now. Nice.

"Colton," Mom scolded. "Be nice, she just got done with finals. Besides, you said you slept in until noon today—at least she isn't lazy."

"He slept in till noon because he was on call all night," Jason defended his friend, and then held up his hand. "Roll me."

Colton tossed the roll.

And so went our normal-ish family dinner. It saddens me to report that I ate at least three helpings of mashed potatoes—all because they were right in front of Colton and every damn time he passed them our fingers brushed.

Maybe Max was right. I needed to either seduce him or abandon the whole idea that he could see me as a potential girlfriend.

I groaned.

Out loud.

"Too many potatoes?" Colton winked from across the table.

"Starving college student." I patted my stomach. Yes, patted it like a frat boy after too many beers. "You understand."

"Aw, they don't feed you down at NYU?"

"I'm an artist." I folded my arms. "It's basically in the curriculum, if you aren't starving, you aren't talented."

"Oh, baby," Mom interrupted. "Of course you're talented. And if you're hungry just tell me and I'll send Colton or Jason down there with some cookies."

Colton at my door? With cookies? Naked? Yes, please.

"Hate to interrupt all this fun talk about starving, but . . ." Jason clapped his hands and leaned forward on the table. "Wedding weekend."

Mom held up her finger and reached under the table, pulling out the biggest notebook I'd ever seen in my entire life and then slamming it down onto the wooden surface in front of her.

Two words: destination wedding. No way was I going to allow my mom to do to me what she was doing to Jason and Jayne. I was going to fly to Mexico, get married, then sip margaritas all week long. No wedding book. Ever.

"So." Mom jerked the book open, using both hands, which was probably necessary, all things considered. A few papers floated to the floor. Sighing, she scanned the page. "The event company gets here at six a.m., so you'll need to be up at five if you want breakfast in time."

"And when you say *you*"—I played with my napkin—"you mean . . . ?"

"You," everyone said in unison.

"Me?"

"All of us." Mom smiled triumphantly. "As a family."

"Yeah, I'd been kind of worried about that."

I wasn't a morning person. How was I supposed to look my best when my eyes were swollen shut?

My mom started firing off instructions, and with each new task my eyes threatened to close out of sheer boredom.

*Peonies?*

*Wedding tent?*

*Cupcakes that needed frosting?*

*Chairs?*

*Centerpieces?*

Well, my mom was a woman possessed. It was the only explanation.

"That's it." She sighed happily. "Now on to Saturday."

"That was one day?" I shouted.

Everyone's head snapped in my direction.

"I mean . . ." I coughed. "Wow, that's all we have to do tomorrow?" I gave a solitary clap. "Yay."

"Very convincing," Colton mouthed.

I flipped him off.

Not a proud moment.

He gasped and pointed. "Your daughter just gave me the bird."

"He's a liar!" I argued. "Need I remind everyone of the pancake incident of ninety-seven?" During Thanksgiving Colton and I had gotten into mom's pancake mix. I'd told Colton that Mom said there was a prize at the bottom—but he had to eat all the mix in order to get it. He didn't believe me. So I got angry. And put the pancake mix down his pants. The funny part was, he was a scrawny kid so I was easily able to overtake him. Unfortunately I didn't know my own strength and gave him a black eye.

When my parents found out, Colton lied and said he gave himself the black eye. My parents told Colton's parents, it was a whole . . . thing. Needless to say everyone found out he was lying and that I was to blame. Our parents were convinced that we had been fighting, so they said we had to learn how to solve our differences through competition rather than beating on each other.

"That was one time!" Jason pushed his chair back as Dad maneuvered himself around an irate Colton.

Smirking, I rose from my chair. "I rest my case."

"There's only one way to settle this dispute." Colton's eyes darkened.

"Oh, hell," I muttered under my breath, my heart hammering against my chest as I recognized the look in his eyes.

• • •

"You ready, squirt?" Colton breathed down my neck. Not how I'd imagined us spending the rest of the evening. I'd had witty banter, romantic movies, and possible kissing on my mind, not . . . this.

"I'm always ready," I fired back. "I was ready last Christmas when you fell on your ass—"

"Mom! Milo said ass," Jason yelled up the stairs.

Ignoring him, I continued. "—and I was ready last summer when we ended the game at a tie because you were bleeding all over the table."

"I broke my finger." Colton threw his hands into the air. "And you laughed!"

"You broke it playing Ping-Pong!" I snapped. "What did you want me to do? Call 911?"

"Guys!" Jason held out his hands between us.

I gripped the paddle in my hand and took my stance.

"Let's have a fair game, all right?" Jason looked at me longer than necessary. Fine, I'd cheated once, but I was ten, give me a break.

"Fair game," I seethed.

"Fair game." Colton blew me a kiss.

"Terms?" Jason asked.

"I win," Colton said, his eyes narrowing, "she promises never to bring up the pancake incident again—or at least for a year, we all know it's hard for little squirt to keep her mouth shut."

I stuck out my tongue.

Colt's eyes heated for a brief moment before he swore and said, "Cute."

"And your terms?" Jason's eyes narrowed. "If you win?"

"I want . . ." I bit my lip. I wanted a kiss. I wanted time with Colton, I wanted . . . "Colton watches *Star Wars* with me."

Colton groaned. He was the only guy breathing who hated *Star Wars*. When he was little he'd had nightmares that Jabba the Hutt was in his closet.

"Four, five, and six," I added.

Jason whistled under his breath. "Tough terms. Tough terms."

"I accept." Colton shrugged as if he didn't have a care in the world. Bastard. "I'm not worried, been training, lifting weights . . ."

Yeah, I'd noticed. Not that he'd needed to before, but damn, now the man was cut.

"Milo?" Jason asked. "You accept Colton's terms?"

"Absolutely." I smiled sweetly. "I always accept his terms—probably because I've never had to worry about following through on them. Once a loser"—I pulled the Ping-Pong ball from the basket—"always a loser."

# CHAPTER FOUR

## MILO

In my mind the Ping-Pong game looked a heck of a lot like the movie *300*, you know, without the swords, blood, and capes.

Grunts and curses cut through the tense air like fireworks. I'd serve, Colton would return, and so the game went, back and forth, back and forth.

A few times I sacrificed my body to gain a point. But my small scratches were nothing next to his war wounds.

Colton struck his head against the table trying to perform a low hit, and I'm pretty sure Jason was going to have a black eye after I accidently slammed the ball in the wrong direction.

"Foul!" Colton shouted.

"No fouls in Ping-Pong, bitch," I yelled.

"Whoa!" Colton held up his hands. "Got a fire under your ass there, squirt? Pulling out the big-girl words?"

"I know big-girl words and I can do big-girl things." I inwardly cringed. Yeah, I should have left that second part out.

He smirked and leaned forward so his hands were pressed against the table as sweat poured from his face. We'd been at it for at least three hours.

Each game had ended in a tie.

"What kind of big-girl things?" He licked his lips.

"Just . . ." My throat went completely dry. "Things."

"Tiebreaker!" Jason removed the ice pack from his eye and set it on the desk behind him.

"Next point wins?" I offered.

"I have a better idea." Colton set his paddle on the table and walked around until he was on my side. "Slap game."

"Are you ten?" I narrowed my eyes, not trusting him for a second.

Colton looked himself up and down and then shrugged. "Do I *look* ten?"

No. Hell, no. He looked . . . well, I wasn't sure, but I needed to snap my mouth shut before I started panting. Sweat soaked through his shirt, and his shirt clung to his abs, which in turn made me want to both cry and thank God that his shirt was tight.

"Slap game." Jason laughed, jolting me out of my stare-down with Colt's abs. "Classic."

Colton held out his hands, pressing them together in front of his body. "Ladies first."

"What a gentleman," I mumbled, holding my hands on either side of his in the air.

"I'm ready when you are," he whispered.

I stole a look at his face; his eyes drank me in.

*Crap.*

He was messing with me.

"Stop it." My jaw clenched.

"What?" He licked his lips again, this time taking extra care to bite down on his bottom lip in such a way that it was impossible not to imagine what it would feel like to have his teeth on my body.

"That." I looked away. "And I'm ready."

"Ladies, we gonna play or we gonna talk?" Jason stepped up beside us and grinned.

"Play," we said in unison.

I flinched. Colton moved his hands, I flinched again and slapped with my right, then my left, but missed on the third time around.

"My turn."

Colton got me once. Twice . . . three times. We usually went three rounds, and Jason decided who won based on how many slaps we got in within the first ten seconds.

"Missed," I taunted, jumping up and down.

A few minutes later, Jason sighed. "Sorry, bro, she's got six slaps to your four, one more round and I'll declare the winner."

With a triumphant grin, I began again. I should have realized my lucky streak wouldn't continue.

I went for his hands and made the mistake of looking at his face, just as his lips formed a mocking air kiss.

I missed.

"WHOA!" Jason shouted. "Missed on the first round, sorry, little sis, but you lost."

"He cheated!" I wailed.

"Don't be a sore loser," Colton scolded, putting his hands down. I didn't even realize I had that much pent-up anger until my hand went flying across his cheek.

"Damn it!" He stumbled to the side.

Jason's mouth dropped open. I covered mine with my hands.

"What the hell, Milo!" Colton kept swearing.

"I, uh . . ."

Jason covered his face with his hands as if I were a supreme embarrassment to the family name and chuckled. "I'll go get you some ice, bro."

"Thanks," he snapped, then looked at me. "Well? Care explaining, Rocky?"

"You made me mad?" I scrunched up my nose and then burst out laughing. "I'm sorry! I shouldn't laugh. It's just, you have a me-size handprint right here." I reached out and touched his cheek. He placed his hand over mine, sealing it against his skin.

"You branded me," he joked, his voice hoarse.

"Yeah, well, now there's no escaping me." I tried to keep my voice light—tried and failed. I really needed to stop staring at his lips. Bad things were going to happen. A girl could only last so long without the opposite sex before she just jumped whoever was in front of her.

"Who says I want to?"

"Want to?" I shook my head in confusion.

"Escape." His eyes went completely black as he took a step toward me, making any space between us nonexistent.

Something shifted in the air. My hand was blazing underneath his. With a curse he grabbed the back of my head, and our mouths met in a violent kiss, one that I knew I'd never forget.

His mouth plundered mine. I arched under his touch and then crumbled under the sensation of the feelings he was creating in me.

"Here's your ice!" Jason called at the top of the stairs.

Colton released me as abruptly as he'd grabbed me. Adrenaline surged through my body, making it impossible to act normal. Breathing was nearly impossible because I was afraid if I inhaled I'd make too much noise and if I exhaled he'd know that what he'd just done to me had physically altered every single cell in my body and left me defenseless and wanting. I stared at him, waiting for him to say the words I'd longed to hear my whole life.

I mean, I didn't expect him to propose or say that he was in love with me. Just admitting a mutual attraction would have been nice.

But he didn't say anything. Instead he looked down at the floor. His face was a mask of indifference, his eyes, once piercing, weren't even looking at me, his mouth was set in a grim line as if he was disappointed.

"Yo!" Jason made it to the bottom of the stairs and set the ice and towel on the table. "Dad needs help with the TV again. I'll be right back—don't kill each other in my absence."

I laughed weakly and waved him off.

Colton still said nothing.

With a huff I walked over to the table, grabbed the ice and slammed it against his face.

"Shit, Milo. Could you be less violent? Please?"

"Sorry." My voice was small. I felt small. There was a damn elephant in the room!

"So." Colton took a step away from me. "I, uh, I'm sorry. I don't know what came over me."

"Sorry," I repeated, my heart dropping all the way to my stomach. "For?"

"Look . . ." Colton swore and rubbed his eyes. "I shouldn't have done that. You're my best friend's little sister—shit, you're like *my* sister, you know?"

My mouth dropped open. No. Freaking. Way. No way was he pulling the sister card again! One day I was going to find that card, rip it to shreds, put a hex on it, and bury it next to his body. Okay, a little harsh, but I hated that card. Hated it more than peas and that's saying a lot. Peas shouldn't exist. Period.

"No, no." He shook his head. "Not like that. I'm just saying, I've known you forever and I'm sorry. I just . . . I overstepped my boundaries. That should never have happened." He cursed again. "If I could take it back, I would."

*If he could take it back he would?* That was worse than saying sorry! I would have preferred getting run over by my own car—or dying in a bull stampede.

My throat felt thick.

I tried to keep the tears in, I really did. Instead they streamed down my cheeks so fast I didn't even have time to wipe them away before Colton saw.

"Milo, shit." He pulled me into his arms. "Don't cry."

I tried to pull away, but he kept me firmly pressed against his chest.

"No, it's not you." I was finally able to wrangle myself free. "It's, uh . . ." *Think, Milo, think.* "It's just that I've never cheated on anyone before, and I feel bad."

*Gold star for Milo.*

"Cheated?" Colton's eyes pinched together in confusion. "What do you mean cheated?"

"Max." Yeah, he was going to murder me. "We've been dating on and off for years and, well, we're kind of back on, and . . . I'm going to have to tell him . . . You're right, Colton, it should have never happened." Yeah, the bitterness in my voice was unmistakable. *And the Oscar goes to . . .*

"Milo—" Colton cursed and started pacing in front of me. "I'll tell him, give me your phone."

"No!" I shouted. "I mean, um, no, it should be in person. I feel bad enough."

The dog bark ringtone went off.

*Damn it, Max!*

"You should answer that." Colton nodded to my front pocket.

"Voice mail."

"It's your guy."

"How do you know?"

"Same ringtone, an unlucky guess."

"So?"

Colton rolled his eyes. "Be mature, Milo, just answer the damn phone."

With shaking hands I pulled my phone out of my pocket and clicked "Accept." "Hey, baby."

"Uh-oh . . . what did you do?"

"Yeah, I miss you too!"

"Milo, say my name if you did something really stupid and unforgiveable like the time you told me I wouldn't get a splinter in my ass for using a wood sled."

"Max . . ." I purred, trying to sound sexy. Colton leaned in like he was trying to listen to our conversation. I glared at him, hoping he'd back off and give me space.

"Shit balls. Oh, look, a bus! What? What was that? You want to throw me under it?"

"So listen . . . you know I love you."

"I hate you so much right now."

I forced a smile. "But I may have done something really stupid . . ."

"Shocked. Really. My heart almost stopped."

". . . and kissed another guy. But to be fair *he* kissed *me*."

"Do you want me to yell?"

"Yes!"

"The pain!" Max shouted. "The misery in my heart! It's dying, I'm dying, you've killed me! You've killed us! Do we mean nothing to you? I bought you an aloe vera plant, Milo! Do you even know what those mean?"

"Uhhh."

Colton held out his hand. "Give me the phone. I'll explain."

"No," I argued.

"NO!" Max yelled. "Well, let me tell you. Aloe vera means healing, it means love, and I gave you a piece of my heart, so you would heal me, not run me over with your Mercedes!"

Colton won the war and jerked the phone out of my hands. "Listen, it's my fault, yeah." His eyes narrowed and then he started laughing. "Well, yeah, that's true. Yeah. Oh, man, you should totally come down. Yeah, that would be great."

*No. No. No. No.* I tried to snatch the phone as Colton walked off with it. "Sure, dude, yeah, and again I'm so sorry, bro, apologies, I just, I don't know what came over me." He smiled in my direction. "Yeah, she sure is. Okay, I'll tell her."

He hit "End," his face still set in a firm smile. "Nice guy."

It was official. I hated all men.

Colton handed me the phone. "Oh, and he said to call him. He said he was surprising you for the wedding, was gonna show up and be your date, now that things are . . . awkward." He coughed. "I told him it was a good idea. Besides, you're probably still pissed at me for mauling you like that—you should be able to have a date for the wedding."

Damn the man for continuing to march all over my heart like I was dirt and he was the freaking army storming some other girl's castle!

"Right." I forced the word out of my mouth, and promised myself I wouldn't cry again.

"Yeah." Colton nodded and looked away. "I should, uh, go help Jason. Thanks for . . ." He stopped talking. "'Night, Milo."

# CHAPTER FIVE
## MILO

Escaping Colton for the rest of the night was not an option. My parents were big believers in doing everything in the evening together—and I do mean everything. So when I said I wanted to go to bed early rather than watch a movie with everyone, the response was yelling until I finally consented to watch half the movie.

Jason was making popcorn in the kitchen—shirtless. That was how he did everything. It used to irritate me that he made food with no clothes on. Then again it wasn't like he had crazy chest and back hair. I could have sworn he waxed but he always denied it.

I tilted my head as he shook his ass in front of the microwave and then continued dancing to the newest demented beat in his head.

Girls had always loved him.

I never saw the pull.

I mean he had the whole olive skin, light eyes thing going for him—compliments of my very Spanish grandparents—but still. To me he was just Jason.

Then again he was my brother, so understanding the whole attraction thing . . . probably a sin.

I turned and rummaged through the fridge for a soda. Really what I wanted was to drown my sorrows in something a bit stronger, but getting drunk in front of the parents all because my childhood crush kissed me and made me cry after we played Ping-Pong and a game of slap? Yeah . . . the idea just made me that much more depressed. Add in the whole "you're like my sister" reference and yeah, let's just say I wouldn't be a nice drunk. That was the last thing my parents needed on wedding weekend.

"Squirt." Colton swatted my ass with a towel and breezed by.

As. If. Nothing. Had. Happened.

I gripped the door to the fridge so hard that my knuckles turned white.

"So, what did she say?" Jason asked behind me.

"She said not a problem."

"Told you she'd be your date."

The soda I'd just grabbed dropped to the kitchen floor with a thud. Quickly I picked it up and closed the door, still listening.

"She's hot," Jason continued. "You two'll have fun."

"I'm sure we will," Colton said, not sounding convincing at all.

"Date?" I interrupted, holding the can in front of my face.

"Yeah." Colton nodded. "You know, since you have Max and all—you were supposed to be my date for the wedding, remember?"

No. I hadn't remembered. In the heat of the moment, I'd survived. I'd made up a huge lie in order to cover up my own hurt feelings and ended up shooting myself in the ass, not that it mattered since technically Max had held the gun and pulled the trigger! I give him one job! Lie! And he goes and invites himself to the wedding! I was going to murder him.

"Right," I said through clenched teeth.

"See?" Jason patted my back. "It all works out."

"Yes . . . it's all working out." I jerked open the can of soda.

And was rewarded with it spraying all over my face and white shirt.

The guys burst out laughing.

And for the second time that night I wanted to cry.

Nothing had changed. Nothing was different. I was like some sexless friend to Colton and even if by some slim chance he did want something more, he was too much of a pansy-ass to admit it.

"Screw you guys," I muttered under my breath. "I'm going to go take a shower."

"Need help getting in there without falling on your face, squirt?" Colton's eyes twinkled with amusement.

"Sure." I glared at him. "You offering to help strip me or just wash me down, Colt?"

His smile fell.

Jason looked at me like I'd just told him I was into chicks.

"Right." I nodded. "Didn't think so. 'Night, boys."

I walked out of the room, embarrassed, sad, agitated, and pissed.

Having Max here wouldn't help, but at least it would take my mind off the fact that the one guy I'd crushed on since middle school had rejected me. And this time, after kissing me.

• • •

I slept like crap all night—proving my point again. All men should burn in hell. I switched between nightmares of Colton's rejection and dreams of Max riding in to rescue me on a giant-ass aloe vera plant.

Groaning, I tossed and turned, finally falling into a deep sleep around two a.m.

"Fire!" A voice penetrated my dreams. "Fire! Wake up!"

I jolted out of my bed to see Max sitting calmly at the end. He had two Starbucks cups in hand and was sporting a pair of black skinny jeans, a blue V-neck T-shirt, and a smile that looked like it belonged on the cover of *GQ*.

"Hey, you're awake." His grin widened.

"Yeah, weird, I thought there was a fire."

He handed me the coffee. "There is. In your pants."

"Pardon?"

"Because you're a liar." He patted my leg and shook his head. "Do I even want to know how this happened? Or was it the usual?"

"Usual?" My voice was gravelly, I took a large sip of coffee—it did wonders for my mood.

"Yeah, the usual Milo freak-out where you speak before you think. Typically involves lots of cursing, yelling, sometimes a fight breaks out, and I always end up having to fix it."

My face burned.

Max nodded. "The usual, then. Gotcha."

"Why are you here? What time is it?"

"Five a.m.," he answered. "Your mom's a fox, by the way, I swear she checked my ass out twice as I walked up the stairs."

"She did not."

"Your dad did the same. Ten bucks says your mom asks where I got my jeans and buys him a pair—oh, and by the way, you owe me big. I finally asked out the Starbucks girl and had to cancel our date on account that my other girlfriend"—his eyes narrowed—"had an emergency."

I winced. "Please tell me you didn't explain it that way to her."

"Course not. I said my asthmatic little sister had an attack and almost died screaming my name . . ."

"You don't have a sister."

"Little Maddie's screams were so loud, all she wanted was her big brother Max."

"Who's Maddie?"

"And I can't deny her the one thing she wants in life, the one thing that makes her go on living." Max wiped a fake tear. "I'm a broken man, Milo, and sisters are more important than dates."

"I'm sure she was understanding."

Max grinned. "You could say that."

"Gross."

"What?" He held up his hands. "I'm a guy. Just because you labeled me your gay friend freshman year does not actually make it true."

Okay, so I was a sheltered kid. Sue me! When I first laid eyes on Max I'd nearly swallowed my tongue. He was gorgeous and dressed like a rock star. Though he'd tried on at least four different occasions early on in our friendship to sleep with me, the rejection didn't keep him from wanting to stay close. Each time I rejected him, it was because I was holding a Colton-size flame. Finally he gave up, and said if he couldn't get in my pants he might as well help others do so. It wasn't poetic, but then, that's Max for you—blunt, to the point, inappropriate, and kind of awesome. Because of his strong metro-sexual tendencies, I finally learned the art of waxing and was always invited to the best parties. Our friendship was mutually beneficial because girls saw him as loyal, when really he was loyal to only two females, his dog Homeslice and me. And when it came to dating he helped scare all the sketchy guys away.

"So . . ." Max set his coffee on the nightstand and pulled me into his arms; we lay down on the bed together. "What happened?"

I groaned.

"Milo . . ."

"He kissed me."

Max held up his hand for a high five. I pushed it down. "What? We aren't excited about this?"

"No, we aren't."

"Continue."

"He said if he could take it back he would."

"Son of a streetwalker . . ." He winced. "Out loud? After he kissed you, he said that?"

I nodded.

"Did you kick him in the nuts?"

I shook my head.

"Grab his balls and give a little tug?"

I shook my head again.

"Damn, my little friend. That blows. So where do I come in?"

"Well." I rubbed Max's arm. "I cried."

"Shit."

"And I didn't want him to think I was crying over him, I mean that's a waste of tears, right?"

Max kissed my temple. "Right."

"So I said I was crying because I'd never cheated on anyone and then I said you and I were dating and yeah . . ."

"Not the most brilliant lie you've ever come up with," Max said after a few minutes of silence.

"I blame the dehydration from the three-hour Ping-Pong tournament."

"Badass, tell me you won."

"Off night," I grumbled.

"Aw, baby." Max laughed and pulled me to a sitting position. "Don't worry, I'll help. Plus, I actually look like competition so it should be easy."

"No offense, Max." I patted his leg. "But you're just—"

"What?"

"I mean, I don't see you like that, so—"

Max threw his head back and laughed. "I'm a guy. I don't care how you see me now, the way you see me over the next three days is going to change. I don't turn it on around you—mainly because I don't give a shit what *you* think."

I laid my hand over my heart and heaved a dramatic sigh. "Such a sweetheart."

"Shut it." He picked up his coffee and tapped it against mine. "Jealousy is the easiest way to get someone to admit feelings. Believe me, by the end of this weekend he's going to be begging for another kiss."

"And if he doesn't?" I slumped and took a huge swig of coffee like it had whiskey in it.

Max tilted my chin toward him. "Then he's an asshole who doesn't deserve you in the first place."

"Truth?" My voice wavered.

"Truth." He smiled that same blinding smile that I'm sure had made the Starbucks lady start stripping. His wide mouth and deep dimples were enough to make anyone stare. Maybe it would work— it *had* to work. Because if it didn't, well, that just meant I was one of those girls, the desperate kind, who had no idea when to quit.

"Okay."

"Now." Max stood. "Let's get you dressed and ready for breakfast. We've got a man to trap."

I laughed. *And he wonders why I pegged him as uninterested when we first met?*

# CHAPTER SIX
## MILO

"Remember what I said," Max coached as we walked down the stairs holding hands. "If I kiss you, you can't push me away . . . and don't do the laugh."

"The laugh?" I squeezed his hand harder. "I don't know what you're talking about."

"When you get super nervous and awkward you giggle like a toddler. It's cute as hell, but he knows you really well—he'll see right through it. Besides, it kind of hurts a guy's feelings when a girl giggles after he has his tongue down her throat."

I rolled my eyes. "You're so romantic, Max."

"So, we clear on the whole laughing thing?"

"Yeah," I grumbled. "Clear as—"

Max's mouth covered mine in an instant. I fought the urge to push him away. It had to be for a reason, right? Like Colton was around the corner, and—

Holy mother of sin. What was he doing with his tongue?

Max stepped back, his full lips curved into a smile. "That'll do, pig, that'll do."

"Please tell me you're movie quoting and not calling me fat."

"The only fat you have on your body is that of your inflated head whenever you play competitive sports."

"Nice."

"Good kiss." Max squeezed my hand.

"Wait!" I turned around, then smacked him on the shoulder. "What was that for?"

"I had to test you before the real thing."

"That was a test?"

"Yup." He dragged me toward the kitchen.

I dug my heels in the carpeting. "Well, did I pass?"

Max turned around, his steel-gray eyes looking me up and down. "I may have to do another test run."

My mouth dropped open as my best friend turned into the player every single girl on campus wrote home about. My heart started racing as every inch of my skin tingled from the expression on Max's face. Even the way he walked made me want to actually kiss him again.

He strutted into the kitchen, pulling me against his body as he did so, and then kissed me again.

Right in front of Colton and Jason.

With a grunt he pushed me up against the same fridge I'd nearly cried into last night and then released me. "You taste sweet," he murmured, his lips meeting mine again.

"And . . . appetite gone." Jason swore. "Mind introducing us to your—" He shook his head. "Friend?"

Max turned around, his eyes sizing up both my brother and Colton, who had fallen completely silent during the exchange.

Too bad I'd never really gotten into Instagram—the picture of the three of them glaring at one another was enough to go viral in seconds.

I'd never noticed how tall Max was. Same height as Jason, about an inch shorter than Colton.

"Boyfriend." Max held out his hand. "And you must be . . . Jason?"

"Right." Jason held out his hand.

Max angled a perplexed stare at Colton as though struggling to figure something out. I had to hide my laugh. He knew exactly who Colton was. "And . . . Carlton?"

"Colton," he said through clenched teeth. "So glad you could make it."

"Well," Max pulled me to his side. "What kind of boyfriend would I be if I abandoned the love of my life during her time of need?" He squeezed my shoulder, while I pinched his side.

With a wince he released me. "So what's on the agenda today?"

"Oh, thank God you're up!" Mom came shuffling into the kitchen looking like she hadn't slept in weeks.

With a flourish she dropped the giant binder back onto the table and started pointing at things.

"Jason, I need you to start setting up the tables in the backyard. Colton, get the chairs. Max, I put you with Milo on the centerpieces for the reception. The tents have heaters but they haven't been delivered yet, and we'll be using the same tent for both the ceremony and the reception so you'll need to break everything down tonight and help the coordinators set everything up tomorrow morning. The bachelor party will be directly after the rehearsal and the bachelorette party is being held off-site at an undisclosed location. I've packed the fridge with water bottles and purchased two boxes of protein bars. If for any reason you start to feel light-headed, sit down on the grass and keep working. Any questions?"

I raised my hand.

"Milo?"

"Where's the bride?"

"Jayne?" Mom nodded. "She's getting ready for this evening. Besides, I told her it was her weekend and her parents agreed. The bride shouldn't have to lift a finger. They pay, we set everything up."

"I knew a Jayne once," Max said wistfully.

I elbowed him in the ribs.

"Any more questions?"

Jason raised his hand.

"Yes." Mom sounded annoyed.

"What's Dad doing?"

"Dad," my dad said upon entering the kitchen, "is going to a bar."

"Dibs!" all three guys yelled at the same time.

*Insert facepalm here.*

"He's kidding." Mom threw him an irritated glance. "He's helping set up the tent." She cleared her throat. "Now, any more questions?"

Max raised his hand even though I tried like the fires of hell to keep it firmly planted at his side.

"Max?"

"Well, it's not really a question, more of a compliment."

"Oh?"

"Has anyone ever told you how beautiful you are when you give orders? Reminds me a lot of Milo. I can see where she gets what I like to call her terror-inflicting skills."

I groaned into my hands while Mom and Dad laughed.

"You know it's true, baby." Max wrapped his arm around me. "Come on, you made a professor cry last semester."

"That's enough." I laughed dryly.

Colton snorted. "You made a professor cry?"

"To be fair he was an adjunct professor and he had a very . . . tender heart," I muttered. I was going to kill Max. Kill him!

"Makes a guy proud." Max nodded. "At any rate, I'm here to help as much as I can."

Mom beamed.

Dad grunted.

And Colton looked like he was ready to shoot fire out of his mouth and singe Max where he stood.

"So . . ." Mom closed the book with a resounding slam that echoed around the kitchen. "Eat some cereal, take some protein bars, and . . ." She checked her watch. "The event planners should be here any minute! Places, everyone! Oops, maybe you guys can eat and walk at the same time?"

"It's like we're in a musical," Max whispered under his breath.

I opened my mouth.

He slammed his hand over it. "Break out in song, and I'm going to make you wish I really had gotten you an aloe vera plant."

"Something wrong?" Colton approached us, hands stuffed in his pockets, jaw clenched.

I bit Max's hand.

With a yelp he pulled back.

"Nope!" I beamed just as Max said, "She likes biting me."

Holy hell.

Colton's nostrils flared before he chuckled and looked away. "I see what's happening here."

"You do?" Max and I said in unison.

"Yup." Colton started laughing so hard he had to grip the table-top. "Milo, why didn't you just say something?"

"Say something?" I was seriously lost. *Was he high?*

"Yeah, Milo."

Max turned on me and mouthed, "What the hell?"

"You're lying about something." Colton's eyes narrowed in amusement. "You always flush when you lie, Milo, and you keep scratching your face. It's a nervous tic thing. What's going on here?"

"Nothing," Max and I said in unison.

Jason came up behind Colton. "You done interrogating my sister's boyfriend?"

"Uh, yeah." Colton stepped back, but not before pointing at Max, then me, and saying, "I'm watching you." Aw, awesome, we were both just given the De Niro.

Once the two of them left the room we exhaled in relief.

"What the hell is wrong with you?" Max gave me a tender shove. "We were fine until you started stepping on my foot and elbowing me!"

"You were hitting on my mom!"

"She's a beautiful lady!" he argued.

"Oh, my gosh." I fell into one of the chairs and moaned. "This is a catastrophe."

"Not true." Max shook his head. "You just have to be more believable. I mean, would it kill you to find me screw-worthy?"

"Screw-worthy? What does that even mean?"

"That's it." Max grabbed my hand and pulled me down the hall. "Where's the bathroom?"

"Uh . . ." I pointed.

With a jerk he had me in the bathroom under the stairs and closed the door. Words and sounds were coming out of his mouth but I couldn't make anything out. Max pushed me against the door and pointed his finger in my face. "I'm going to kiss you, damn it, and you're going to like it. And I'm going to take off my shirt and you're going to manhandle me, and you're going to stop being so damn nervous or so help me God I'm going to bend you over that sofa in the living room and spank your sexy ass."

Shocked, I was paralyzed in place. "Where did that come from?"

"Inside." Max looked at me and smirked. "I have lots of feelings and I'm sick and tired of you looking at me like I don't have a penis. I may be used to your innocence, but for my own pride, at least try to be attracted to me. Now close your damn eyes."

"Stop cursing at me."

"Stop being difficult! I'm trying to help you. And stop squirming. Shit, take a Xanax or something."

"Max." I closed my eyes and huffed. "This isn't going to—"

My hand was on something hard.

I blinked my eyes open.

Since when did he have a six-pack?

I tilted my head, you know, to get a better look. His skin was really smooth but bumpy, each muscle defined so much that there was enough of a ridge for my hands to play with.

"Oh, look, he's a man after all," Max said, sounding bored. "I'm not your sexless friend. I'm not your damn brother. I'm not your gay friend. And I sure as hell am not thinking about anything right now except that your hands feel really good against my skin. So I'm going to kiss you, and you're going to respond like the idea of my mouth on yours doesn't make you want to cry—and you'll like it."

"I'll like it," I repeated.

"There's my girl." His eyes flashed, and then he was kissing me again, only this time his body was on fire as it pressed against me. I felt every ridge of his abs; the length of his body was beyond devastating.

Slowly I wrapped my hands around his neck and pulled him closer.

# CHAPTER SEVEN
## COLTON

"I don't like him," I said for the tenth time while Jason and I set up the tables.

"Dude!" Jason rolled his eyes. "Why does it matter? She's like a sister to you. We'll protect her if he goes all ape-shit."

"Right." Because that's exactly what I was worried about. Her virtue. That was why I'd spent the better part of the night reliving that kiss and woken up so sexually frustrated that I threw my pillows across the room.

Because I was being protective.

Hilarious as hell.

*Little sister. Little sister.* It was a no-poaching zone. And once you went in for the hunt, you either didn't make it out alive or you wished you had gotten mauled.

We would never work.

Ever.

Never. Ever.

"Uh, you okay?" Jason asked, his eyebrows arching with what I could only assume was curiosity as to why I looked ready to rip a tree in half and throw it at all men named Max.

"Yeah, why?"

He pointed. "You look like you want to punch the shit out of that table and your hands are balled into such tight fists that I'm a bit concerned you're going to pass out from blood loss."

"On edge," I snapped.

"Shocker," Jason mouthed, just as Max and Milo came around the corner. Holy shit, I was going to lose my mind.

Her hair was tousled.

Lips bruised.

Well, that was it. Jason was going to have to arrest me. I was going to prison. At night I was going to sneak into Max's room, beat him senseless, smother him with a pillow, and then dump his body into the pool.

Just kidding . . . the pool wasn't deep enough.

A pond.

A large pond.

A lake.

The ocean.

"Colt?" Jason waved in front of my face. "I asked you a question."

"Sorry," I mumbled. "What was it?"

"Max says he's terrible with arrangements so he's going to finish up with the tables and you're going to go help Milo, okay?"

"Sure. Whatever." I dropped the table, hard. Unfortunately it landed on Jason's foot.

"Shit!" He hopped around on one foot cursing a blue streak.

"Sorry?" I winced.

"Ice." Jason glared. "Get me ice."

I ran toward the house, Milo close on my heels. "What happened to Jason?"

"I dropped a table on him," I said calmly, searching for ice. The guy already had a black eye and now he was going to have a broken toe. Yeah, I was the worst best man ever.

"Why would you do that?" Milo grabbed a towel and held it out as I put ice in it.

"Oh, you know, for shits and giggles."

"Ah, I see—you're in love with the bride," she teased.

I rolled my eyes. "Jayne? No thanks."

Milo's face fell. *Shit.* Now she knew for sure her brother was marrying Satan.

"I didn't mean it like that . . ."

"Yeah." She shrugged. "You did, but maybe she's different now, more mature, not as—"

"She's a whiny bitch," I said honestly. "But he loves her and that's all that matters, plus she's always been a bit spoiled."

"Yeah." Milo looked miles away.

"Thanks for helping me with the ice."

She beamed.

That smile slammed through my body. I used to live for her smiles, used to live for her visits. When she first went away to college, it had felt like a part of me left with her, but it wasn't like I was able to ever actually say that out loud.

I'd wanted her for years.

But wanting and having were two very different things.

I'd rather never have her—than lose her as a friend. And I'd come so damn close to losing her last night. So yeah, I shoved my foot into my mouth and nearly suffocated to death—but at least we could go back to normal. Right?

"So, Max . . ." I held open the door as we walked out into the brisk morning air. "He's . . . nice."

"Liar." She nudged me in the shoulder. "But I appreciate you trying."

"Maybe I'd respect him more if he didn't maul you in front of me."

"Hmm." Milo shrugged. "You didn't seem to mind any mauling last night."

"Milo—"

"No." Her smile appeared forced. "It's fine. Friends, right?"

I knew that look. She was still pissed. But she had a boyfriend! She'd cheated; so if anyone had a right to be pissed it was me—not her.

I grabbed her hand with my free hand and tugged her against me, leaning down so our foreheads almost touched. "Right. Friends."

Her eyes flashed.

Hell, the pull she had on me was otherworldly. I wanted to close the distance between our mouths. I was desperate to touch her again, even with her boyfriend a few feet away.

"Ice!" Jason yelled. "In pain over here!"

With a chuckle I tossed the ice pack in his direction and turned back to face Milo. But she was already walking into Max's waiting arms.

I'd done that.

I'd forced her hand, it was the only explanation my pride would allow me to come up with. I'd always felt something between us, and now that something was sizzling into nothing—fast. I'd successfully pushed her back into the arms of her idiot boyfriend because I freaked out over a kiss.

All because I was afraid.

# CHAPTER EIGHT

## MILO

Max whistled. "Well done."

"I'm sweating."

"As you should be with the way he manhandled you."

We were standing side by side, talking in hushed tones while I waited for Jason to stop hopping around on one foot, and for Colton to come back and join me. It had been Max's idea to switch jobs.

I had argued.

He'd firmly told me he was going to get me into Colton's pants if it was the last thing he did.

Guys were confusing. One minute Max was pissed that I didn't see him as a sexy, available man and minutes later he was plotting ways to get me laid.

"Tell me again," Max mumbled under his breath.

"No."

"Milo." He grinned. "I need to know that you know the instructions I've so tirelessly given you over the past few minutes."

"Smile, act evasive, brush his arm . . ." I coughed into my hand as I mumbled the final point.

"What was the last one?" Max winked. "Come on, Milo, let's hear it."

Heat rushed into my face. "Bend over."

"Atta girl."

"Not a dog."

"You have a nice ass." He shrugged and crossed his arms. "And guys are turned on by sight. It's a scientific fact. He's not blind, believe me, he'll take the bait."

"If he doesn't?" I asked in a small voice.

Max leaned over and kissed my temple. "Then you and I can always make out and watch chick flicks while you cry into your ice cream, and then I can beat his ass."

"I do like kissing you." It didn't give me butterflies or anything but he had nice lips, and if I tried really hard I could see what other girls saw, but there wasn't that pull, just friendship, nothing more.

Max sighed and rolled his eyes as if he'd heard my declaration a million times before. "Everyone likes kissing me."

"Not a humble bone in your body, is there?"

"Not a one." He saluted. "Looks like lover boy's on his way over. Have fun!" He ran off toward Jason, who looked like a gang had just jumped him, and started setting up tables.

"He gonna be okay?" I pointed at Jason.

Colton turned around and winced as Jason fell out of his chair. "Yeah, he'll be fine, it's just a bump."

"Ha, a bump." I laughed it off and shifted my weight between both feet like a middle schooler during recess. "Kind of like the black eye."

"All accidental," Colton snapped. "Okay, how do we do this shit?"

"Wow, weddings just bring out the romance in guys, don't they?" I pulled out the fake flowers and started grouping them on the table.

"They're flowers. Do I look like the type of guy who wants to arrange flowers?"

"Yes."

"Milo," Colton growled.

"Show me your tattoo and I'll say no."

He lifted his shirt.

I gave him a nod. "No, Colton. You're a muscled badass with a tattoo—you don't do flowers."

"Somehow I imagined that compliment feeling better," he mused, picking up one of the silk roses.

"So." Ignoring him, I pulled out the instructions. "Three red roses go in the middle and then we're supposed to fill the rest of the vases with this . . ." I lifted the white tulle into the air.

"What is that?"

"Err . . . decorations?"

Colton picked a piece up and held it as far away from his body as humanly possible, like he was afraid if it got close to his man parts it would wrap around and squeeze his balls off. His lips curled in disgust as he rolled his eyes and set it on the table.

"Fine." I pinched the bridge of my nose. "Stick the pointy things in the green foam thing that looks like SpongeBob and then stuff the white crap into the glass thingy and make sure it's full."

Colton's smile was blinding. "Got it. Why didn't you just say so?"

We worked in relative silence for the next half hour. I did every single thing Max suggested. I dropped at least ten roses, and bent over trying to pick them up so Colton would notice, but the man was a machine. It was like he couldn't wait to leave!

With a flourish I dropped another rose and went to retrieve it only to have Colton grab my hand so hard that I winced in pain.

"Leave it."

"But—"

"I said . . ." He was so close my exhalation tangled with his inhalation. "Leave it."

His jaw flexed as he pulled my hand closer to his body and then released it as if I'd hurt him.

"I think we're done." He cleared his throat. "Yeah?"

"Sure."

"Jason!" A high-pitched scream broke the cloud of confusion. "Baby! I need you!"

"Speak of the devil," Colton muttered under his breath.

I hadn't seen Jayne Harrison in years. But I still hadn't forgiven her for telling me my Barbie lunchbox was stupid in the first grade. She also said I smelled like tuna.

Sometimes during school I imagined her getting eaten by a giant octopus or falling off the swing set and bruising her perfect little face.

Peering around Colton, I noticed nothing had changed since high school. She had a blonde A-line bob and wore enough makeup on to open up her own Sephora.

Her tight, black leather dress looked more appropriate for a dance club than for during the day—maybe she was one of those daylight vampires or something.

"Where are you?" she wailed, looking around the yard, her eyes finally settling on Colton.

He grabbed me and pushed me in front of him.

"Brave," I muttered under my breath.

"Self-preservation," he snapped back. "I'm not sorry. My balls actually retreat back into my body when I hear her voice."

"Milo!" Jayne's heavily mascaraed eyes grew wide. "Is that you? Oh, look at you! How cute! You're still wearing your brother's clothes!"

I clenched my fist at my side and nearly decked her, but Colton's light touch on my shoulders calmed me down—enough for me to know that it would be a mistake to give her a black eye to match my brother's.

"Oh, you know me. I just love boy clothes," I said through clenched teeth.

"Yes." She eyed me up and down. "Well." With a bored look she glanced behind me. "Colton, looking great."

"There they go," he whispered, then said louder, "Thanks, J, you too."

"Where is he?" she demanded loudly enough to make me jump.

"Baby!" Jason limped toward us, followed by Max. "How are you?"

"Jason!" She covered her face. "What happened to your eye? And your leg! Are you okay?"

"Fine." He grinned. "You know how things get when Milo comes home."

"I know." She sent me a glare and then pinched my brother's cheeks with her talons. "We'll get you all better."

Colton started coughing wildly behind me.

All eyes shifted to him.

"Bug," he wheezed, giving his chest a few strong pats. "Sorry."

"Hey, what's going on over here?" Max ran up to the group and then froze, all color draining from his face.

"Max?"

"Jayne?"

"Oh, no," I muttered, my heart sinking at Max's wounded expression.

"I thought you were finishing up school." In a gesture of shyness, she tucked a piece of hair behind her ear. The woman didn't have a shy bone in her body.

Max blushed. He *blushed*! "Yeah, well, I'm here with Milo."

"Oh." Jayne nodded, her voice icy. "Are you like one of her Big Brothers? You know that program for kids?"

"What the—" I lunged for her, but was stopped by Colton's arms. He was shaking. From laughter. Awesome.

"Actually . . ." Max eyed me. Oh, no, he was going to do something bad, really, really bad, and I was going to want to punch him in the throat.

"I'm here with Milo because . . ."

Here it comes.

"They're dating," Colton interjected smoothly, releasing me so I could run into Max's arms.

He chuckled and whispered in my ear, "Broke my heart, broke my heart, make it better."

*Damn it.*

"Small world, huh?" I kissed Max on the cheek, and then the mouth, latching on to him like he was the only man in the world. He responded with a growl low in his throat as he pulled my hair and then lifted me into the air. Okay, now he was getting a bit carried away.

Not that I hated it.

No sane girl would hate it. I don't care WHO she was crushing on.

Jayne laughed loudly as if trying to take the focus off of us. "Um, excuse me? Can you guys not do that in public?"

"Sorry." Max placed me on my feet. "I just can't help myself."

I looked into his eyes adoringly.

His eyes reflected the same look.

"Max, we should, uh, catch up." Jayne fidgeted with her purse.

"Sure thing." I watched the light fade from my friend's eyes. "We should do that."

"Great." Jayne grabbed my brother by the hand, having already forgotten Max. "Let's go have some coffee and you can tell me all about how you got a black eye."

They walked away, leaving me clinging to Max and Colton shaking like he'd just gotten drenched in water. "Sorry, man, that woman freaks me out," he explained, looking down at himself as if he wanted to make sure his body was still intact after a run-in with Jason's fiancée. He shuddered and then pinched the bridge of his nose. "I have to go . . . shower or something."

Max and I stayed quiet until we were the only ones outside.

"Spill," I finally said a few minutes later.

"I don't want to talk about it."

"I almost just got pregnant with your love child out here on my parents' lawn—the least you could do is tell me what happened."

He shrugged and looked down at the ground. "I wasn't enough."

"Enough?"

"To keep her." Max frowned. "I wasn't enough."

# CHAPTER NINE
## MILO

"Sit." I pointed to one of the chairs by the pool.

Max sat and leaned back in the chair, closing his eyes for a few seconds before cursing and leaning forward on his knees.

"She denied you?"

"For my brother," Max said sharply.

Shock radiated through my body, making me stagger. "Whoa. Back up, you have a brother?"

"He's old." Max looked up and then shrugged. "Graduated like five years ago from NYU. He's on Broadway."

"Cool. Have I seen any of his shows?"

Max's eyes went completely cold.

"Not the time. Got it." I shook my head. "So Jayne's a bitch."

Max burst out laughing. "Yeah, something like that. I was in love with her my senior year of high school."

"How did you even know her?"

"Summer camp."

"You're kidding."

"Nope." Max grinned. "I went to one of those really stupid theater camps during the summer."

"Aww."

"Shut it."

"And?"

"And she was there, as well as my brother, though he was an instructor. Apparently she led us both on. I fell hard. At the end of camp I told her I wanted to see her again. She strung me along for an entire year. It wasn't until the following summer when I was making plans to visit her for a week that she told me she'd been screwing my own flesh and blood behind my back, Reid had no idea so it wasn't like I could be pissed at him."

Wincing, I reached for his hand and squeezed. "Well, look at the bright side."

He gave me a doubtful look.

"Now I'm stuck with her and while you dodged the bullet, my brother stood there and let it hit him square in the eyes."

"He's probably still bleeding, poor bastard," Max grumbled.

"Tell me you don't still like her." I released his hand and stood. "She's crazy."

"Of course I don't still like her." Max rolled his eyes. "You know nothing of men."

"You keep saying that, but—"

"Rejection's a bitch, okay? It doesn't matter if the girl goes batshit crazy on you—it's a pride thing. She led me on, and she cheated, then she dumped me. While she was the one to blame, I never got to yell at her, slam a door in her face, call her a bitch, tell her she had lipstick on her teeth . . ."

"Yeah, you've thought about this way too much."

"It just sucks. When you see your ex you want to win."

"Win?"

Max sighed and patted his knee. "Have a seat while I explain how the world works, Milo."

I sat on his knee and crossed my arms.

"Boy meets girl. Boy and girl break up. Boy and girl go separate ways. Fast forward ten years. Boy meets girl at supermarket. Boy wants to look like man, have balls of steel, sport a six-pack, and be driving a Ferrari. Now, tell me girl doesn't want the same thing."

"I've never wanted balls of steel."

Max pressed his lips together and waited.

"Fine, if I was supermarket girl, I'd want big boobs, a tiny waist, killer outfit, sick car, and one of those credit cards that has no limit."

"I rest my case." Max popped his knuckles. "All I'm saying is, I want to win."

Jayne's screechy laughter pierced the peaceful morning air. Max and I cringed simultaneously.

"Winning," we said in unison, falling into fits of laughter.

Max kissed my forehead and helped me off his lap.

"Max?"

"Hmm?" He put his arm around me.

"You're not going to like . . ." I felt my cheeks heat with embarrassment. "I mean you won't . . ."

"Spit it out, Milo."

"Fall in love with me."

"Damn." Max pulled away, his face pinched. "It's like you can read minds! I love you, okay? I've loved you for years! I just want to be in your life. God, don't shut me out! Don't love him! Love me instead! The plant, Milo! The aloe vera! How can you deny me?"

Somehow in the middle of his speech he'd adopted a British accent.

"Shakespeare theater camp?" I crossed my arms.

"I was the best damn Hamlet they'd ever seen." Max's grin spread across his face, his dimples damn near making me want to let out a girlish sigh. "And sorry, I may be a great kisser, and yeah, you turn me on—you're hot, so what else is new? But love? Yeah, I don't do that. I'm like one of those guys who girls write about. The rogue."

"Rake?"

"Yeah, that."

"Awesome."

"I'm probably going to die alone." Max exhaled and put on what I can only imagine was supposed to be a brave face. "But I'll always have memories of us."

I pulled him in for a hug and giggled. "We should probably make one of those pacts that if both of us aren't married before we're thirty we walk down the aisle hand in hand."

"Deal." He shrugged. "I could totally wake up to you for the rest of my life, but I'm pretty sure that it won't happen."

"Oh, yeah?" I rolled my eyes. "What makes you so certain?"

Max pulled me in for a tight hug, then whispered in my ear, "Because Colton's been watching you from the upstairs window for the past twenty minutes."

# CHAPTER TEN

## COLTON

"What are you doing?" Jason asked, scaring the shit out of me. I cursed and banged my forehead against the window, then pulled back, elbowing him in the jaw.

"What the f—"

"Jason!"

Mrs. Caro, his mom, came around the corner and folded her arms. "That is terrible language!"

"I was going to say fu—"

"*Fudge.* Yes, I know. Been using that excuse since you were in middle school. What happened to your face?"

"Black eye from last night." Jason shrugged.

"No, no." Mrs. Caro leaned forward and placed her hands on his jaw. "Your chin, it looks like you're bleeding."

"Son of a—"

Mrs. Caro frowned.

"Whore."

"Better." Mrs. Caro grunted and held out her hand. "Now let's go get you cleaned up."

"Better not," Jason grumbled under his breath. "I swear at the rate I'm going I'm probably going to get hit by a car before I get married."

"One can only hope," Mrs. Caro mumbled under her breath.

"What was that?" Jason asked.

"I hope we have Dial soap." She winked at me and then patted Jason's back. "It disinfects."

"Oh." Jason followed her down the hall, so I was able to return to my stalking post. Why the hell did she and Max look so damn happy? I could have sworn I almost ripped the guy's head off when he kissed her again.

"Shit," I mumbled under my breath. They weren't on the lawn anymore. I leaned in closer and tried to peer to the left to see if they'd walked around the house.

"Bird-watching?" Milo's mocking voice invaded my ridiculous stalking session.

"Yup." I didn't move. "Early spring, lots of . . . birds returning from . . . Florida."

"Oh, yeah?" Milo stepped right next to me and pressed her face against the glass. Damn, she smelled good. "Wow, look at all of them, it's like a freaking Hitchcock movie out there."

Yeah. No birds. None. Not even the fake kind people put on their lawns. Awesome.

"They left." I cleared my throat. "You probably scared them off with your loud walking."

"My loud walking didn't seem to scare you off."

Damn, she had me there.

"So." I moved away from the window. "Where's Max?"

"Eating. He's hungry all the time. It's incredible the amount of food that guy puts away."

"Cool."

*Cool?* Wow, I'd just made things so much more awkward. I shoved my hands in my pockets and waited for her to say something to break the silence. I didn't know how to act normal or how to act interested without first scaring her and second ruining everything. Then again, acting interested wouldn't be right. What was I thinking? I had to act indifferent but not so much that she thought I was an ass.

Which left me looking like a complete loser as I watched her smile grow.

"Colt . . ."

"Yeah."

"You sure you're doing okay?"

"Course!" I laughed it off. "I just didn't sleep that well last night." Visions of your best friend's little sister dancing through your head didn't exactly scream R and R. "Tired."

"Me too. I wish we didn't have to work."

I nodded.

Milo's head jerked upright. "Holy crap! I know what to do!"

"Huh?"

She grabbed my hand and dragged me down the hall to the guest bedroom that led into the attic. "Uh, Milo?"

"Shh!" She pressed her fingers against my lips.

That shut me up.

It also shut off all functioning systems of my body except for the one that screamed, *Kiss her senseless and lock her in the attic for a few days.*

"We're hiding until break time. By the looks of it, Mom is going to let us have coffee and doughnuts at nine."

"So we're going to hide in the guest room?" I looked around the empty room.

"Nope." She grinned. "Attic time. Up you go!" With a grunt she pulled open the door to the attic and turned on the light.

And immediately I was transported back to my childhood. Milo always made me play dragon slayer. I had to be both the dragon and the slayer, which usually proved a problem when at the end of our playtime I had to die, but she hadn't cared. The only mission I'd had, as one of her best friends, was to kill the dragon, save the princess, make it to the castle (aka the top of the stairs) in time, and offer her my sword. In reality, it had been a wooden sword. She'd then knight me and we'd sit at a table that was square instead of round, and we'd make Jason King Arthur.

"Come on." She tugged my hand, leading me up the stairs. Funny, when I was little I couldn't care less about being the guy who got knighted.

Now? Now I'd kill just to be a contender.

# CHAPTER ELEVEN

## MILO

Colton's face fell as he made his way slowly up the stairs. Funny how life happened. I spent half my childhood waiting for him at the top of the stairs.

And now? Now I was waiting for him again.

Not to slay the dragon, but to do something more heroic.

"It's smaller than I remember," he mused once he reached the top; his green eyes took in the room. The toy trunk was still in the corner along with my princess gowns and the giant family portrait from when I was born. My parents held me up between them like I was freaking Simba from *The Lion King* while an irritated Jason made a face at the camera. Priceless.

Dusty boxes lined the walls. The boxes had been there since I could remember. We used to build castles out of them.

The dragon always—and I do mean always—got slain before he reached the box castle. Colton was good like that.

I shrugged. "You're just bigger."

"Guess so." Colton walked around to the tiny window and took a seat on the toy box. "So we're just going to hide out until break time?"

"You have any better ideas?" I teased, wiping my hand across the dusty surface of one of the boxes. "My mom's losing her head over this wedding—don't shake your head, you know it's true. It's not even like she likes Jayne anyway!"

"No." Colton patted the spot next to him. "But she loves Jason and if Jason loves Jayne, then your mom loves Jayne, which means she wants everything to be perfect."

"You're right."

"Sorry, I didn't quite get that." He grinned, making my stomach drop to my feet.

"I'm not saying it again for your benefit, Colt."

"Fine." He sighed and picked up the wooden sword by his feet. "Tell me, how badass of a dragon was I?"

Laughing, I took the sword. "You always got the dragon. Meaning you did a really good job of killing yourself and then turning back into the knight. And I must admit the dragon always made really cool dying noises."

"Why'd we stop?"

"Hmm?" I was too busy watching his mouth to pay attention to the words actually coming out of it.

"Playing dragons and knights."

"Um, I got boobs?"

Colton dropped the sword and swore.

"Sorry, but it's true."

"You had . . ." He pointed and looked away. "You've always been a girl." The tips of his ears burned a bit pink. Was it possible that the great Colton Mathews was embarrassed?

"Right," I said slowly. "But the minute you realized I wasn't just a girl, that I was turning into a young woman, you went from playing and slaying the dragon to slaying all my friends."

Colton glared with disapproval. "I did not slay your friends. And by slay I'm assuming you mean lay because it rhymes and you're ridiculous like that."

My stomach clenched. I could still remember what it had felt like to go to Jason's and his graduation party and see Colton locking lips with Jenna. They'd been behind the garage, kissing in the shadows. When Colton saw me, he tried to run after me, but I went and hid like a total loser. My heart had been broken. After all, Jenna and I were in the same exact class, which meant he was interested in girls my age. Just not me.

"There weren't that many girls, Milo. I think you're exaggerating. Besides, I'm reformed. I haven't dated seriously in . . ."

"What?" I interrupted, folding my arms across my chest. "Thirty days? Having problems counting that high?"

"It's been a while."

"Look . . ." I stood. "It's not like it's any of my business."

The attic fell silent.

"Isn't it, though?" he whispered, his eyes searching mine. When I didn't say anything, he stood and pulled me into his arms. "Tell me it's not your business."

"It's—"

"Jayne, seriously, back off!" Max yelled.

Colton and I froze, then silently padded down the stairs to the door and listened.

"What?" Jayne whined.

I made a face at Colton while he put a pretend gun to his head and pulled the trigger.

"Come on, nobody has to know . . . for old times' sake."

"Run away!" I whispered. "Run!"

"No, no, I'm good. Thanks for the really inappropriate offer, though," Max said in a stern voice.

Cursing, she walked off and slammed the door.

I pushed open the attic door and yelled, "What the hell, Max?"

Whoops! Now I looked like a lover scorned.

"She came on to me!" Max held up his hands. "And you heard what I said! The bitch has got to go! I'm serious, guys. She tried grabbing me under the table! And when I swatted her hand away she took it as an invitation to get more aggressive." He groaned and closed his eyes. "All I kept thinking was if I can just spill orange juice on her shirt then she'll freak. Instead she thought it was an excuse for us to go somewhere private."

I walked over and put my arm on his shoulder.

"Wait a second . . ." Max looked between me and Colton. "What were you guys doing in the closet?"

"Attic," Colton said quickly. "Just looking for . . ."

Oh, hell, if he said birds again we were done for.

"Something old, for Jayne, for the wedding."

I nodded and winked at Max.

"It's almost break time, I'll just . . ." Colton walked out of the room, leaving me alone with Max.

I smacked him on the chest. "You ruined our moment."

"I almost ended up on a milk carton!" Max shouted. "She wasn't taking no for an answer!"

"You're a man, make her!"

"I may be a man, but she terrifies me. Yeah, she broke my heart, but holy shit, it's like she got a brain transplant. She asked how much money engineers make!"

I laughed. "What did you tell her?"

"I told her I was going to be a lifer. You know, go to school and just keep learning because learning was the foundation of life and I wanted to give life back into the world."

I tilted my head and squinted at him. "You come up with that crap ahead of time or does it just pour forth out of those wise lips of yours?"

"It's a gift." He shrugged. "Unfortunately I grossly miscalculated her ability to understand complicated sentences and big words, so from that lovely explanation she took that I had enough money to just go to school for the rest of my life."

"Damn."

Max sighed. "Thus the milk carton theory. No doubt she would have kidnapped me and you would have dreamed of my kisses for an eternity."

"No doubt."

"You should tell Jason."

"You tell Jason!"

"Okay." Max held up his hands. "We're not doing this. I refuse to engage."

"What's that supposed to mean?" I blocked his way to the door.

"This!" He held up his hands. "This is what you do. You're picking a fight because you're frustrated, albeit sexually. A little hint, take off your shirt and stare him down, works nine times out of ten."

"And the one time it doesn't?"

"You may have a repeat of your sixteenth birthday and get laughed at."

"Are you saying I have a bad chest?"

"Aw, shit. There you go picking fights again." Max went over to the bed and took a seat. "Let's get this over with."

"What?" I looked around the room. "What are we getting over with?"

"Let's have a look." He motioned to my shirt with his hand and sighed impatiently. "Come on, we don't have all day. It's like prison, your mom expects us to be back at work in fifteen minutes."

"Fine." I fidgeted with my shirt. "Just, don't laugh, and be honest. I want to know if I'm going to be that ten percent or the ninety, all right?"

"Okay."

I lifted a bit of the shirt, and stopped. "And if it's bad, maybe just . . . let me down slowly, like say something like, 'Oh, wow, at least you have really pretty lingerie.'"

"Fine."

Lifting the shirt higher, I almost punked out when Max groaned and shouted, "Damn it, Milo, take off your clothes!"

Irritated, I lifted the shirt all the way up to my head.

When the door opened.

"Hey guys, Mrs. Caro wants—"

The shirt was still over my head. Max was probably staring, and that was Colton's voice.

"Er, I mean when you're, um, finished . . ."

"This isn't what it looks like!" I turned toward the door and barreled in the general direction as I tried jerking my shirt down.

When the shirt was finally dislodged, I stumbled into Colton's arms, sending him crashing against the door, and my shirt fell enough for me to see that he'd banged his cheekbone.

"Shit!" He pulled away from me, but my shirt was still slightly up around my bra, so his hands went directly to my naked stomach. "Shhhit!" He pushed me away and tried to turn around but was clearly disoriented because this time he ran into the other side of the door, stumbled, and then hobbled down the hall holding one hand to his cheek.

After a few moments of silence, during which I prayed someone from the future had created time travel and was coming back to save my sorry ass, Max finally clapped. "Or you could just take off your top, give him two head wounds, and chase him down the hall. Yeah, that works too."

"Oh, no." My eyes filled with tears.

"Hey, hey." Max came up behind me and helped me pull my shirt back down. "If it makes you feel better, your boobs looked awesome."

"You mean it?"

"Comes from my heart." He grinned. "Right here." His grin widened as he placed his hand low on my chest.

I groaned as he fell into fits of laughter.

"All right, little girl, let's go do damage control and face that drill sergeant mom of yours."

"He's never going to want me," I whispered under my breath.

"Course he will." Max held me close. "If he doesn't, I'll just kill him."

# CHAPTER TWELVE
## COLTON

I was so disoriented that I stumbled into the kitchen and just stood there for a few seconds. My head pounded something fierce, and my body? Well, let's just say that even though nothing below the waist had been hit—that didn't mean I wasn't feeling the effects.

Everywhere.

"Damn it!" I pulled out a chair and sat.

Jason walked into the kitchen, took a look at my face, and pointed. "Milo get you too?"

"What the hell is wrong with her?" I blurted.

"Several things." Jason winced as if remembering the pain of his black eye. "She's an accident waiting to happen. You need ice or bandages or . . . something?" He examined my jaw and cheek. "Looks like she clocked you good."

"She didn't punch me," I said defensively.

Jason sat down next to me and leaned back in his chair. "Then how'd she hurt you?"

Hah. Right. Um, that's something I wanted to explain to her older brother, *You see she didn't have her shirt on, I walked in on her, almost shit my pants, walked into the door, almost shit my pants a second time, then stumbled down the hall Hunchback of Notre Dame–style.*

Oh, and I'd thought about her naked at least seven times since Jason had sat down.

Clearing my throat, I waved him away. "Misunderstanding. I tripped, she tripped, and you know how those things go."

"Hey," Max's voice called from behind me. Every nerve ending was waiting to hear Milo's voice chime in. "We on break yet?"

"Coffee's on and Mom went to buy fresh doughnuts from town."

"She gets to leave?" Max sounded irritated as he walked over to the coffeepot and poured himself a mug.

I snorted.

He drank coffee like a pansy.

Was he pointing his pinky finger?

No, wait.

Ah, well played. Not his pinky finger, definitely a middle finger directed at me. Nice.

Milo wasn't usually into his type—you know the kind, metrosexual to the extreme, tight pants, tight shirts, smooth skin.

Oh, good. Smooth skin? So I was what? Noticing his skin now? I must have hit my head harder than I'd thought.

"Uh . . ." Jason pointed at my face.

"What?"

"You're bleeding."

"Where?" I patted my chin and then my lips, and my fingers came away wet with blood.

"Nosebleed!" Max shouted and then took a step toward the table, only to fall onto his knees, then his back. Out cold. He was completely passed out.

"Someone help me!" Milo shouted from the doorway.

"I'm bleeding!" I retorted.

"He could have a concussion!"

"Good!" I roared.

Jason and Milo stared like I'd just told them I poisoned Max's coffee and smiled while doing it.

Cursing, I got up from the chair and grabbed a towel. Holding it to my face, I moved Milo out of the way so I could help Max.

"He's seriously out cold." Jason poked Max's face.

"Is that normal?" I whispered.

"You're the firefighter!" Milo hit me on the back of the head. "Don't you have any EMT skills?"

Hell, yeah, I did. I just didn't feel like exerting myself—not for Max. Because he'd seen her naked. *Naked!* Damn she'd looked soft, all creamy, and smooth, just begging for a man's hands to—

"Hey!" Milo swatted the back of my head again. "Help him!"

"Right." Without thinking I slapped Max on the cheek.

His eyes flew open. "What the hell!"

"You okay?"

"Why'd you slap me?"

"Looks good." I pinched his cheek, slapped it again, and then got up. "He'll live."

"That's it?" Milo stomped her foot. "He'll live? What kind of public service employee are you?"

I shrugged as Max tried to sit up. "I'm going to puke," he said.

"Scared of blood?" *What a pansy-ass!*

"Yes," he said through clenched teeth.

"Here, I'll help you to your room." Milo got the guy to his feet and started walking with him down the hall, only he was clearly too heavy for her.

Rolling my eyes, I stepped between them and grabbed Max by

the shoulder even though I wanted to grab him by the balls and give an unfriendly tug. "I got it."

Max's eyes widened. "Actually I'm feeling a lot better."

"No," I said smoothly, as I took him down the hall, "you aren't."

He met my gaze, then smirked. "Well, well, well, it seems I've found your weakness, Clark Kent."

"Huh?"

"You like her?" Max asked.

I was so shocked I almost dropped him. "Nope."

"Oh." He nodded. We were almost to the bedroom door. "It's cool. I mean, what's not to like? Killer body, beautiful smile, tight little ass—"

"Keep talking and I'm going to break your jaw."

"A tiger in—"

I let my fist fly, knocking him off his feet and into the bedroom. He hit the floor with a thud. "I warned you."

Max smiled through the blood running from his nose into his mouth. "Cute. Little. Ass." He made a spanking motion with his hand. I saw red. As in completely lost my shit and charged toward him, only to hear Milo scream my name just as I was ready to land another blow to his face.

"Colton!" She wrapped her arms around my body and pulled me back. "What the hell are you doing?"

"He was—" I pointed at the bastard only to see him give her an innocent smile, then wipe his cheek. Holy hell, was he fake-crying?

"It hurts," Max said with a pout. "Kiss it and make it better, baby?"

"You've got to be shitting me," I muttered under my breath.

"Of course!" Milo released me and went to Max. "What happened?"

Max's eyes gleamed. "I fell, Colton tried to catch me but he wasn't fast enough. Weird, huh? It seems to be his thing. Not being first, not being fast enough . . . losing things." Max's middle finger saluted me as he gave Milo a tight hug.

"Just stay here." Milo kissed his forehead. "You deserve a break."

"My ass." *Didn't mean to say that out loud.*

"And you!" Milo stomped over to me and pinched my arm. "Leave him alone!"

"Fine!"

"Fine!"

"Fine!" Max repeated after both of us. I lunged for him again but was blocked by Milo. She quickly shut the door and crossed her arms. The hallway was too small for one of our fights.

"What?" I shifted nervously.

"You punch him?"

"He was talking about your ass." I leaned in and pressed her back against the wall.

"At least *someone's* talking about it." She tilted her chin in defiance and glared.

"What the hell is that supposed to mean?"

"You know exactly what I mean!" She poked my chest, and I had to admit it felt like Mighty Mouse had taken possession of her finger; it hurt like hell.

"Stop." I grabbed her hands.

She fought against me, struggled as I tried to pin her arms to her side, and then lost complete control of my body.

And kissed her.

Again.

# CHAPTER THIRTEEN

## MILO

He was kissing me.

In the hallway.

My fake boyfriend was in the guest room a few feet from me, and Jason was down the hall.

It was one of those kisses that girls talked to their friends about—possessive, dark, hungry. I loved it—I wanted to wrap my arms around his body and pull him against me.

Instead I barely kissed him back.

Because that wasn't how I wanted him.

Out of anger? Out of jealousy? Because he was pissed that I was finally out of his reach? As his lips moved across mine, I pondered— almost like time stopped—I let myself wonder. Would I ever be okay with half of him—the jealous half—when I wanted the whole package? The sucky thing about unrequited love is you're never quite sure where the other person stands—you can only make assumptions based on your own feelings and then hope to God it's at least better than all-out rejection. Yeah, they may say they want you, but is the want as strong as yours? Does it hurt? Does it ache?

Gently I pushed Colton away. "We shouldn't."

"Sorry." His voice was hoarse. "I don't know why I keep doing that."

"Yeah, you do," I said as the cold weight of sadness and rejection settled in my stomach like a bag of rocks.

"He's not right for you."

"And you're the expert because . . . ?"

Colton touched his forehead against mine. "We've been friends since first grade—when you used pink marker to write your name all over my bedroom walls."

Tears threatened, making my throat close up. He was being kind—what I'd actually done was write "Colt+Milo=Love."

"I know you." He put so much emphasis on the *you* that I started to shake. "Trust me."

"How can I trust a guy who doesn't even know what he wants?" I pressed against his chest. "What do you want from me?"

His eyes darted back and forth with uncertainty.

And that was the thing.

I wanted him to be certain. No hesitation.

"I want—"

"I'm home!" Mom called from the kitchen. "Doughnuts! And time to regroup! The decorators are here so we'll need everyone to pitch in! Let's go, troops!"

Colton stepped away from me and walked down the hall toward the kitchen.

With a sigh I went back into the guest room to rescue Max.

He was sitting on the bed texting.

"Wow, miracle recovery," I joked.

He looked up from his phone and grinned. "Theater camp. Admit it, you totally dig my acting skills."

"Those acting skills earned you a punch in the jaw."

"False." Max crossed his arms. "My acting skills got you and Colton to talk. Geez, you two are so boring. I swear he wears his thoughts on his face. I'm surprised Jason hasn't figured it out and murdered him already."

"Jason wouldn't do that."

Max rolled his eyes. "Um, he would, he'd even ask for my help to dispose of the body. You're a no-fly zone, get it? Trust me on this. Oh, and P.S. Colton thinks you have a nice ass."

"He said that?" Nerves exploded in my stomach.

"No." Max's grin grew. "I did and then he punched me."

"I'm confused."

"If he didn't care, he wouldn't have punched me."

"Maybe he was defending my honor."

"Honor my ass. He wants to plow into said honor and make little babies and name his firstborn Max."

"Huh?"

Max got to his feet and winced, his fingers grazing his jaw. "Good right hook, though, I'll admit. It hurt like hell too. The things I do for my friends."

"Best friend."

"Best friend." Max gripped my hand in his. "Trust me on this, Milo. I know what we're doing is working. We have the rest of the day to get him to drop his pants."

"Um." I raised my hand.

"Question?"

I nodded.

"You may ask."

"Can he keep his pants on?"

"Why the hell would you want his pants on when you want them off? Girls are weird."

"Max." I tugged him toward the door. "Pants stay on."

"Off."

"On!"

"Pants off!" he roared, pushing open the door.

Jason stood there, his hand raised as if to knock, a look of complete embarrassment washing over his features. "I, er, uh, Mom's back and, I think, um . . ." His eyes darted between us. "Continue." He shoved his hands into his pockets and shuffled down the hall.

"Yeah." Max nodded. "Pretty sure your family thinks you're a whore now."

"Thanks." I snapped my teeth together.

Max put his arm around my shoulder. "Stop being so argumentative and I'll stop raising my voice."

"No deal."

He sighed. "Well, can't say I didn't try. Now, listen to me very carefully."

We stopped right before the kitchen. Max turned me to face him and cupped my face with his hands. "Eye of the Tiger."

"The song?"

"The focus comes from the song." He snapped his fingers. "Now, who's the tiger?"

"Colton?"

"Good!" He patted my cheek. "Now, I want you to envision a doughnut."

"What—"

"Envision the doughnut, damn it!"

"What flavor?"

"Does it matter?" He sounded irritated.

"To me it does!"

"Chocolate. You're a chocolate doughnut."

"Got it."

"Now," Max whispered. "Become the doughnut."

"Huh?"

"Speaking English here. Become the doughnut."

"I'm a . . . chocolate doughnut . . . I taste . . . good?"

"Sell it!"

"I taste awesome!"

"There you go!" He slapped my butt. "Now when you walk in there, be the delicious chocolate doughnut, all right? You taste good to him, you smell good, you look good. Be. The. Doughnut."

We walked into the kitchen hand in hand.

Mom was eating a doughnut and talking animatedly with my dad. Jason had both a chocolate and a vanilla doughnut stacked on top of one another, and Colt was sitting at the end of the table reaching for a vanilla one. He looked up, our eyes locked.

Colton lifted his vanilla one to his lips and bit in. Yeah, I was so-o-o-o that doughnut, my entire body tingled.

Max smirked and slapped my butt again and whispered low in my ear. "Like I said, be the doughnut, feel those teeth, get your man, bitch."

# CHAPTER FOURTEEN

## MILO

"Now." Mom dabbed the corners of her mouth with her napkin and made eye contact with each and every one of us before setting her napkin back down and clearing her throat. "The rest of the decorating crew should be here any minute and—"

"No!" A shrill scream erupted from the front room.

Max started choking on his doughnut. I hit his back and gasped as Jayne stomped into the kitchen, murder in her eyes. "It's all wrong!"

"What is?" Dad asked, calmly setting his cup on the saucer and sending her a bland glance.

"The colors!" She stomped her foot.

Colton made eye contact with me and Max and shook his head.

"Honey, you said you wanted red." Aw, poor Mom. The situation was like trying to calm a hippo. It was going to charge you regardless of how nice your words were. It would charge you, and then either drown you or sit on you.

"I said," Jayne screamed, angry crimson blotches staining her cheeks, "*watermelon* red!"

"Red's red," Max muttered.

"What?" Jayne glared at him. "What did you just say?"

All color drained from Max's face. "Jason's dead, he's going to be dead, because it's always the groom's fault, right? Ha, ha." He forced a smile while Jason glared at him from the opposite end of the table.

"I can't believe this!" Jayne started pacing. "The wedding's tomorrow! Everything has to be perfect! It's not going to match!" She stopped pacing. Yeah, any second now, the hippo would charge. "What are you going to do about it?" And there it was.

She directed the question at my mom.

Max slid a knife toward Jason and nodded encouragingly.

Jason eyed it like he was seriously contemplating cutting the bitch, while Colton calmly picked up the weapon and put it in his lap.

Mom stood. "Now, I understand you're upset."

Jayne flinched, a look of utter disbelief etched into her features.

"But you need to calm down."

"Ooo." Max shook his head. "Bad call, real bad call. It's like telling the shark you're a surfboard. It's gonna bite you to make sure you aren't a seal, then it's going to kill you anyway. My leg, my leg!" I swatted him on the stomach.

Jayne's eyes narrowed as she zeroed in on Mom.

The chairs around the table made a resounding *screech* as we all pushed away.

"You said you would take care of things," Jayne said in a low voice. "*This* is not taking care of things!"

"Listen, sweetie—"

"We're getting married!" Max yelled.

"What?" Colt roared as a doughnut went flying out of his hand, missing Jason's bad eye by a centimeter.

Everyone fell silent.

"Surprise!" Max lifted his hands into the air. "You know this is as good a time as any, babykins." He reached for my hand; I pulled away and glared. Son of a monkey! What was he doing?

"Oh, honey!" Mom ran around the table and pulled me in for a hug. "We never thought it would happen for you!"

"Gee, thanks." Nothing more encouraging than your own parents assigning you to spinsterhood and a childless future. "But we're not—"

"We are!" Max gritted his teeth and nodded toward Jayne.

The fire left her.

She slumped into her chair. "Max? You two, you're really getting married?"

"Yup." He gripped my body so tight I wheezed. "Come here, baby."

He kissed me hard in front of everyone.

I could have sworn I saw the knife in Colton's hand twitch.

"A toast!" Mom clapped and pulled out a bottle of champagne.

"But it's like ten thirty in the morning?"

I received four stares that would have frozen hell over. "I mean, sounds great!"

Max whispered in my ear, "If we don't have alcohol, we'll all per-ish. I'm fully convinced that I may not make it to my next birthday if I have to stay in this house any longer. Keep an eye on Jayne, make sure she stops harassing your mom, and I'll go fix things."

"How the hell are you going to fix things?"

He shrugged. "I know people. Now, toast to our future, and stand close to Colton. Oh, and remember our talk."

"Doughnut, I know, be the doughnut."

"No." He rolled his eyes. "Eye of the Tiger!"

With that he snuck out of the room, taking my dad with him.

"Where are they going?" Mom asked, setting the champagne on the table.

"Boy stuff, wedding stuff," I lied.

"This has just . . ." Mom wiped a tear from her eye. *Oh, crap.* "Turned into the most . . ." And here comes the chin-trembling. "Beautiful . . . wonderful . . ." And the waterworks. "Day!" She wiped her cheeks.

"Mom, don't cry." I said it like an order.

"I'm sorry." She sobbed harder.

"Mom, seriously, stop crying."

"I'm just so proud of you!"

"Well, I did just solve world hunger by way of marriage to Max." I clenched my teeth.

"Really?" Jayne perked up.

"Yeah." I nodded enthusiastically. "Because that's what weddings do, cause peace, not war."

Jason choked on his champagne.

"Milo?" Colton handed me a glass of champagne. "Can I talk to you outside for a minute?"

"Sure." I grinned, knowing full well he was going to want answers. *Great! Just more lies to cover up more lies. Fantastic.*

# CHAPTER FIFTEEN
## COLTON

*Married. Married! Married?* Right, however I said it, however I looked at it—all I saw was freaking red. The color of rage, and if I was being completely honest with myself? Pain with a hefty dose of regret. *Damn it.*

I downed the rest of my champagne and set the glass on the table just as a decorator came by and set down a large contraption that I'm sure they patterned after a medieval torture device.

"What is that?" I pointed.

"Holds the cake." The guy shrugged and walked off, just as Milo came up and eyed the same thing.

"Is this an S&M wedding or what?"

Yeah. My thoughts totally went there.

Milo with a whip.

Dressed in head-to-toe leather giving me bedroom eyes. My groin tightened as a vision of her waving the whip around floated around my head. Damn, was it wrong to love the violence as much as I did?

I mean, come on, the woman was walking violence, she practically ran into that one!

Coughing, you know, to hide my embarrassment and make sure her eyes weren't anywhere but my face—lest I embarrass myself and have to jump in the subzero-temperature pool—I got her attention.

"So what's up?"

"Married?" I squeaked. "You're shitting me, right?"

Obviously I missed my calling as a therapist or a motivational speaker.

"I guess so." Milo's cheeks burned red. "I mean, I guess . . . yes?"

"You guess so?" I snapped, my temper taking over. "You guess so? You freaking *guess* so?" I stomped over to her and grabbed her by the shoulders. "You don't guess about marriage, Milo, it's for life! What the hell is wrong with you? You're still as immature as ever. Shit."

"What?" Her shrill voice made me want to duck and cover.

*Whoops.* I was about to get punched again—this time purposefully.

"I'm not immature." She tried jerking away from me, but I wouldn't let her. Pissed as hell, I held her firm.

"Yes. You are. You don't just marry an asshole because he asks you!"

"He's not an asshole!"

"You were naked!"

"What?" Jason roared, coming up from behind us. "Who was naked?"

"Should I tell him or will you?" I sneered.

"Everything okay?" Max jogged over, hands in the air as if he was innocent, the bastard, the perverted bastard!

"Well?" Jason crossed his arms.

"She had her shirt off . . ." I nodded. "For him!"

"You looked too!" Max pointed.

Jason's eyes widened and then narrowed in on me.

"No." I clenched Milo harder against me. "No, it's not like that."

"It is," Max said helpfully. "Totally like that. I was innocent in the whole thing. Honest, I don't even know what he's talking about."

I was going to strangle that guy with my bare hands.

"You saw my sister naked!" Jason shouted.

Everyone poured out of the house, including Jayne. *Oh, good, witnesses.* At least everyone would know how I was murdered. See, and this was why I never made a move! It wasn't about just losing her friendship—but also about losing his.

"No." I swallowed. "You've got it all wrong."

"He stared at my boobs," Milo said triumphantly.

Jason lunged for me. I released Milo a bit abruptly, and she went sailing into the cake stand metal thing.

Lots of crunching and cursing followed.

Jason froze.

I closed my eyes.

And Jayne started crying—wailing was more like it.

"My cake stand!" she shouted into the sky like a howling were-wolf, her feet stomping all over the grass, killing any seeds that hoped to sprout into beautiful greenery. "You ruined everything!"

"Thank God," Jason said under his breath.

"Arrest her!" Jayne pointed at Milo. "Arrest her now!"

"For shit's sake, she's injured!" I went over to grab Milo; instead she pushed as I pulled, making me lose my balance and fall backward—directly into the pool.

When I resurfaced, I saw Jason pull out handcuffs.

"What the hell are you doing?" I shouted as I tried to get out of the pool.

"Destruction of private property!" Jayne sniffed. "And Jason's a good cop, a fair cop, so he's arresting her."

Max, the bastard fiancé, covered his mouth with his hands.

And Mrs. Caro, having just arrived with the champagne bottle, started sipping directly from it.

Now *she* had the right idea.

"Son." Mr. Caro stepped forward. "Maybe this is—"

"No." Jason nodded. "Jayne's right, fair is fair, I'll just take her into town. I may be gone for a few hours, but—"

That rat bastard! He was going to get out of all the wedding decorating!

Not my proudest moment, but once I was on my feet I charged at full speed toward one of the wedding decorators, knocking the candles out of her hands. They hit the ground with a thud.

"Uh-oh." I said dryly, holding out my hands. "Arrest me too, Jason, looks like I destroyed more property."

Max walked over to me and whispered under his breath, "Kind of defeats the purpose when you jump on the bomb after it's gone off, but carry on." He stepped back.

"Fine." Jason grabbed me with his right hand and Milo with his left.

"Max, do something!" Milo shouted.

"Right." He nodded and then reached for the champagne bottle. "May I?"

Wordlessly Mrs. Caro handed it to him and he took a big swig.

"That's not doing something!"

"It's all I've got. I'll bail you out in a bit, Milo, just try not to hurt them—after all, they're stuck in the car with you, not the other way around."

Jason seemed to think about this for a moment, if his wincing was any indication. Yeah, that's right, he was probably recalling all the violence done to him in the past twenty-four hours.

"Second thoughts?" I asked.

"Get in the damn car, both of you."

Rachel Van Dyken

I went to the front.

"Oh, no, hell, no." He opened the back. "You were arrested, friend, you get to ride in back. The guys at the station are going to give you hell for this."

"Let them." I smiled from the backseat as Milo scowled. "We leave prison and go to jail. I choose jail."

The car fell silent.

"Hey, can we stop at Starbucks?" Milo asked as we pulled out of the driveway.

# CHAPTER SIXTEEN
## MILO

"When I said be the doughnut . . ." Max leaned across the bars of the county jail. "I didn't mean to literally *be* a doughnut and get your ass arrested by some doughnut-eating copper."

"Hilarious."

He looked behind him and smirked. "Hey, they were hungry."

On the officer's desk was an entire box of doughnuts. Max thought it would help lower the tension while he tried to work his magic and bail me out of jail. Then again, it wasn't like we hadn't been treated nicely.

And it wasn't the first time I'd been in jail with Colton.

All in all we'd been in jail at least three times together; our own parents called the cops on us once. Embarrassing to say the least. I knew Jason wouldn't have put us behind bars if there had actually been criminals in the small prison, but it was just us, which meant he either was trying to make a point or needed our undivided attention away from the family.

He was in the corner smiling—happy as a clam, that one.

Max's cell phone rang. "Be right back."

"Max, don't leave me!"

"Hey, I have a wedding to save. You come second." He blew me a kiss and walked off.

"Real winner you have there." Colton snorted. "Seriously, I think sainthood's in his future."

"Cold?" I tilted my head as Colton let out another shiver. He was still wet from his swim in the pool. He'd been given a blanket, but I could tell he was still suffering from the chills.

"Nope. Hot. Sweating. Sweltering. On fire." He glared.

"Fine, drop your pants and prove it."

"That proves nothing!" he roared, turning bright red.

"It proves a little bit of something." I winked. "Wouldn't you say?"

"I hate you so much right now."

"Funny." I took a seat next to him. "You said that last time we landed in jail."

"Again." He scowled. "Your fault."

"Please!" I pushed against him. "That was not my fault and you know it!"

"You set the church on fire."

I picked my fingernails and looked down. "In my defense, you pushed me into the candles."

"Because you taunted me!" His voice rose. "You kept saying, 'Colton, jump! Colton, jump!' It was the frigging balcony!"

"Ten feet." I fought to keep my voice even. "I told you to jump ten feet."

"It was more than ten."

"*No*, it wasn't."

"Was." He held up his hand. "Can we not argue?"

"Why? You gonna shut me up by kissing me again?"

He froze and then stared at my lips like a man starved. "That depends, are you going to kiss me back like you have been? Every. Damn. Time."

If he thought I was kissing him back that second time then he was in for a rude awakening.

"Are you blaming me for kissing you back?"

"I'm just saying it takes two." He shrugged. "That's all."

"Right, that's all you're saying."

"Damn it!" He grabbed me by the shoulders. "Do you have to have the last word all the time?"

I didn't say anything.

"Well?"

"I was trying not to have the last word."

He released me and ran his hands through his hair. "Damn it to hell, you irritate me."

I flinched and slid away from him.

"Milo," he growled. "Not like that, it's not—"

"You're free!" Max appeared in front of the cell, dangling handcuffs in front of his face. "Oh, and I'm keeping these for later."

He winked.

I made a face. "Gross."

"Gross?" Max and Colton said in unison.

"Er, metal. I don't like metal during—" Yeah, I couldn't finish that sentence.

"Sex." Max nodded. "Sorry, babe, I know I should remember you don't like to be handcuffed to the bed, it's just I always seem to forget, you know? Maybe it's because most of my fantasies involve— oh, look, there's Jason, be right back!"

I stole a glance at Colton. He was gripping the edge of the bench so hard I thought he was going to go all Hercules on me and break it off.

"You okay?"

"Please don't talk," he said in a hoarse voice.

"Look, he's kidding, Max and I haven't . . ." I shook my head. "We haven't."

"You haven't?" His eye twitched.

"Done that."

"Handcuffs."

"Sex."

"I bet he's terrible at it. I bet he cries afterwards and sucks his thumb," Colton said, laughing, and then he swore. "Said that out loud, didn't I?"

"Yup."

"Shit."

"You okay?" I touched his shoulder.

"No." He bit down on his lip. "I'm either going to kill your fiancé by the end of the day or just drown myself in the pool. At this point it's a toss-up."

"If I punched you, would you feel better?"

"No." He swallowed. "But you could kiss me again."

My head snapped up.

"Sorry, guys!" Max walked back up to the cell and laughed. "That Jason's hilarious. Oh, and P.S. We're sending the local Russian mafia after Jayne." He made a cutting motion at his throat.

"He's kidding." Jason came up behind him and slapped him on the back.

"Pity," I grumbled.

"Dude, why are you even marrying her?" This from Max.

Jason paled and looked down at the ground, shuffling his feet. "It's complicated, and it's kind of also why I wanted you guys away from Mom and Dad for a bit."

"Could have done without the whole prison thing," I said sourly.

Jason shrugged. "Jayne would have followed us to a bar, plus she has spies everywhere."

"Shocker." I grumbled. "So un-complicate things for us."

"I have to marry her."

"No you don't!" Colton shot to his feet. "You really don't!"

"I do!" Jason yelled. "She's pregnant, okay?"

After a few seconds of tense silence, Max spoke up. "Why does that matter?"

Okay, so he voiced what everyone was thinking.

"Because," Jason said through clenched teeth, "It's a small town and everyone knows everyone's business and if I jilt her at the altar while she's pregnant, I'll never get to run for mayor."

"You want to be mayor?" I squeaked out.

"Eventually." He sighed. "Look, I've tried to get out of it, but no matter what I do, I look like a bastard. What type of guy gets a girl pregnant and then doesn't stay with her?"

"Question?" Max raised his hand. "How do you know she's telling the truth?"

Jason's eyes narrowed. "Because she told me."

"Do you have a picture of the love child? Have you gone to the doctor with her? Is she really sick? Gaining weight? Losing weight? Does she pee all the time? Has she started shopping for maternity clothes? These are the things you need to know."

Squinting, Jason cursed and then looked down at the ground. "No to all of the above, but—"

"Theater camp." Max shook his head. "I'd bet my nonexistent cat on it. She's playing you. Girls are careful about who they sleep with, and it's possible that I have it on good authority she's on birth control."

"What the hell?" Jason roared.

"A little bird named Reid told me. Don't worry about it." Max waved him off and let out a long sigh. The type of sigh I was beginning to notice meant he was going to do something really stupid.

"A guy's gotta do what a guy's gotta do." Max shook his head. "Man, that bus just keeps driving by and your whole family just keeps pushing me under it. Milo, you get that, right? Like I'm going to need psychological help after doing what I'm about to do."

"Uh-oh, what are you about to do?"

"Save the day. I've always wanted to be a superhero."

"Max—"

"Nope." He held up his hand. "I'm going to need a hell of a lot of Gatorade, a camera phone, and a saw."

"You can't kill her!"

"The saw is so I can break out of the wooden box she's going to put me in once she realizes what I'm doing. Geez, Milo, I'm not a psychopath."

Colton grunted.

"Hilarious," Max said dryly. "Okay, Jason, punch me."

"What?" we all yelled in unison.

"I'm fighting for her honor. Trust me, the girls like a guy who fights for them. She'll see the black eye and hit on me again. " Max shrugged. "Punch me."

"I'm not going to punch you!" Jason looked horrified.

"I'll do it!" Colton shouted.

"Not helping," I moaned.

"Punch me, you pansy-ass, good-for-nothing, backwoods, doughnut-eating son of a—"

Jason's fist flew across Max's face.

He stumbled to his knees and sighed. "Grandmom, is that you? I can feel her, she's so cold . . ."

"Hell, Jason, you could have killed him."

"What's going on in here?" The chief walked in and looked around.

We just pointed to Max.

"Damn bus," he muttered.

# CHAPTER SEVENTEEN
## MILO

"Okay, you have two hours to save his life." I gripped Max's shoulders. "Can you do this?"

He rolled his eyes. "Blindfolded." Max shivered in disgust. "Not that I'm wanting to be blindfolded anywhere near that girl."

"You're pretty cool, you know that?" Jason nodded, apparently they were friends now that they weren't behind jail bars anymore. "Oh, and P.S.: If she finds out it's a setup, I'm denying all charges and throwing your ass in jail. Again."

"On what charge?" Max asked.

"Illegal prostitution," Jason answered.

"Wouldn't look so good on my job applications . . ." Max tapped his chin, then turned to me. "Okay, spray me."

"You're really letting him go through with this?" Colton grabbed me by the shoulders and pulled my body away from Max. "He's your fiancé."

Max raised his hand.

"Not now, Max," I snapped.

"No, I think he should get to talk. After all, he's going to go whore himself to Jayne and sacrifice his manhood on the altar of skank."

"Thanks, man." Jason exhaled. "Good to know I could still be stuck with that altar every freaking day of my life. Anyone have any whiskey? Anyone?"

Max reached into his back pocket and pulled out a flask.

"Seriously?" I smacked him in the chest.

"A dying man's wish," Colton said defensively. "If he wants to bathe in whiskey while mermaids sing to him—let it happen."

"Mermaids don't wear tops," Max apparently felt the need to point out.

"Focus!" I clapped my hands. "You go in, you get out."

The guys burst out laughing, then Max added, "Aw baby, that'll leave her frustrated, now won't it?"

"I hate men," I muttered.

"You love us," Max declared loud enough for me to want to punch him in his perfect face. He put on his leather jacket and grabbed the keys to his car. "Wish me luck!"

"Good luck!" we said in unison.

"Dude has balls." Jason stared after Max like he was some sort of Greek god or football legend.

"Of actual steel," Colton agreed once Max had gotten into his Jeep.

"Cheers, to the man we all hope to be one day." Jason lifted the flask into the air and drank, then passed it to Colton.

"Unbelievable. He's not going to war, people! He's going to a bachelorette party. He's surrounding himself with horny bridesmaids and trying to get the spawn of Satan to admit she isn't pregnant, which by the way we still aren't sure of. Most likely he'll be drunk within two hours and end up in prison."

"Have you met her friends?" Jason asked.

"Well, no."

"Yeah." His jaw flexed. "Let's just say their idea of a party involves tea, biscuits, gossip, and a hell of a lot of perfume."

"But it's a pre-bachelorette party?" I watched as Max drove away.

"Pre-bachelorette party? Hell? Both are interchangeable." Jason nodded. "Trust me, the guy's going to hate women for at least a week, hope that's not a problem."

"Nope."

"Thanks, Sis."

"Huh?" I was too busy hoping my friend came back safe, and not in a box like he assumed. "For what?"

"Letting us use your fiancé." Jason nodded. "I have to admit Colt and I were worried that you jumped into things—but he's pretty straight, you know?"

"Yeah." I didn't know what to say so I just agreed. "He's pretty awesome."

"Anyway, I guess, without getting too sappy, Colton and I are proud of you for settling down with such a stand-up guy, right, man?" He hit Colton on the back, but Colton didn't say anything for a minute. Instead he stared right through me, and then he seemed to collect himself.

"Thrilled." He cleared his throat. "Tickled abso-freaking-lutely—pink."

"All right." Jason clapped his hands. "I'm going to go take a quick nap in the guest room so Mom can't find me, then get ready for the rehearsal dinner. You coming, Colt?"

"Give me a second." His eyes didn't leave mine.

I shifted nervously on my feet.

We were standing in front of the house. The afternoon breeze picked up, making me shiver.

"What's up?" My ability to sound unaffected as he continued to stare was basically nonexistent. I scratched my arm nervously and waited.

"You and me."

"You and me, what?"

"It's time."

"Huh?"

"I cheated too."

*What. The. H.*

"You have a girlfriend!" I shouted, fighting the tears as they pooled behind my eyes.

Instead of answering he took my hand and led me back into the house, then downstairs into the basement.

I needed a damn paper bag or something! *Girlfriend! This whole time! What the crap?*

Shaking, I sat down on the couch and waited for him to give me the talk. You know the one, where the guy pats your hand, tilts his head two degrees to the right, gives you the pity smile, then angles your chin and does the soft punch across your jaw, like "Here's lookin' at you, kid."

I had that speech memorized.

He gave me that stupid speech when I was sixteen after I mauled him with my lips.

To be fair, the whole underwear incident killed whatever romance could have been there, and, well, technically, I mean he was eighteen, meaning it could be considered, er, slightly illegal. But not really, I mean who actually paid attention to those laws?

"I cheated," he began again. My heart dropped. *No. No. No.* "At Ping-Pong."

My head snapped up. "Come again?"

"You had a few points that I didn't count, you couldn't tell because it looked like it missed the table—the ball hit the table three times that I said it didn't."

"You sick bastard!" I roared, launching myself across the couch as I beat him with my fists. "You took an oath! An oath to always be honest and true when we play games! We shook hands, asshole! We exchanged spit—"

"My favorite part," he grunted from underneath me, as I continued to beat on his back. He turtle-shelled me so I couldn't actually hit anything of substance. "You worn out yet? Or you wanna go another round?"

Heaving, I fell back onto the couch. "I'm gassed out."

"Losing your touch."

I raised my hand then dropped it when Colt started talking.

"Do it," he challenged. "Slap me, see what happens."

Not one to back down—no matter how gorgeous the taunting face might be—I raised my hand again, but Colt intercepted it, flipped me off the couch onto my back, and pinned me to the floor.

Cool air hit my stomach as my shirt hiked up toward my bra. Colton kept his hands pressed against mine—which were still pinned to the floor like freaking thumbtacks.

"Easy or hard?" he breathed, lips an inch from mine.

I refused to answer.

"That's what I thought—for you—always hard."

I smirked and arched underneath him.

He cursed and looked away. "Right, so I cheated, sue me. At least I apologized, and I'm willing to spend the next two hours watching one, not three, *Star Wars* movies, so take your pick."

"You will?" I couldn't keep the excitement out of my voice. When we were little Colton and I had had movie night every night of the summer. Jason always fell asleep so it was always me and Colt eating popcorn, playing games, getting sick off candy.

The two things I missed more than anything in the world while I was away at school? Colton and movie night.

My throat got all thick as I tried to rein in my emotions, but that's the thing, when you want something so bad that you ache— you can't help but respond with raw emotion.

Forget wanting the guy to kiss me—those feelings would always be there. But having him as my friend? My lifelong friend who used to do the Chewbacca voice for me so I wouldn't be scared of Storm-troopers in my closet?

Colton was always there for me when I needed him, maybe that was part of my driving force, part of my desperation. He was every-thing I'd always wanted.

We fell asleep together on the couch—always.

Until I started to grow up.

And then we sat in separate chairs, until finally we stopped movie night altogether.

"You okay?" he whispered, gently releasing my hands and brush-ing some hair from my face.

I nodded, not trusting my voice.

"I'm sorry." His eyes searched mine. "I'm sorry that the minute we started getting older these things, these moments, stopped. I'm sorry I stopped playing dragon slayer. But I'm not sorry for fighting with you."

"What?"

His forehead touched mine. "I'd rather fight with you, bicker with you, every damn day of my life than have nothing at all. I'm selfish enough to want any piece of you—even if it's the bad, the ugly, the ridiculous. So even if you hated me, I'd still die a happy man—because I'd still be on your mind."

"Yeah?" I said weakly. My heart soared, even though I told it to stop getting its hopes up. Colton wasn't being romantic, he was just reminiscing about childhood.

"I'd rather be on the receiving end of a black eye from you—than the receiving end of a kiss from another." He kissed my cheek, his five o'clock shadow rubbing against my skin. "Truth."

# CHAPTER EIGHTEEN
## COLTON

There are moments. Moments that, for some reason or another, God gives us in order to help move us forward toward our destiny.

She was my destiny.

And somehow I'd missed it—I'd missed *her*.

Instead of choosing her every chance I was given, I justified the reasons I should walk the other way, or ignored the fact that I was given a choice in the first place. I made excuses and blatantly ignored those precious moments.

The other thing about the moments that are given to us? They're limited. We don't get an endless amount. If you miss them, they're gone. Time machines don't exist; you can't go back and fix what's been broken.

I hated to admit that I was afraid—terrified that because I'd done the wrong thing for twenty-three years of my life, I wasn't going to be given the chance to make it right.

She was getting married.

To Max.

Though I didn't want to throw stones, their relationship seemed at odds with itself: one minute they were all over each other, the next they looked—funny, almost like they were best friends more than lovers.

Sighing, I tried to focus my thoughts on the movie.

Not Max.

Not Milo.

And definitely not the fact that the reason I canceled movie nights so long ago—was that I couldn't control myself anymore.

She remembered things differently—she was innocent.

I, however, knew exactly how things had gone down so long ago. She'd kissed me, and I'd thanked God that she embarrassed herself in the process so I didn't end up taking her virginity in the basement.

Jason would have killed me.

I would have killed me.

Movie night was never the same. I couldn't sit next to her without thinking about her soft lips—I couldn't breathe the same air without her scent floating into my personal space.

It was a living hell and I felt like a sick pervert for being a senior and crushing on a sophomore, and not just any sophomore, but Jason's little sis.

"Hey, this is the best part!" Milo smacked me in the shoulder as the movie started. She used to make me read the beginning to her because she said my voice sounded cooler.

I swallowed the dryness in my throat as I tried to lean back and relax. Yeah, it was going to be the longest two hours of my life.

Milo reached forward and paused the movie. "We have to go back, you missed the beginning. You're supposed to read it out loud."

"Shit."

"Huh?"

"Nothing." I tried not to sound tense as I waited for her to rewind the movie. I read as fast as I could, allowing the hum of my own voice to block out the arousal I felt at her arm grazing mine.

One hundred and thirty-six minutes of hell. I knew exactly how long the movie was because, though I wasn't a fan of math, it was the only thing keeping me from ripping her clothes off.

If she moved one more time I was going to lose my shit. We were at the very end of the movie when things shifted. With a sigh she leaned on my shoulder and tucked her legs underneath her.

I looked down—I swear it was only to see what she was doing.

And saw directly down her shirt.

*Shit balls.*

She shifted a bit more; I still stared.

I was going to burn in hell.

And the way would be paved with two very perky, very round breasts. There were worse ways to go, right?

"Luke!" Milo yelled, then shifted closer to me; my body hummed as her head rubbed against my chest.

I imagined her screaming my name.

And suddenly developed a not-so-little problem.

Gently I tried to move away to hide any evidence of where my thoughts were going. I sure as hell didn't want her to think I had a thing for Luke Skywalker or—God forbid—for robots.

"No." She yawned and burrowed farther into my chest. "I'm comfortable."

I almost yelled, "I'm dying!" Instead I smiled like an ass and said, "Yeah, me too, this is nice."

The hell it was.

I could have sworn my body parts were yelling at me as my muscles strained against my clothes. *Free me, free me!* I shifted again. *Take her, take her!*

When I didn't think I could take it anymore—when I honestly contemplated faking a seizure so I could get some relief from her hot little body—the lights went out—along with the TV.

"Sorry!" Mrs. Caro called from upstairs. "My fault! We blew a breaker! Hold tight."

I was tight all right . . .

The holding was the issue; any holding and I'd make a fool out of myself.

With a sigh I tried to shift away again, but Milo grabbed my hand. "I'm still scared of the dark."

"Yeah, well, I'm still scared of sharks, so we can still be friends."

"I hate that word."

All I could hear was my own heartbeat in the silence. "Yeah," I whispered. "Sometimes I do too."

The lights flickered back on. I turned my head and saw that Milo's mouth was right next to my chin. Damn it, that woman had never understood her own beauty. She was the type of girl who terrified guys. Her features were too perfect, soft where you wanted them, and sharp where it mattered. Her high cheekbones and pouty lips made me nervous enough—add in her caramel-colored eyes and I was basically a man hypnotized.

I was the damn snake in a basket—in more ways than one.

Ah, if only she had a magic flute.

"You guys down here?" Jason called. The sound of his feet hitting the stairway reminded me of a clock ticking. With each step I pulled farther and farther away from Milo, and in return, her face clouded—as she pulled further and further into herself.

Another moment I'd missed.

Another moment I'd purposefully ignored.

My heart clenched as I wondered if that was the last one I was going to get.

# CHAPTER NINETEEN

## MILO

"*Star Wars.*" Jason shook his head. "I thought you won at Ping-Pong?" His brows drew together in confusion.

"He cheated." I punched Colt in the shoulder and received a blank stare in return. What was wrong with him? His skin was so flushed it looked like he was feverish.

I'd thought he was going to kiss me.

Weird, because when I thought he was going to yell at me he kissed me, and when I thought he was going to kiss me he pulled away.

Men. I would never understand them. Ever. Colton was hot and cold, we'd share a moment and then he'd change, acting like he was irritated with me.

My phone went off.

"Max?" I all but yelled. The guy had been silent as the dead for the past two hours. I could only assume he was finding success.

"Ax." His voice sounded like gravel churning in a washing machine. "Tell Jason and Colton to have the ax ready, I'll be there in five." The phone went dead.

"Er, guys, that was Max."

"He's alive!" Colton shouted, seeming genuinely surprised at this revelation. "Damn it."

"Pardon?"

"Nothing." He looked away.

"He said he needs an ax?"

"An ax?" Jason rubbed his chin. "What the hell would he need an ax for?"

I shrugged.

"Well." Jason nodded toward the stairs. "We owe him for going into the lion's den balls to the wall—lets go get the ax from the garage and wait for him outside."

Five minutes later Max pulled up to the house.

Nothing could have prepared me for what I saw when he stepped out of the Jeep.

His shirt was half ripped from his body, he had scratches up and down his arms, his eye looked slightly puffy, and lipstick stained his collar. To add insult to injury I could have sworn he was missing a substantial amount of hair on the right side of his head—and he had a limp.

"Ax," he mouthed, then he cleared his throat. "Give me the ax."

Jason's mouth opened and closed as he handed Max the ax.

Max didn't say hi.

He didn't smile.

He gripped the ax in his hands, and walked right by us, like a man on a mission.

"What the hell is he doing?" Colton asked aloud.

"Beats me." Jason shrugged.

Max continued to walk. He finally stopped in front of a giant oak tree—and started swinging.

"I'm a man, damn it!" He swung again, pieces of bark flying as he massacred the old tree, swing after swing after swing.

"Ahhhh," the guys said in unison as if they suddenly understood why my best friend had lost his mind.

"What? What's this ahhh?" I shrieked. "Max grew up in the city. Until today I didn't even think he knew what an ax was, let alone how to use one!"

"Manhood." Colton shook his head. "Poor bastard, he's trying to find his manhood. Damn, that pre-bachelorette must have been hell."

"The things he's seen." Jason's voice cracked. "And actually survived." He removed his baseball hat and bowed his head. "He's a hero."

"He had tea," I argued.

"Some wounds . . ." Colton agreed. "They're on the inside? And that's what's going to be the hardest for him, you know, when he pulls through."

"Pull through, big guy!" Jason shouted. "You pull through!"

As if Max had just earned a Purple Heart, he dropped the ax onto the ground, fell to his knees, and gave out a war cry.

"Let it go, buddy." Colton nodded. "You let it go."

You know that whole *Men Are from Mars, Women Are from Venus* theory? Yeah. I was living it. It was as if they were from a different planet.

Slowly we walked toward Max as he rose to his feet.

I opened my mouth to talk but Colton put his hand over my lips and said softly, "Give him a minute. Victims of this type of assault usually need to be the first to speak. It gives them their power back."

I rolled my eyes as Colton removed his hand.

Max lifted his head and shuddered. "I . . . I . . . I think I need to take off my pants, make sure my balls are still there and all, you know, just in case."

"Dude." Jason put his hand on Max's shoulder. "You do what you gotta do, you hear me?"

Max nodded, then looked at me. "You're one of them."

"Huh?"

"A girl," he spit. "You're one of them."

"Uhhh." I reached out but was nearly tackled to the ground as Colton grabbed me from behind.

"They touched me," Max whispered.

"Good touch or bad touch?" I asked, struggling in Colton's arms.

"Safe to assume, it was probably all bad touch." Jason nodded knowingly like he was an authority on the topic. "By the looks of the marks on his arms, there was an obvious struggle."

Max nodded.

"Yeah." Colton released me and went over to Max's side. "A few pieces of hair missing—catfight?"

He nodded again as Colton leaned in and sniffed.

"They marked you."

He whispered. "At first it was fun—"

"Always is." Jason whistled.

"And then . . ." Max swallowed. "They all wanted to hang out and I couldn't keep their names straight, and then I was hit with this wall of expensive perfume, and someone put something in my drink, I swear I'm not making this up! I swear they drugged me. The room started spinning, they all wanted to talk, and then a few of them started asking me why men were stupid, and then they said we hate men . . ." His lower lip trembled as he repeated in a weak voice, "We hate men."

"Dude, you don't have to keep going," Colton said tenderly. "We got you."

"No." Max stumbled away. "This needs to be said, damn it!"

Colton held up his hands in defeat.

"Then they . . ." Max rubbed his arms. "They touched me, ripped my shirt open, said that I was the only one who understood them, that I wasn't like those other men and then . . ." His eyes found mine. "They kissed me, like seven of them, all bridesmaids. A few were married. I tried to pull away but they have claws masquerading as acrylic nails. They dug into my skin, and the crazy part, when I tried to run—they liked it!"

"They do, man, they always do. It's like getting attacked by a bear, you just cover your head and pray it will be over soon."

I raised my hand. "Hate to break up whatever this is, but I gotta know, did Jayne own up to it?"

All eyes flashed to my face like I'd just told Max to go back to the women and offer himself up as a male sacrifice.

"No." Max's shoulders slumped. "Every time I tried to get her alone, another girl would follow. Jayne just wasn't into the whole scene. She was on her phone half the time talking to some chick about the bachelorette party." He rolled his eyes and mimicked her voice. "'Oh, it will be so fun, shooters! I can't wait for shooters.'"

I jumped into Max's arms in excitement.

He dropped me and started screaming, "Get away, get away!"

"She's not pregnant!" I yelled.

"How do you figure?" Colton pulled me away from a shaking Max.

"Would you be excited about shooters if you couldn't actually drink them?"

"No," the guys said in unison.

"So it wasn't all for nothing!" I said in a chipper voice, then added more solemnly, "You'll be honored for what you did, Max."

He closed his eyes and nodded.

"So." I clapped my hands. "Who's going to infiltrate the bachelorette party?"

All the men pointed at me.

Yeah, no way was I getting out of that one.

# CHAPTER TWENTY

## MILO

Two shots of vodka, a strong cup of coffee, and a shower seemed to bring Max out of his crazy mood, though he was still pretty jumpy. When I handed him the coffee he hissed.

I smacked him and told him to behave, and then he looked like he was ready to cry. *What the hell did those women do to him?*

"You sure you're going to be okay?" I took a sip of my own coffee.

"Of course," he said smoothly. "But, er, the only way I was able to actually *leave* was because I told them I was gay."

The coffee spewed out of my mouth directly onto his face and crisp white shirt.

"Worst. Day. Ever." He reached for a towel and wiped the coffee dripping from his chin. "And now I have to change."

"Sorry," I mumbled. "So now not only are we hopelessly in love, but engaged, and you're gay? How does that work?"

"Oh, no worries." He set the towel down. "I was gay until I met you—then I fell in love and decided to try to be straight."

"Try?" I repeated. "Can't we change the story to something like you play both fields but mine is more fun?"

"Hmm." He rubbed his chin and considered it for a moment, then nodded. "That works too."

"My mom's going to freak out." I pressed my hands to my temples and pushed away the beginning of a headache.

"Chill, it's not like anyone's going to say anything. Besides, they were drinking so much wine it'll be a shock if half the bridesmaids even make it to the rehearsal dinner. You'll see."

An hour later the entire wedding party—including both families and the nice pastor—were seated at the table.

I kept getting looks of pity from the bridesmaids, as if they knew my dirty secret.

Max mouthed, "Sorry" as he took a sip of wine and then dug into his salad.

Honestly, things had progressed pretty well; everyone was getting along. Jayne was doting on my brother enough to make me want to puke up shrimp cocktail and Colton was sitting on my right.

Our arms kept brushing.

I swear I only contemplated throwing him onto the table and having my way with him like three times. Maybe four. Or five. Or six.

"Milo?" Colton nudged me. "You okay?"

"Yeah, why?"

"You were counting out loud and gripping your fork like you wanted to impale someone."

"Stress," I said through clenched teeth.

His eyebrows drew together in concern. "Drink more wine."

"Good advice."

We tapped glasses just as my mom stood at the head of the table and clinked her crystal water goblet with her fork. "I just wanted to take some time to say thank you to everyone who helped us set up today."

*Everyone* being the three of *us*. But whatever.

"And, I'm so . . . glad." She totally choked on the word *glad*. "That Jason has found someone worthy of spending his life with."

I grinned at Jayne: ah, true love.

She wiped a few honest-to-God tears and stood up to give my mom a hug. The same woman she'd bitched out a few hours ago.

Her parents hugged my parents.

Let's just say there was a lot of hugging.

"I have something to say . . ." I pushed out of my seat and stood.

Jayne smirked in my direction. I smiled politely back. "Jason, I'm so glad that after all those years getting high in the garage, you finally saw the light, and instead of growing pot, like you originally intended, went to college and came back a better man. It honestly"—I wiped my own fake tears—"makes a sister so proud to know that you chose to be drug-free and dumped that really pretty Victoria's Secret model in pursuit of more homegrown"—I sighed—"options." I looked around. "Because let's be honest, that girl would have led you back down that rabbit hole. Instead of the high life, you're here. In the suburbs with Jayne. It sounds so idyllic, don't you think? At any rate." I lifted my glass. "I'm just proud of you for pulling your life together and marrying such a winner!"

I sat.

Nobody raised their glasses.

Finally Max stood and said, "Cheers."

Everyone drank while Colton pinched me under the table.

Jayne was seething; I could practically see smoke billowing out of her ears as she glared at me from across the table.

As Max opened his mouth to speak, one of the drunken brides-maids sputtered out, "Aw, I wish you weren't gay, Max."

My mom dropped her wineglass and gasped as my dad swore graphically in front of the pastor.

The pastor held up his hands and said something about how all God's children were welcome at the table.

Max's wide eyes found mine.

I pinched Colton. "Make it better!"

His chair tipped over as he stood and shouted, "I kissed Milo!"

And silence.

"That was making it better?" I whispered.

"You bastard!" Jason yelled.

"Oh dear, oh dear." The pastor reached for his wine, then made the sign of a cross in front of his chest as my mom reached for my dad's shoulder and gripped his tie instead, which formed a noose around his neck.

I think he wanted her to pull.

# CHAPTER TWENTY-ONE
## COLTON

"Jason!" I held up my hands. "Calm down!"

Wrong thing to say. Milo tried to stand in front of me, but Jason easily moved her out of the way.

I should have run.

Instead I faced him like a man.

And got punched in the face.

Yeah, the wedding pics were going to hell in a handbasket.

"Damn it!" I fell over my chair and continued swearing until I made eye contact with the pale pastor across the table. "Sorry, uh, sir."

He shook his head and took a substantial drink of wine.

"Mom, we'll be right back," Jason yelled as he grabbed me by the collar of my shirt and booted me out the door. Once we were in the yard, I turned to face him only to receive another punch in the face.

"What the hell, man?" I tasted blood in my mouth.

"You kiss her after she's engaged?"

"Wait!" I held up my hands. "What?"

"You waited until she was taken before you kissed her, you bastard!"

I backed up and shook my head. "I'm confused."

"Why couldn't you have realized you loved her before she got engaged? She's probably confused as hell and it's all your fault! And she doesn't deserve that and neither does Max, and you're a bastard for waiting twenty-three years to finally see what the hell was in front of you all along."

"Holy shit," I whispered. "You knew?"

"Dude." He shook out the hand he'd used to punch me. "I thought you were going to cry when she left for college, and then all those other chicks you were trying to date . . . I bet they paled in comparison. Then, when you knew she was coming back for the wedding, you wouldn't leave me alone! You kept asking if you looked okay, was your hair too long? When was Milo coming? Was she bringing anyone? Hell, you're a wreck."

"I love her," I blurted.

"No shit."

"She's marrying the wrong guy."

"Well, apparently he's gay, so at least you got that going for you."

I laughed. Like really laughed. How the hell had things gotten so screwed up? Jason joined in until we were almost rolling on the ground.

"I thought it was one of those unspoken rules," I finally said. "I thought you'd be pissed."

Jason folded his arms across his chest. "It's my job to be protective—which I was—but I trust you, man. If I was really against you guys hooking up—do you think I would have left you alone as much as I did? I swear I gave you so many chances to tell her and every single time you punked out."

"Yeah," I said, irritated as hell with myself. "I did."

"So." Jason shrugged. "Now what? Are you going to pull your head out of your ass or are you going to let her marry Max? Because frankly, they don't act like they're in love, and let's be honest, that guy is as metrosexual as they come. Don't get me wrong, he's nice, but . . . I always pictured her with a homegrown guy, not a city one."

"He likes nice clothes." Why the hell was I defending him?

"He was also taken advantage of by women today—women!" Jason laughed. "If he can go into the lion's den and come out alive—you can admit to Milo you have feelings. Hell, you don't even have to drop the L-word."

"And if she rejects me? And I ruin our friendship?"

Jason was silent for a minute.

I waited.

"Love is never a sure thing, man. You're never going to be totally certain that the person you offer your heart to will accept it with open hands, but if you don't take that risk you'll never reap the benefits of what it has to offer. If she rejects you, at least you can move on with your life. Because right now you're in a hell of your own making. Any movement on your part, whether it's towards her or away, is better than staying where you're at."

"Hell," I mumbled. "That was a lot of wisdom you just spouted right there."

"Yeah, well." Jason laughed. "Clearly that weed I used to smoke didn't kill all my brain cells."

We burst out laughing.

Jason sobered first, his eyes flickering to the ground as he shoved his hands in his pockets. "I screwed up."

"No."

"Yeah." He rolled his eyes. "I dated her because I was bored, screwed her because she was hot, and proposed because I was trapped. So much for love, huh?"

"We'll figure it out." I tried to sound convincing even though I knew the odds were stacked against him. "You ready to head back in?"

"You go." Jason turned away and started walking toward the end of the backyard, where the swing set stood. "I need a few minutes."

"All right." I walked back toward the house. Instead of going in the back door I went around the front, with the idea of avoiding the watchful eyes of the wedding party. Hopefully the rehearsal dinner was winding down—I'd rather set myself on fire than sit one more minute at that table.

The bachelor party couldn't come soon enough. Jason had one best friend, me, and a dozen other friends we all hung out with regularly. He'd picked six of the closest ones to stand with him at the wedding. The ones not in the wedding would all be at the bachelor party, which meant I could get away from Milo for a few hours and try to figure out what to do. Being next to her was too distracting . . . and I was pretty sure if I tried to kiss her again she was going to knee me in the balls. I needed a better plan of action.

"Max!" Milo whispered. "What are we going to do now?"

"I want to go home," he said in a low voice. "Bitches be crazy and I don't have enough strength to say no. I don't have it in me, I'm juiced out, my number's been called, Milo. Shit, the things I do for my best friend."

Milo clapped her hands. "Focus, Max. What's the story?"

"I love you," he said in a bored voice.

Curious, I stepped around the corner. No chance in hell I was sticking around to watch them make out. But they were by the bathroom under the stairs, apparently strategizing, so I paused, remaining hidden in the entry. Seemed I wasn't moving any time soon after all, especially considering I'd heard Milo say, "What's the story?" Indeed. What was the story? My ears strained to hear their conversation.

"Make it sound more convincing."

"My heart," he drawled. "Oh, how it beats for you. Thump, thump, thumpity thump—"

"I'm not Bambi!"

"Aw, Thumper, what a guy, I used to love that rabbit—"

"Max!" she snapped.

"Fine. You're beautiful, I want to screw your brains out and—oh, look, cake."

"No cake until you make it more convincing."

"Remind me of this moment," Max said in a lofty voice, "when I ask you for a favor, and trust me, it's going to be huge. I mean I'm pretending to be your fiancé."

"Your fault," she said in an irritated voice. "You were only supposed to be the boyfriend."

"And now I'm gay . . ." he continued.

"Again, your fault."

"And now they want to hear our engagement story."

"Again," Milo snapped, "your fault!"

"I panicked!" he said in a strained voice. "I'm still not myself . . ."

She groaned and reached for his hand. "Fine, we'll just say we met at school, fell in love, and you proposed under the stars."

He scoffed, "Please, I have more romance than that in my pinky finger."

"You proposed during poetry class?"

"No." He released her hand and tapped his chin. "They'll never believe I would be so unoriginal."

"Need I remind you . . . They. Don't. Know. You."

"A concert." He snapped his fingers. "A concert I put on for the homeless—"

"Oh, hell."

"—and I wrote a song for you. The last song, and I asked you to come onstage. You cried. People in the audience wept, I mean full-on wept when I told them the story about how you rescued me from my nasty drug addiction and involvement in the Mafia."

"You're Canadian."

"And then." He snapped his fingers again. "As I held your face, like a mother holds her newborn babe close to her teat . . ." He nodded. "You whispered, 'Max is the love of my life. I'd die for him, and yes, yes I'll marry you, and bear you seven children to fill the house with laughter. Yes, I'll sleep with you every night—naked, because you hate clothes—and I swear, nay, I vow . . . '"

Holy shit! Were his lips trembling?

"'To make dinner for you. Every. Damn. Night.'" He lowered his head. "Yes, it's perfect. All right. I'm ready. Let's do this."

"If I could go back in time, I'd burn down that theater camp."

"Wasted opportunities." The guy winked. "Besides, you freaking love me. I saved your ass from a boring existence pining away after Colton these last four years."

"Yeah." She nodded sadly. "That's true."

My entire body froze, my heart shattered in my chest. She was sad. I'd made her sad. She'd done this because I was too afraid to speak up. Then again, Milo had really outdone herself to convince me she didn't want me, but that didn't matter. Her face fell as Max wrapped his arms around her in a gesture of comfort.

Screw that. Dragon slayer was back, and look, I actually had one to slay now—his name? Max.

# CHAPTER TWENTY-TWO

## COLTON

No, flipping, freaking, bloody, damn way!

Hell.

Hell.

Hell.

That little brat!

It was a tie between wanting to strangle her with my bare hands and wanting to swat that tight little ass for putting me through twelve hours of hell. There I was, hiding beneath the stairs like some lovesick bastard and she'd been playing me the whole damn time! While I was elated that Max was nothing more than a friend, my fingers itched to do something violent as they shared an easy smile with one another and a parting hug. I'd been ready to go to PRISON over their kissing. I could have been someone's bitch for no reason.

"Hey." Jason came up behind me. "You okay?"

Pure evil filled me, and I didn't bother to hide it. I smirked as I imagined all the hell I was going to put them through. "Oh, I've truly never been better."

"You look homicidal."

"I may be . . ." I said, my body humming with excitement. "You know we never fully congratulated the happy couple."

"Huh?" Jason's eyes pinched together. "What are you talking about?"

"Follow my lead." I couldn't have hidden the grin even if I'd wanted to.

Milo and Max were sitting in their seats at the table, drinking wine, pretending everything was peachy as shit, and I was about to not only rain on their parade, but shoot thunder and lightning out of my ass.

Okay, maybe not my ass.

Too far.

So I'd been under a lot of emotional stress—it ended tonight. And I was going to put her through—I looked down at my watch—about twelve hours of the same type of hell she'd put me through.

Then I'd kiss her again.

Marry her.

Lock her in her room and think of about a million different ways I could punish her—as well as make her remember that she wasn't anyone's but mine.

"So." I rubbed my hands together and cleared my throat to get everyone's attention. "I would just love to hear how you two got together."

"Who?" Mrs. Caro looked around the room in confusion.

"Max and Milo."

"What?" Milo coughed.

Max grinned. "You see, it really is a funny story."

"Max . . ." Milo warned.

"Really?" I crossed my arms. "I'd love to hear it."

Max's chest pumped up a bit and then his eyes narrowed in my direction. Shit, he knew. *He* knew that *I* knew.

"I sang a song." He stared right through me, and then broke eye contact as he addressed the table and stood. "You see, I love to do charity."

"No he doesn't." Milo laughed, trying to get Max to sit down. "He hates charity, really, just . . . hates . . . helping people." Her voice died at the end a bit as she stared into her wine, most likely wishing she were drunk already.

"My little love muffin's so humble." Max patted her head, then pinched her cheek. She hated being pinched. Pinching Milo was the equivalent of attaching a piece of raw steak to your ass and running full blast toward a tiger.

Needless to say, it wouldn't end well.

Unless you were the tiger.

"That's so sweet." One of the bridesmaids leaned over the table, her cleavage almost dipping into her chocolate cake.

"That's me—sweet." Max winked. "Anyways, as I was putting on this concert for charity, inspiration hit."

"I'd like to hit something," Milo muttered.

"Why not propose onstage?"

The girls giggled.

Max returned their grin and shrugged. "I invited her onstage, played the song I wrote for her, and got down on bended knee. It really was romantic, I—"

"I wanna hear it," I shouted.

"What?" Max covered his choke with a cough. "Hear what? The proposal?"

"The song." I grinned. "I want to hear this . . . romantic song. I mean, shouldn't we all get a chance to share this special moment?" I looked around the room.

Mr. and Mrs. Caro sighed into each other's arms, the bridesmaids all but swooned out of their chairs, and Milo killed me with her eyes.

I blew her a kiss.

Her cheeks stained red. "Um, guys, Max is probably tired from . . . earlier today, and it's getting late. We don't want to miss the bachelorette and bachelor parties."

"We have time!" Jason said from behind me.

I loved that man. No, seriously. Loved him.

"See?" I clapped. "No problem."

"Great," Max said through clenched teeth. He walked toward the middle of the dining room and then paused. "You know, I, uh, noticed you don't have a piano, and it's really difficult without the proper, um, notes."

"Oh." I walked up to him and patted his back. "No worries, man, you just sing from the heart. A cappella is fine. Right, everyone?" I started chanting, "Max! Max! Max! Max!"

With each shout Milo sank lower and lower into her chair.

When the noise died down, Max cleared his throat and looked heavenward. Yeah, both he and Milo deserved what was coming.

"Milo," he crooned in a voice that wasn't at all terrible, *damn it!* "My special girl! I want you to know, if I could, I'd give you the world." He paused dramatically, then fell to his knees.

*No freaking way.*

"My heart and soul are yours alone my special, pretty, pretty"— he paused again—"lady. So promise me now you'll forever be my baby."

He ended on a high note that I'm pretty sure no man can reach unless he's been castrated. Then he got up from his knees and bowed.

Bastard.

Milo was the first on her feet, clapping wildly. "It's even better than before."

It was on. They had no idea of the war they'd just started. They might have won one tiny battle—but I was going to be the ultimate victor.

So without thinking, without really even realizing I was talking out of my ass, I said, "When did you propose?"

"A few months ago."

"What day?"

Max grinned. "Tuesday."

"What Tuesday?"

"March fifth."

"Was a Wednesday."

"How do you even know that?" Milo snapped.

"Whoa there!" Jason reined me in for a hug. "Sorry, he's been hitting the bottle."

Just kidding. I hated Jason.

"Bachelor party?" He pinched my neck so hard I was going to have bruises.

"Yeah." Defeated, I started to walk away, but stopped. "Hey, Max, you should come too!"

"He can't!" Milo blurted.

"He should," Jason agreed. "Come on, Max, come hang out with the guys."

Max took a few steps away from Milo but kept looking back as if to ask permission. I wrapped my arm around his shoulders and squeezed so tight I was pretty sure his back popped. "We're going to do some male bonding and shit."

"You know," he whispered under his breath, "I don't know how you know, but you know . . ."

"'Bye, guys!" I yelled over his voice, then whispered, "Yup, and you're going to help me or I'm sending you into the bachelorette party with some Skinnygirl Sangria and a box of chocolates."

He gasped, his eyes round with horror. "You wouldn't!"

Ha, I had him by the balls. Time for a twist. With a malicious grin, I waited for him to keep arguing. "I've already done my time!"

"Then play by my rules," I said coolly. "Agreed?"

"Milo's going to kill me." Max reached for my hand and sealed all our fates.

# CHAPTER TWENTY-THREE
## MILO

"Milo?" Mom came into my room, took one look at me, and burst out laughing. Tears streamed down her face and a few hiccups followed.

"Do I look that awful?" I pulled the red leather dress lower, but it was useless. Every time I tugged it just snapped back to where it had been before, which was so inappropriate I probably wouldn't be able to bend over without getting arrested.

"No," she sighed happily. "It's just—you have it on backwards."

I swear. Sometimes it feels like I'm not even a girl. Colton doesn't think of me as a woman and now I can't even put on a dress right? I was being overdramatic, but still. It was the stress speaking.

I felt like crying.

See? This was why Colton didn't notice me! I wasn't sexy! I wanted to be sexy! And Max went and sang that nice song and now Colton believed him, but if they got him drunk—God help us all if they got Max drunk.

He was one of those emotional drunks. You know, the type who sits at the bar and makes friends with everyone, then continues to buy shots for people, until he bursts into tears and exclaims in slurred language that he loves everyone so much that he wishes he could just give the world a hug.

"Crap." I sat on the bed with a huff and crossed my arms.

"Let me help." She pulled me to my feet.

Fifteen minutes later the dress was on the right way, with the plunging neckline in the front and the high part in the back. I suddenly remembered why I'd bought it in the first place without trying it on. It was gorgeous. It fit really tight—I'd probably have three bruised ribs come morning, but it was worth it.

"Shoes." Mom clasped her hands. "You need something tall."

"But that'll make the skirt look shorter!"

"Exactly." She waved. "Oh, look! You still have your shoes from homecoming."

I winced.

Homecoming. The senior homecoming I attended with my own brother. Awesome, like I wanted to relive that sad moment.

"Put them away, Mom."

"No." She put them by my feet and held them stable while I stepped in. They were strappy black six-inch heels—at least they still fit. "Now twirl."

I twirled lamely on the heels, nearly toppling over.

"You need makeup."

"Mom, I don't—"

"Sit!"

After another twenty minutes, I was convinced I could make a good living as a prostitute.

Eyeliner thicker than sludge? Check.

Short tight dress? Check.

Stripper heels? Check.

Bright red lipstick? Check.

"Perfect!" she shouted. I'm pretty sure she was slightly inebriated. "Now go have fun!"

I hobbled down the hall and then hobbled down the stairs and out the door, and made my way to my car.

Our town might not have had a lot of places to eat but it had a crap-load of bars. The girls wanted to do a bar crawl from one end of Main Street to the other, finally meeting up with the guys around midnight.

I locked the car, jumped out, and nearly sprained my ankle. Yeah, I was going to be that girl at the end of the night—the one who carried her shoes and caught a foot disease from the dirty sidewalk.

I would rock it in Vegas.

I continued to tell myself that the evening was going to be fine; it had to be fine. All I needed to do was make sure Max kept his hands to himself and Colton actually noticed I was wearing a dress and had boobs. Yes, that was my mission: make Colton aware of boobs. If all else failed, I'd have some drinks, stay silently in the corner, and pray that Max practiced self-control. He was an adult, after all.

• • •

"Drink! Drink! Drink!" the bar patrons shouted as Max downed his third shot in a row.

The dude could party—had to give him that.

We'd been at it for at least three hours and he was still as solid as Fort Knox—never slipped up once about the engagement.

It wasn't that he didn't talk about it.

He talked all damn night. Milo this and Milo that. I almost ran my head through the bar.

"So . . ." I waved my hand at the bartender and pointed at the empty glass. "Tell me about Milo. What's the deal?"

"Uh . . ." Max looked away. "I gotta go to the bathroom and—"

I grabbed the collar of his shirt and tugged. "Sit."

"Drinking game!" Jason came up behind me. "Cups!"

"Did someone say cups?" Jayne shouted, coming into the bar with a few of the bridesmaids, and finally Milo.

Shoes in hand, Milo, my newfound nemesis, walked into the bar, cringed, then set eyes on me. Her smile grew until she saw Max. She looked beautiful. Her short dress didn't hide an inch of her legs. I drank my fill and then cursed when I realized I was supposed to be paying her back for all the hell she'd been putting me through. Did payback include licking those thighs? The bartender dropped a shot in front of me. Bottoms up. Something told me I wouldn't be doing any licking for quite a while. Not if I had any control over it. Pain first, pleasure second.

She mouthed a curse and stomped over to us, crossing her arms over her really, *really* nice-looking chest, and glared. "Max?"

"Wazzup?" He swayed on the barstool. I held him steady and prayed he wouldn't reach for her purse and puke in it. "You're super pretty tonight, Milo, so . . . cold."

"Cold?" she repeated.

"Yeah, like, you must be freezing since you're naked!" He laughed at his own joke, then yelled, "She's naked, she's naked!"

"Strip poker!" Jason shouted above the music. "Back room!"

"Yay!" Max clapped his hands and slid off the barstool, swaying on his feet as he pulled Milo in for a hug. "You smell like . . . happiness."

"What's that smell like, big fella?" She sighed, helping him walk with us toward the back of the bar.

"Sex."

"What?" She laughed nervously.

"Never. I never did it, Colton. Never. Ever. Ever. Ever. She said no." His face drew into a tight pout. Holy shit, was he crying? "'No, Max!' She yelled at me, Colton." He was enunciating my name like a three-year-old. "'No, Max, I don't want the sex like that!'"

"Max, maybe you should drink some water—" Milo's gaze searched around the bar.

"No." He pulled away, collapsing against my chest, then reached for my shirt and gripped like a freaking vise. "And you know what happened?"

I shook my head.

"I say okay Milo, you don't want to ride the gluteus maximus."

"He's drunk," Milo said in a desperate voice. "And that's not how you—" She stopped talking.

"How you what?" I leaned in. "What, Milo?"

"How you . . ." She chewed her lower lip.

Max patted my face with his hand. "She's a virgin," I think he meant to whisper. Instead he said it so loud that the rest of the people walking to the back room with us paused.

"I want to die," Milo muttered.

"Naked time!" Max launched himself from my arms and stumbled into the room. Poor guy was going to be puking his insides to his outsides come tomorrow morning.

Milo and I followed the herd into the room. I grabbed her hand and held her back. "So, you've never slept with your fiancé."

"Nope," she said tightly. "He's, uh . . . Catholic."

"Really?" I nodded.

"Very, very, very devout." She looked down.

"Interesting. Is that why his Jeep has one of those Star of David stickers on it?"

"He's a Catholic Jew," she said in a desperate tone.

"Oh . . . I wonder what that's like . . ." God, she made it so easy.

Jason whistled loudly and pointed at the group of people filing into the room. "Who's in?"

"Milo is!" Max shouted, jumping into the air, his landing missing the chair by an inch.

"Me too." I winked. "I love a good game of poker."

"You gonna keep your pants on this time," Milo teased, "or are you gonna freeze your balls off like the Christmas of 2010?"

"There's a difference between choosing to lose and actually losing," I snapped back.

"You still lost."

"Milo, it was four in the morning! I had to be at the firehouse at five! I was exhausted!"

She grinned saucily. "Still lost!"

"Girls against boys!" Max danced around the table. Great, so he just got his second wind. "Shots!" I swear his yell shook the walls.

"Oh." Jayne smirked in our direction. "Milo's not drinking."

"She's pregnant too!" Max yelled.

The noise died.

Jason groaned into his hands while Jayne stiffened and set down her bottled water.

"Jason," she said in a stern voice, "I thought we weren't telling anyone yet."

"Well." He looked pissed. "They all know now, don't they?" *Uh-oh, drunk Jason was going to make an appearance.* "Now everyone knows why the hell I popped the question! God knows I wouldn't have done if you hadn't trapped me."

Oh, shit.

Max's eyes widened. "So no game?"

"No game," Jayne said in a stern voice. "Ladies, let's go."

With that they walked out, leaving Milo and Max with us and the rest of the guys.

Milo started walking toward the door, but I grabbed her hand before she could make it very far. "And just where do you think you're going?"

"Home?"

"Milo bought a goldfish once." Max felt the need to pipe up. "She was drunk. She loved that fish." He snorted. "I ate it." With a laugh straight out of a low-grade horror film, he collapsed into giggles, then yawned. "I'm so tired."

The next thing I heard were snores.

And he was still standing.

Shaking my head, I pointed at him. "Real winner you got there."

She tilted her chin up. "He's sweet."

His snore turned into more of a growl, getting louder by the minute.

"I can see why you're waiting to have sex with him—waiting for that special moment, huh?"

"I told you he's religious!"

"Bullshit." We were standing nose to nose.

"Are you calling my bluff?"

"Sweetheart, you can't even keep your lies straight anymore."

"You can't tell when I lie." She poked my chest with her finger.

"Fine." I stepped back. "Let's play a little poker. Winner takes all. Shake on it?"

She slammed her hand against mine and tried to let go, but I pulled her in until she hit my chest. "Oh, and by the way, it's strip poker, with shots, and I haven't lost since I was sixteen."

"What the hell were you doing playing strip poker at sixteen?"

I smiled. "Care to find out?"

# CHAPTER TWENTY-FOUR
## MILO

A sudden chill enveloped me as I tried to hold my head high—they say that even whores still have their dignity when they first start their profession. Great, so now I was comparing strip poker to selling my body.

The world around me was fading in and out. Every time I blinked at Colton, my body swayed slightly to the right. Fine, so it had been a really long time since I'd actually drank. Wasn't that a good thing? I mean, I'd only been twenty-one for a year!

"You fold?" Colton leaned forward, his naked chest touching the table like an erotic kiss. I licked my lips to keep from drooling and focused on his abs as they rippled with each breath he took.

It would probably be inappropriate to reach across and touch them—you know, like a comforting touch. I bet he'd be warm and hard, so damn hard. My fingers tingled as I reached into the air. Good thing the room was swaying because the next thing I knew, my hand was on his warm skin.

A few male chuckles erupted around me.

In the distance I heard Jason's voice. "She's done, man, let's go."

"No!" I shouted, standing. Another gust of cold air slammed against me. I'd lost both shoes and my dress. So I was basically standing in front of them naked.

Then again, they were all in their boxers—I was a pretty good poker player, no matter what Colton said.

"We're finishing this round!" I swayed a bit, then flipped my cards over. "Hah!"

I had a flush, high card was king of clubs, which basically meant I was going to wipe the floor with his ass!

"So classy," Colton muttered.

Apparently I'd said that last part out loud.

"You're right." He fidgeted with his cards, then threw them in the pile. "You win. Good job, Milo."

He was too calm. My eyes narrowed as I leaned my hands against the table and stared him down. "Let's see the cards."

"No." He crossed his arms. "You win. Game over."

"The hell it is!" I reached for his cards, but was intercepted by his hand before my fingertips could graze the edges.

"Can't you just win like a normal person?" he yelled.

"Colt." Jason yawned. "The guys are gonna drive me and Max home, you got Milo?"

"Yeah, I'll take her drunk ass home. I've had one beer—I think I can manage." I waved them off as they all staggered out of the room, leaving me and Colt completely alone.

I scowled. "I'm not drunk and you're a cheater."

"Good God, woman!" Colton shouted. "You won the freaking game. Why can't you just do one of your triumphant winner's dances and be done with it?"

"Because you're a liar from the pit of hell!" I swung my hand into the air and nearly toppled over. He grasped me again, but this time I collapsed purposefully against his chest, then slyly snaked my hands down to the table.

"Remind me to hide all tequila next time we hang out." His breath was hot on my body.

"Next time we hang out, you're going to be the one naked, mister!" Wait, how was that a threat?

He smirked, his eyes taking me in from head to toe. "You promise?"

I shivered—but it wasn't because I was in nothing but my bra and panties, nope, it was because he was looking at me—like really staring at me, not through me, but at me, like he was about to devour me.

I almost forgot about the cards in my hands.

Quickly I glanced down, and swore a blue streak as I turned over the cards, revealing a royal flush.

"You lying"—I pushed against his chest—"lying, lying, lying, lying pants-on-fire bastard of a whore!"

"Huh?"

"A royal flush!" I squeaked.

Colton groaned. "Calm down, Milo."

FYI, telling me to calm down after I've had a few shots, been cheated out of a good card game, and had enough sexual frustration to make a priest weep . . . not the best idea the man ever had.

Without thinking I simply launched myself into the air. In my mind I was graceful, like a gazelle frolicking across the Sahara.

What I probably looked like? A half-naked prostitute with mascara smudges under her eyes strangling a nice young man with good intentions and a kind smile.

"Milo!" Colton grabbed my arms but it was useless, my hands had already grabbed his neck and started to squeeze as I wrapped my legs around his body and fought against him.

I don't know at what point it happened—but within a few

seconds, my body realized that there wasn't much clothing separating us from each other.

The air shifted as Colton's face changed from irritated to starved. His hands tightened around my waist as our eyes met for a heartbeat.

"Colt—"

I wasn't allowed to finish.

Partially due to the fact that the end of his name was drowned out by his mouth. Growling, he threw me onto the poker table and hovered over my body.

Chips went flying to the floor.

Cards fluttered in the air.

And I kissed him back—I kissed him back so hard that my mouth ached. My body ached—every damn thing ached.

• • •

*Stop!* I yelled at my body. *Stop, damn it!* I was ruining everything! How was I making her suffer if I was kissing her?

Hell, she had a way of discovering every single nerve and exploiting like it was her job to drive me insane.

Her body arched under my hands as I slid them down to her hips. Everything I'd wanted from her was being presented to me—on a literal table. All I needed was the silver platter.

But she was drunk.

Which made it unfair.

It also made it not count.

With a feminine sigh, she wrapped those tight little arms around my neck and pressed herself against me.

Yeah, it was going to take the power of a god to push her away.

She tasted like tequila—and I was pretty sure I was going to kill Max, because all I kept thinking was that she tasted like happiness, which made me think of sex.

And tasting her.

Over and over and over again.

My fingers dug into her flesh as my mouth left hers and started blazing a trail down her neck toward her bra strap.

"Don't stop," she mumbled.

Let this be a lesson to every lady out there. The minute you open your damn mouth. Poof. Magic moment? Gone.

It was enough time for me to pull back and realize.

I didn't want her on the table, not like this.

And if Max was an honest drunk—which I'm assuming he was, considering he'd admitted to eating her pet goldfish—she was a virgin.

To hell with that.

Taking her virginity on a poker table after she'd drunk enough tequila to breathe fire? No. Not her. Not the girl I'd loved for my entire life. Not the girl I dreamed about when I closed my eyes. Not the girl I lived for when I woke up.

"Milo." I kissed her one last time across the mouth, my lips brushing hers, memorizing her taste just in case it was longer than a day before I would be able to partake again. "You're drunk."

"I'm not that drunk," she pouted.

"What's six times seven?"

"Unfair!" She laughed. "You know sevens were the hardest for me to learn."

"Milo . . ."

"Forty-something."

"Close enough," I grumbled, then slowly removed my body from hers, which felt like leaving a part of my soul and walking in the other direction knowing that I would never be fully complete without what I left behind.

But I wasn't leaving her.

I just didn't want her *that way*.

Actually I wanted her in every way—repeatedly. Except this one.

Milo's eyes snapped open and with a curse she scurried off the table and reached for her dress. "S-sorry."

"Ah." I put my hand through my hair. "No worries, I'm used to hot girls mauling me for allowing them to keep their clothes on."

"What?"

"That's why I lost." I shrugged, reaching for my discarded shirt on the floor. "You would have had to take off either your bra or your—" I pointed, yeah, lame, but I couldn't actually say the word lest I spontaneously combust and lose my shit.

"Oh." She stepped into her dress. I watched every move. Slowly she turned and I reached for the zipper, cautiously zipping all the way up when my body demanded I tug down. All. The. Way. Down. "So I guess that means, you have to lose an article of clothing."

"What?"

She stepped away and turned, crossing her arms over her chest. "Well?"

"Uh."

"The shirt was already off, so take it off again." I did as she said, mainly because she was so damn hot when she was telling me what to do that if she said that her favorite song was "Kumbaya," I'd not only sing it but make up my own hand motions. "So." She licked her lips suggestively and started circling me. *Oh, divine. Lovely. Torture.*

Her hands reached around to my front and paused on the button of my jeans. "I think these have to go."

Holy hell.

Was it wrong to thank God in a situation like this? Was it? Really, though? I mean I didn't want to be blasphemous, but . . . yeah, I was feeling a lot of gratitude at the moment.

"Okay." I reached for my button and froze.

Happy moment gone.

I wasn't wearing boxers.

I wasn't wearing a damn stitch underneath the jeans. I was free-balling.

"How about another drink?" I offered in a hopeful voice.

"Pants," she said in a low voice. "Now."

"You're sure?" I cursed a blue streak in my head. I was about to show her my ass. Our first naked moment was about to happen at Goldy's Bar and Grill, which was like the equivalent of an Applebee's. Rock on.

"Do it." She smacked me in the shoulder, then walked back around to face me. Bad idea. Really, really bad idea. In the history of bad ideas—this one fell at least at a one or two.

"Fine." I told my body to stay relaxed, but the minute it heard *relax* it thought of the opposite. Rigid.

Great, so I was going to salute her.

Naked.

A naked salute.

Would crying make me seem less masculine?

"We don't have all night." She rolled her eyes, still a bit unsteady on her feet. Maybe she would be too drunk to remember? One could only hope.

With a jerk I pulled my jeans down to my feet and waited.

Milo gasped and covered her mouth. But her eyes didn't leave me. She drank me in like I was a freaking Greek god—and my body responded like Marvel had just written my name in one of its comic books, I could have sworn I felt my shoulders broaden, my chest grow to epic proportions.

"What the hell!" a male voice shouted.

I looked up.

A horrified Jason stood at the door, his eyes taking in the scene around him. "What the . . ." With an abrupt turn he tried to leave the room and slammed into the door, then stumbled backward, just as Max appeared.

"Hey, you find my wallet?" He swayed. "Holy shit! Do you take pills or something?"

Needless to say I pulled my pants up at the precise moment that Milo held her stomach and then ran over to the trashcan and started puking.

I flinched, hoping it wasn't my nakedness that had caused the nausea.

"Badass." Max laughed. "You have that effect on all women or just mine?"

I glared.

Jason rubbed his jaw. "Worst. Wedding. Ever."

# CHAPTER TWENTY-FIVE
## MILO

"I'm dying!" I shouted for the third time as the cold air hit me in the face. "Seriously, my stomach is churning."

"Maybe you shouldn't have drank that much," Colton said in a fatherly voice that made me want to jump out of the moving vehicle and flag down a semi.

"You taunted me."

"Ah, so it's my fault."

"Keep your pants on!" I snapped, and then giggled. "Oh, wait . . ."

"Hilarious, Milo."

"Tell me." Yeah, the alcohol was totally talking at the moment. "Do you always wear pants without boxers or is that new?"

"We should have this conversation when you're not sticking your head out of the car window like my golden retriever."

"Colton." I reached for his arm and squeezed. "Damn. Do you live at the gym or something? And how is that even fair to people like me?"

"People like you—"

"Women everywhere!" I threw my hands into the air. "How do we compete? How do we settle when the bar's so damn high we have to get a freaking ladder to even touch it?"

Colton cleared his throat. "I don't necessarily think that—"

"And then when you dropped your pants!"

The car swerved to the right.

"I mean holy shit, Colt! It's like you want other men to hate you!"

The car hit one of the rumble strips on the right, then swerved to the left.

"Ah, cat, I saw a cat."

"And really." I let out a heavy sigh, finally feeling better about getting everything off my chest. "What do you expect, huh? What do you expect from us girls? Of course I'm going to be obsessed with you! You're just . . ." I shook the fuzz from my head as my vision doubled, then tripled. "You're just . . ."

"What?" he whispered.

I couldn't have kept my eyes open even if I'd tried. Instead I slumped into the seat and closed them, but not before whispering, "Mine, Colt. You've always been mine."

• • •

We rounded the corner of her parents' house. Milo was completely out—as in I'm pretty sure she was dreaming of a giant tequila monster and wishing she hadn't had that last shot.

Sighing, I turned off the car, got out, and went over to her side. Crazy how peaceful she looked when she slept. Of course that was a total false representation of how Milo actually lived day-to-day life. She was like a freaking bomb that went off for twelve hours straight only to reset itself every night so it could repeat the process the next morning.

"Come on, sweetheart." I pulled her from the seat and carried her inside the house. The lights were turned down low—so nobody had stayed up to make sure she was all right, or that I was all right, for that matter.

Jason and Max had quickly left the bar, both of their faces red as they mumbled something about seeing me back at the house.

Wasn't that the story of my life, though? In the end, it was always me and Milo. Jason had always trusted me with her. And in return? She'd always trusted me with herself. Never once having to worry about being safe or protected.

I took the stairs one at a time, a heaviness settling on my shoulders as I fought with two desires: to just tell her I knew everything and kiss the hell out of her, and to make her suffer.

Kicking the bedroom door open, I nearly dropped her when I realized Max was lying across the bed reading.

"Aren't you drunk?"

"I recover very quickly," Max said with a snort, his eyes not leaving the page of the book. "Besides, a guy happens to sober up pretty fast when he sees his best friend drunk and staring at a guy's naked body like she was a doctor studying the human form."

"Look, about that." I set Milo on the bed.

"No." Max set the book down and folded his arms across his chest. "She may have played you but she did it because she can't handle all the feelings in her, okay? She's Milo, for shit's sake. *Normal* isn't really in her vocabulary. I don't even think she knows what that word means."

I chuckled. "Yeah, well, it wasn't what it looked like. I mean we didn't . . . do anything."

"It doesn't matter." Max shrugged. "If you don't have the balls to take what's been yours for this long . . ." He picked up the book again. "Then maybe you don't deserve her."

"I don't deserve her." I cleared my throat. "But I want her anyways."

Max threw the book onto the bed and jumped to his feet. He swayed a bit, but his eyes were clear as a freaking sunny day. "I was hoping you'd say that, so this is how it's going to work."

"Huh?"

"What?" He punched me in the arm. "You want Milo, I'm going to help you get her. Because I'm a stand-up dude and I'm sick and tired of her pining after you, and besides, if I help you win her over then I can move on with my own dating life. The waters are rough when she's always there killing my game."

"Uh . . ." I raised my hand. "I have her."

"Aww." Max patted the same shoulder he'd just gotten done punching and sighed. "You cute, misinformed, innocent little lamb."

"Pardon?"

"She's going to eat you alive."

"What?"

"Milo." Max pointed. "Doesn't do declarations of love. She's not like most girls. You can't just break down and cry and say you want to have a bazillion babies with her."

"One, maybe two," I said hoarsely. "A bazillion? Who says that?"

"Stupid men. Ones that are in love and dig their own graves for sport. If you want to catch one in the wild all you need to do is turn a bit . . ." He smiled. "And there you go! Look!" He pointed at the mirror. "Shh, don't make any sudden movements."

"You calling me stupid?"

"Yes." Max nodded. "But chin up, we'll fix you."

"No fixing."

"Then no girl."

"How do you even know this?"

"I'm not really gay." Max rolled his eyes as if that were the reason I was hesitant about taking his advice. *Right.*

"Dude." I tried explaining. "I have her—I just need to tell her how I feel."

"She'll run." Max popped his knuckles. "She's afraid of her own feelings. She's been after you her whole life. The minute she has you in a corner, she'll panic. Girls are weird like that. They overthink everything. *Holy crap, what if he isn't the same man I thought he was? What if I don't love him as much as I think I do? What if he sucks at kissing? What if his—*"

"I'm good at all things sexually related. Let's just clear the air."

"You sure?" Max rolled his eyes. "I mean how do you really know?"

Well, shit, he had me there. I averted my gaze. "I just know."

"Is that hesitation I see in your eyes? Kiss me."

"Hell, no!" I shouted.

Max shrugged. "Fine, don't kiss me, but at least hit on me. Okay, so pretend I'm Milo and you're about to make your move and declare your love, blah blah blah."

"No." I stood my ground. "I'm going to do it my way."

"Your way is going to be another two years of cat and mouse. You gotta play her game to win it."

Damn him. He had a point. Milo *wasn't* most girls. What if he was right about everything else too?

"I see the wheels of your mind turning—fascinating. Tell me, do you actually feel the smoke coming out of your ears?"

"You're a jackass."

Max grinned. "I've been called worse. My mom hates me."

"What?"

"Thirteen-pound baby. *Hate* isn't a strong enough word. When I came into the world, she told my father our family was cursed. Anyways, over-share. Okay, so I'm Milo . . . you do what? What do you say first?"

I shuffled my feet.

"Stop looking down."

*Shit.* "Fine." I licked my lips nervously. "Milo, I know that things have been—difficult, and . . ."

Max winced as I kept going.

"And, um, I know that . . ." And just like that, my mind went blank.

"Wheels stopped moving, didn't they?" Max nodded in understanding.

"Yeah." I covered my face with my hands. "How the hell am I going to do this?"

"Follow my lead."

I nodded as Max put his hand on the back of my neck and pulled me forward. "You irritate the hell out of me, but I can't stand it any longer. I want you, and only you, for the rest of my life. I want to kiss you, I want to make love with you, I want to have children with you. I want a life with you. And if you try to run I'm just going to hunt you down. You and me. Forever."

"I really need to start knocking," a voice said from the door.

Max and I jumped away from each other, I hit my chest, he burped, and I'm pretty sure there was some ball scratching and shifty eyes.

"Found the Advil." Jason lifted it into the air. "Anything you boys need to tell me?"

"He loves Milo!" Max shouted.

"Shh!" I smacked him on the chest as Milo moaned in her sleep.

"No shit." A bored expression crossed Jason's face. "So why are *you* hitting on him, Max?"

"He wasn't," I said defensively, my voice cracking. "He said that I couldn't just come out and tell Milo how I felt, that she may overthink things and freak."

Jason nodded. "Yeah, shit-for-brains is probably right."

"And again, been called worse," Max pointed out. "Not a big deal. Just trying to help a friend so I can finally go on a date where I don't feel guilty that Milo's home watching *Star Wars* and eating her body weight in ice cream."

"You're a good friend." Jason pounded Max's back in appreciation.

"I'm the best friend," Max said crisply. "And I don't care how much you love her, Colt. Or that you want to make fireman babies—I'm still the best friend, you feel me?"

"Actually it was more like you were feeling him earlier . . ." Jason piped up.

"Yeah." I held out my fist and bumped his knuckles. "I feel you."

"Good." Max looked at the clock on the nightstand. "Now let's go over this again. She put you through hell. You need to make sure she understands that regardless of what she's done to you, you'll still fight for her. Think you can do that tomorrow?"

I nodded, and then inspiration hit. *Jenna.* "Oh, yeah, I think I can manage."

"Awesome."

The room fell silent.

I looked at Jason; he was leaning against the wall, head hung.

"Still going through with it?" Max asked what I was thinking.

"Got any bright ideas in that head of yours for me?" Jason laughed humorlessly. "After all, the bridesmaids said she didn't drink all night."

"Actually." Max snapped his fingers. "I think I do."

# CHAPTER TWENTY-SIX
## MILO

The first thought that came to me as I tried to remove my sandpaper tongue from the roof of my mouth?

*Tequila may have been a bad idea.*

The second thought?

*Colton. Naked.* A naked Colton standing before me in all his godlike glory and me staring. Like a psychopath. I mean, I should have said something, right? Like "Oh, you're hot," or "Wow, work out much?" Instead I'm pretty sure I said something inappropriate and then yelled at him in the car.

I believe puking was also involved in my night of fun, as well as a heavy dose of shame.

"Ugh . . ." I moved to a sitting position.

"Feeling better?" Max held out a cup of coffee.

"Don't shout!"

"Trust me, you did plenty of shouting in bed last night." He winked.

Holy crap.

I set the coffee down on the nightstand and looked under the covers to make sure my clothes were still on.

Was I that girl?

The drunk hussy who slept with her best friend?

"Was it good for you?" Max leaned toward me.

"Yes?"

"Wow, I expected you to be more enthusiastic."

"It was awesome."

Max rolled his eyes. "You didn't even taste it."

"P-pardon?"

"You have to put it in your mouth to actually experience the flavor."

I felt my cheeks turn about seven shades of red before Max grabbed the discarded coffee.

"Now, taste."

"The coffee?"

He frowned, then offered a sly smile. "Of course the coffee, why? What did you think I was talking about?"

The smolder in my cheeks was going to light my face on fire.

"Aw, sweetie." Max laughed and pulled me in for a hug. I winced as my pounding head made contact with his chest. "Believe me, if we would have slept together, you would remember, even drunk, you would remember."

"Someone's cocky."

"Confident." He released me. "So are we upset or are we okay?"

"We?"

"Partners." He winked. "For life. You and me, we're a we." He lifted the coffee to his lips. "Hey, that rhymed. How badass am I, after getting drunk last night?" He nodded his head. "Sharp as a tack."

The coffee slid out of the cup and onto his hand.

Lots of cursing followed.

Then flailing.

"Yeah." I took the coffee away. "Sharp as something."

"So." Max reached behind him and pulled out my diary. "Curious minds want to know, when you drew that picture of the house you and Colton were going to live in once you got married in front of the queen of England, did you purposefully draw the dog without a tail or were you just confused?"

"Give me that!" I lunged for the pink diary. "How the hell did you find it?"

Max held it above his head and took a sip of coffee. "People always hide interesting stuff under their mattresses, though I had you pinned for more of a signed 'N Sync poster, considering all the stupid hearts around JC Chasez's face on the torn-up poster in your closet." The freak had gone in my closet too? "This is just as good. Though I have to admit, I'm a bit disappointed that you chose Prince Harry to walk you down the aisle. Do I mean nothing to you?"

"I had a thing for royalty!" I shouted, my headache making a fierce pounding in my temples.

"Mmm." Max set his coffee down but kept the diary above his head. "One last question."

"If I answer, will you give it back so I can burn it?"

"I'll give it back." He held up his hand. "But burning this would be a crime. It's like reality TV only worse, I seriously cried real tears and it wasn't because the story was sad. Oh, and P.S. It took you five years to spell *nightmare* right, just thought I'd let you know."

"What's the question?" I ignored his teasing and focused on calming myself so I didn't throw up again.

"Did you mean it?"

*Aw crap.* "Mean what?"

"In here." He shook the diary. "Did you mean it about Colton?"

"How am I supposed to even remember—"

"No worries, I folded the page." He cleared his throat. "'Colton is my favorite, he is like my best friend. He reminds me of my dad only I want to kiss him all the time. Colton is like my superhero. Sometimes when I watch movies I imagine I'm the princess and he's rescuing me. Today we played dragon slayer. He rescued me and then said I was pretty. I hope he means it. Because one day I'm going to marry him. He's going to be mine forever, and then we'll play dragon slayer again and it's going to be real—because everyone knows you're playing pretend until you get true love's kiss. And I'm going to get mine. In my castle.'"

I looked down at the blankets, not trusting myself to actually look Max in the face. How could words I'd written years ago make such an impact on the way my heart slammed against my chest?

"Not gonna lie, I'm kinda pissed about the whole 'best friend' part, and I may have red-penned that bitch, but the rest of it looks about right." Max slammed it shut. "So, let's toss you in the shower, throw a hell of a lot of cover-up under those eyes of yours, save your brother's ass, then get you a groom!"

"You watch too much TV."

"I cut my teeth on daytime soap operas growing up." Max shrugged. "I can't fight my true nature. Now, let's do this."

# CHAPTER TWENTY-SEVEN
## COLTON

"I'm not wearing this under my tux." I held the offending shirt out and dropped it onto the floor. I was half tempted to step on it too, but Jason rescued it in time.

"I'm marrying Satan," he seethed. "The least you can do is put on the damn R2-D2 shirt with a smile!"

I grimaced. "It's too tight."

"Again, let me repeat, I'm marrying Satan. Wear the shirt."

Sighing, I threw on the black robot-looking shirt, then buttoned up my dark-gray dress shirt over it. "We don't even know if this is going to work."

"It's Milo." Jason pulled out a flask. "It will work."

"How long until brunch?"

Jason checked his watch. "A half hour."

"Which means we only have . . . ?"

"Two hours until pictures, four hours until the wedding." He started pacing, then stopped. "You think it's a bad sign that it's my wedding day and the only thing that makes me smile is a vision of my hands around Jayne's neck?"

"Just tell yourself you're into BDSM—makes it totally acceptable."

"Good call." He held out his fist for a pound just as someone knocked on the door.

It could be anyone, though I was hoping it was Max. He was supposed to be bringing us our victim.

As expected, it was Max—and the man I could only assume was his brother.

"Fellas." Max slapped the guy's back. They looked nothing alike. His brother had curly blond hair and green eyes. I assumed Max was adopted and the guy in front of me was the product of good genes at work.

"Reid." He held out his hand. "I hear you guys need my help."

"He's an actor." Max nodded. "Broadway, soap operas, big time. He's like a big fish—no offense to your homegrown small-townness, Jason, but you're like a sad goldfish just waiting to go belly-up. We need a betta or something."

"None taken." He held up his hands. "To bait Jayne we need a big fish or, er, a betta."

Reid laughed. "One word, man."

We all waited.

"How?" He shook his head. "How? Jayne?" He whistled.

"That was two words, actually." Max cleared his throat.

"How the hell did you and Jayne even get together?"

"Yeah I lost count at eight words." Max shrugged.

Jason cringed. "Long story. Lots of mistakes, lots of—"

"It goes like this," Max interrupted. "Boys are told since they're little that pretty things are good. Pretty things equal happy things. So when we grow up and see a shiny pretty thing, we're drawn like moths to a flame. We keep flying toward the light until it's too late. You know, like that *Sleeping Beauty* chick with the spinning wheel?"

I chuckled. "Are you seriously comparing us to a Disney princess?"

Max waved him off. "'Oh, look, it's so pretty, I want to touch it. I want to touch it, and kiss it, and make love to it'—*boom*!" He slammed his hands together. "Trapped. You're trapped in her web of lies. Oh, no, your body's going numb, help! You yell! You gnaw off your own leg in order to escape, you bleed out, and just when you think you've made it, the spider returns and offers you food. 'Aren't you hungry?' she says. And then come the compliments, 'You're so strong, look how great you are.'"

"So we're flies now?" I asked.

"And *boom*!" He slammed his hands together again. "Not only are you trapped all over again, but you feel guilty that you even tried to escape."

Something happened in that moment, as if a light were suddenly turned on in my brain. I looked around at Jason and Reid, and an expression of awe marked their faces, as if we'd just experienced greatness but were unable to describe how or when it had happened.

It was official. Max was a certified genius.

"So." Max cleared his throat. "You ready, spider? Ready to get out of that web and become a free man? Just think, *I'm not the fly, I'm not the fly*. Come on, repeat after me, 'I'm not the fly.'"

Jason whispered, "I'm not the fly."

"Again."

"He likes metaphors, huh?" I asked Reid.

"You have no idea." He rolled his eyes.

"Again!" Max shouted. "Let me hear you!"

"I'm not the fly!" Jason's voice could have shattered windows.

"Good." Max slammed him on the back. "Good work here, boys. Good work. I feel like we made progress. Now, stick to the plan, and we'll be toasting our success tonight. Hands in."

He held his hand out. With a curse I put mine on top, Jason followed, and finally Reid.

"Feel pain, no Jayne!"

"Feel pain, no Jayne!" we shouted, and lifted our hands into the air. A rush hit me like we'd just won the Super Bowl or something. We'd save Jason, and then . . .

Then I was going to kiss my girl.

But not until I'd served her a bit of jealousy—after all, it was so much more fun kissing her when she was pissed as hell.

# CHAPTER TWENTY-EIGHT
## MILO

I took a seat in the dining room and grimaced as the smell of food wafted into my nostrils. I had been able to shower without Max's help—though he did try to walk in on me a few times just to be sure I hadn't passed out. I put my foot down when he tried helping me apply makeup because, he said, my eyeliner needed to be darker and my perfume wasn't strong enough.

It had been three hours since I'd woken up, and I still wasn't feeling better, especially if my reaction to the smell of food was any indication.

Gross.

"Eat," Max said from behind me. "Eat so you don't puke your little lady guts out later this afternoon."

"I can't believe I used to think you were hot," I grumbled.

"Still hot." Max took a seat. "Still your best friend." He held up a croissant. "Now eat."

I took a bite.

"Chew."

I chewed twice.

"And swallow."

With a gulp, I chased the croissant down with a cup of coffee and slowly took another bite.

"So, we're going to kill Jayne."

Coffee spewed out of my mouth onto the plate in front of me. "I'm sorry, what?"

"Nothing. I just love keeping you on your toes. Hey." He touched my cross necklace. "This is nice . . . Think if we tie a bit of garlic around it and stuff it down her wedding dress she'll melt?"

I had opened my mouth to respond when Max suddenly stood and held out his hand. "Reid, meet my best friend and lover."

I rolled my eyes and held out my hand. "Milo."

"Nice to meet you, Milo." The guy's grin screamed movie star as he held my hand in his, then kissed my knuckles.

"Never gets old." Max sighed.

"Huh?" I shook the fog from my head. The guy was gorgeous.

"He's like that *Twilight* vampire guy, the one with sparkles. I swear he says hello and women's clothes, they fall right off. Amazing, really."

"He's lying." Reid winked.

I heard a thud and turned around. "Grandma! Grandma, are you okay?"

"It's his eyes," Max said from behind me. "Magic powers."

"Ma'am." Reid rushed to Grandma's side. "Are you okay?"

"Heaven." Tears pooled in her eyes as she reached up and caressed his face. "I've died, haven't I? I just . . . I never fathomed it would feel so real." Her hands moved down his chest, and dipped into his pants. Holy crap! Someone needed to get Grams away from the young man before she took advantage of him in a bad-touch way.

"That's enough," Max grumbled, pulling a laughing Reid away. "Sit and behave before you give her a stroke."

Shrugging, Reid took a seat next to me and Max. I helped Grandma to her feet and set her down toward the opposite end of the table so she couldn't attack Max's brother.

"Where is everyone?" I looked around at the empty seats. Weddings were always stressful; people rarely had time to eat, so my mom had decided to do a wedding brunch instead of just putting out snacks.

"Oh." Max reached for his mimosa. "Jason should be right down and Colton had to go pick up Jenna."

"J-Jenna." Paper bag, I needed a paper bag. It couldn't be the same Jenna. Could it? No. I was being silly. Ridiculous, really. I clenched the glass so hard my hand shook.

"One more squeeze and I think you may shatter it," Max said, his voice laced with approval. "Come on, give it a go, I wanna see if you could actually do it."

"Max." I released the glass and placed my hands demurely in my lap. "This Jenna, is she an old friend?" Guys talked, right? So Max, being a guy, would know.

"Not sure." Max reached for a Danish. "I think Colton said something about her living around here. Yoga instructor. Very flexible. Hell, I dated one of those once . . ." He sighed with a dreamy, faraway look. "Couldn't move for days." I thought he was going to stop talking but he didn't take the hint when I pinched his thigh. "It was amazing the way her body was able to—"

"Max," I snapped through clenched teeth. "Not now!"

"What?" He shrugged and leaned over to whisper, "It's just a date because you made up a white lie about having a boyfriend. On second thought, to say what you did was lying would be like saying Grandma isn't imagining what Reid looks like naked." He shuddered and took a sip of water. "Your white lie grew into an elephant the size of Canis Majoris."

Panic welled in my chest. What if he fell in love with her?

"That's a star, by the way," Max whispered.

"I know what Canis Majoris is," I seethed.

"Well, you flunked astronomy, so—"

"Let's not focus on that right now!" I tried to keep my voice even. Laughter bubbled out from the hall, and then Colton appeared.

With my worst nightmare.

*Hah, spelled it right in my head!*

Take that, Jenna "Ugly Face" Urtin!

Yes, her last name was Urtin.

How was I the girl who got passed over? At least my last name made sense!

Why couldn't she be fat? And ugly? And tall. Not short. Guys liked short. No, I wanted her to be a candidate for the freaking WNBA. Instead, perfect height, perfect pretty brown hair, perfect braces-free smile. *Damn her!* I slammed my fist onto the table, gaining the attention of every person in the room.

"Milo!" Jenna exclaimed, her face erupting with joy.

"Jenna!" I said in an equally excited voice as I clenched the fork in my hand, ready to wield it as a weapon if need be. "So nice to see you!" I clenched the fork harder.

Max reached under the table and pried it from my death grip as Jenna walked around the chairs. Awkwardly I stood without my weapon, and pulled her in for a hug.

Oh, great. She smelled good too.

"You look amazing," she gushed. "And, oh, my gosh, is this your fiancé?"

It was on the tip of my tongue to say it all. To blurt the lie out and just be finished with the whole masquerade.

And then I met Colton's challenging glare.

So I put on my big boy pants and went ovaries to the wall. "Sure is! Max, meet my dear old friend Jenna."

I was counting on Max being on my side.

Instead his eyes widened, his smile turned deadly, and he pulled her in for a long hug—the type that screams, *I'd like to get to know you better*. "Beautiful, great to meet you. Any friend of Milo's is a friend of mine."

"Yay," I said weakly.

I was in hell.

# CHAPTER TWENTY-NINE

## COLTON

Her expression? Priceless. I was glad that Jenna had ended up being a cool chick. Luckily she and Jason had a bit of a history, so when I asked her to come help me win over a girl and ruin Jason's wedding?

She was all for it.

Apparently Jayne had burned a lot of bridges in her short life.

"This is so nice." I laid it on thick. "So glad you two remember each other." I winked at Milo.

Her hand reached for the knife.

Max removed every single piece of silverware within reaching distance, like she was a three-year-old ready to inflict self-harm. Though I'm pretty sure he was more concerned about her accidentally impaling one of his boys.

"Jason?" Mrs. Caro called.

He and Jayne were the only ones who weren't seated at the table. Shit was going to hit the fan—and soon.

They stormed into the room. Jason smiling so wide I was afraid his face was going to freeze in place, and Jayne pouting like she'd just been told that her fur coat wasn't real.

"Good, now everyone's here." Mrs. Caro looked around the table. "We're so glad you could all join us for this"—she cleared her throat—"very joyous union." She reached for her mimosa glass. "How about a salute to the happy couple?"

We lifted our glasses.

And showtime.

I almost felt bad for Jayne—*almost* being the key word.

"Actually," Reid piped up, "I'd love to say a few words."

All the color drained from Jayne's face, leaving her a hideous pasty white, and then she flashed over to red. It was like watching a confused chameleon.

"Oh." Mrs. Caro looked confused, but sat and let him take the floor.

"I've known Jayne since I was in high school." He laughed softly. "She used to wear the funniest cat T-shirts. That girl had an obsession. One time during se—I mean during, uh, on set, she even meowed." He coughed wildly.

*Oh, my hell. Forget Jason, Reid is my new best friend.*

"At any rate, it's been such a joy to see her grow up over these past years. Jayne, I'm sorry we've grown apart, those monthly visits just got too hectic with my schedule, and now I feel bad that last month, when you called I wasn't able to answer. I hope you can forgive me for not being there when you wanted to gush about your new sex—I mean, sorry, your new fiancé. But, hey, we'll always have New York, right?" He chuckled and looked around the table to make sure what he'd said had actually had time to sink in. You could hear a pin drop in the room.

Milo's eyes went wide as saucers.

And Max was filming the entire thing.

"I think . . ." Reid sniffled. Hell, this was a long speech. "I think what gets me most, is I think I would have been a good father." He wiped a fake tear. "He would have called me 'Da-da,' and I would have chased him around the house, and I think, I think we could have been happy, Jayne. You, me, and little Anvil." Classic. He wiped another tear. "Family name, I would have given him my family name, and now, now another bastard's poaching on my land. The land I claimed, plowed, planted, and grew over and over and over . . . and over." He sighed and took a drink. "And over again. Well, when you lose you lose. Am I right? So cheers to the happy couple. May you find happiness with your new family."

Reid sat.

I nodded at Max, who mouthed, "Theater camp, bitch."

Jayne's mouth fell open and then closed as she reached for her mimosa and lifted it to her lips with a shaking hand.

All we needed was for her to take one little sip.

As if realizing what she was doing, she set the glass down and smiled happily at Jason. "Sorry, thought it was my water."

Water, my ass.

I kicked Max under the table. It wasn't going as planned. She was supposed to freak out, and we were supposed to push her over the edge by bringing in an ex, not make her commitment to Jason more solid.

I kicked again.

Max let out a howl and jumped to his feet. "I too have some things I'd like to get off my chest."

"Abort!" Milo mouthed. "Abort."

I ignored her and said loudly, "Max, that would be so wonderful. Gosh, it's so nice hearing from friends and family."

"Weren't really gonna do the toasts until this evening, but—" Mr. Caro sputtered as Mrs. Caro smacked him and nodded her consent.

"Growing up with Jayne—"

"Did everyone grow up with Jayne?" Mr. Caro asked.

"Oh, we went to theater camp together," Max explained. "Back when Jayne wanted to be an actress." He sighed. "Now look at her . . ." Heads turned as everyone looked. "A homemaker, just waiting for the little oven to ding so Anvil can pop out and cry 'Mama!'"

"We haven't discussed names yet," she said smoothly.

"What's wrong with Anvil?" Max asked midtoast. "My grandfather was a POW in Vietnam—his name was Anvil, you saying my grandfather's name isn't good enough?"

Jayne's eyes narrowed. "Your grandfather's name was Stan."

"My other grandfather, the blind one with the tic in his right eye."

"Oh, dear!" Mrs. Caro gasped. "Was he injured in a war?"

"No." Max smiled. "Circus accident."

"The toast." I coughed.

"Right." Max straightened and lifted his glass. "As I was saying, I too knew Jayne when she was a social-climbing little monster. Hell, even in high school she was always dating guys she thought were gonna be famous someday. I was passed over—well, that's not entirely true. I had her first, then my brother." Mrs. Caro spit out her mimosa all over the table while the ancient grandma suddenly woke up from her nap and began listening with a hand cupped to her ear.

"Speak up, Max!"

"So!" Max yelled. "SHE SLEPT WITH MY BROTHER!"

"Who, dear?"

"JAYNE!" Max pointed. "AND MY BROTHER REID!"

"Oh." Grandma fanned her face and waved at Reid. He hid behind a stunned Milo. Smart man. Smart man.

"BUT!" Max continued to yell, "ALL'S WELL THAT ENDS WELL! THAT'S WHAT GRAMPS SAID ON HIS DEATHBED! He said, 'MAX, YOU MARRY A GOOD ONE!'" He looked down. "And I've got her right here."

Too far. He just went too far.

Max leaned down and reached for Milo's face. "I'm so glad you're not pregnant, forcing me to marry you before I'm actually ready for such a huge commitment where we fight over paying the electricity bill and make sacrifices like eating hot dogs every day while you clean out the baby's dirty reusable, homemade diapers. It really, really makes me feel happy we waited and saved ourselves." He addressed everyone at the table. "SAVE OURSELVES FROM THE PITFALLS OF SIN!" He sat and then, as if remembering he was toasting, not condemning, raised his glass and said in a chipper voice, "Cheers to the happy couple. May this day be the worst of a lifetime of happy days!"

Yeah, pretty sure he got that quote wrong.

"On that note . . ." Mrs. Caro reached for her pearl necklace and pulled. "Shall we pour more champagne?"

Glasses lifted around the table, all but Grandma's because suddenly she wasn't in her seat anymore.

*What the hell?* I looked around the table. Had the woman passed out again? I scanned the room and finally located her behind Reid.

I yelled his name.

But I was too late.

She launched herself into his lap like a rabbit in heat. There was no time, no time to save him. The only thing I could do was watch in horror as Grandma grabbed him with her freakishly strong hands and kissed him square on the mouth.

"Grandma!" Milo shouted, knocking her chair backward just as Mr. Caro was returning with the champagne. Naturally he tripped over the toppled chair, and the bottles went sailing over the table. Max caught one; the other knocked Jason in the face.

The dude was a freaking punching bag.

Once it fell from his eyeball, it landed on the table and popped, sending sticky liquid all over.

Jayne screamed.

The bridesmaids screamed.

Mrs. Caro started to cry.

And Reid was turning blue.

"Let him go!" I was leaning across the table and candles to pry Grandma off him when Max started hitting me across the ass.

"What the hell?"

"You're on fire!" Cold water followed the beating; my hands were still latched on to Grandma's shoulders. I lost my grip and grabbed whatever else I could find.

Which just so happened to be her wig.

Good ol' Grandma was bald.

Screaming, I tossed the wig into the air.

It landed on Max's head.

"HOLY SHIT, A CAT!" Max froze, like totally froze in place. "Milo, get it off, get it off, Milo, I'm allergic. Milo, get the damn cat off my head!"

"QUIET!" someone shouted.

Grandma finally released her grip, and fell backward across Max's lap. The wig slid off his head onto her face.

*May she rest in peace.*

I made a crossing motion with my hand.

Reid had tears in his eyes.

Without saying anything I grabbed the champagne from Max's grip and handed it over.

"JUST STOP IT!" Jayne wailed. "I hate you! I hate all of you!"

With a huff she ran off and burst into tears.

There really wasn't anything left to do except lift my glass into the air and say, "Cheers."

# CHAPTER THIRTY

## MILO

"So." Max leaned across the sticky champagne table, his eyes locked on Jenna. "That's a pretty dress."

He was kidding, right?

Grandma moaned in his lap.

Jayne had just run out of the room sobbing.

My mom was crying softly into my dad's shoulder while Dad sipped champagne straight from the bottle.

The bridesmaids had gone after Jayne.

And Jason had a piece of meat pressed against his swollen eye. On the brighter side of things, at least he wouldn't have to make eye contact with Jayne when he said his vows.

"Um, thank you." Jenna blushed. Interesting, I didn't know whores were still able to blush after the things they'd seen.

Grandma moaned again in Max's lap. He patted her head and continued his conversation with Jenna. "I just love yoga."

"Great." Jenna's eyes locked on Max's lap. "Um, I think she's stirring."

Reid flinched in his seat, his eyes locking on Grandma's body. Maybe he thought if he stared hard enough she'd just stay that way?

"Up you go!" Max helped Grandma to her feet. "There you are, right as rain."

"Oh, dear." Grandma shook her bald head as Max handed her the wig. "What a rush!" She turned to face a pale Reid. "And you, my dear, the things you do with that tongue of yours—divine. I'm in the last guest bedroom at the end of the hall if you get bored."

With that she grabbed a glass of champagne and sauntered off.

Reid went from pale to purple.

"Shit, he's going into shock," Colton murmured. "Quick, someone do something! He's not breathing."

"Committing suicide." Max exhaled and closed his eyes like he was in pain. "By holding his breath. Brave little tyke, well, we had a good run, Brother." Max slapped him on the back. "A good run."

Reid shrugged, still holding his breath.

"Dude!" Colton yelled, then ran around the table and slapped Reid across the face.

Max whistled loudly and burst out laughing. "I think this is my favorite weekend ever."

Reid cursed and started breathing again, though I was pretty sure he was still going to be scarred for life.

"Get it together, man!" Max followed up Colton's slap with one of his own. "Forget Grandma—you have a bride to seduce."

"I don't know," Reid croaked, licking his lips. "Holy shit."

"What?" I leaned forward and placed my hand on his muscular thigh.

"I'll never wear ChapStick again, my lips taste like ChapStick."

"Huh?" I asked.

Reid held my gaze, his lower lip trembling. "I wasn't wearing ChapStick."

"Oh," we all said in unison.

The scraping of a chair being pushed out gathered all our attention as Jason slowly moved from his end of the table to ours, the meat still held against his eye.

Without words, because really what could the guy say—"Sorry my grandma took advantage of your man parts?"—he reached into his jacket and pulled out a flask.

Reid took it.

And drained the thing.

"Better?" Jason asked.

"Sure." Reid's voice was hoarse. "I may never be able to perform sexually again without Viagra and a prayer, but sure, I'm ready."

"Go get 'em." Jason nodded.

"You can do it." Max seemed totally confident. "Just walk up to Jayne and let her believe you want in her pants, do that sexy look you do, and all will be well."

Reid tilted his head to the side, still not talking.

"Bro, show me the look, show me you're ready."

With a grimace Reid stood. "Can't, man. I may only have one look left in me and I'm not wasting it on my brother."

Max reached out and gripped Reid's hand. "We're proud of you. What happens at the dinner table stays at the dinner table—now go steal the bride."

"Roger." Slowly he walked away.

"Well." Colton clapped his hands. "This plan is going to hell fast."

"Too many unpredictable players." Jason shook his head. "And I would have never imagined Grandma would—attack."

"Ever since HBO," I whispered in a low voice. "It's poisoned her mind."

"Well." Colton shrugged, then reached for the whore's hand. "I guess one good thing has come out of this weekend, huh, Jenna?"

Grinning, she leaned against his chest and laughed. "I'd say so."

I was cutting off his balls and feeding them to him if his lips touched hers.

"Ouch." Max winced. "Could you please release my arm?"

"Sorry." I let go and counted to five, so I didn't throw a knife at her face.

"So what now?" Jason set the meat on the table. "We just continue to pretend everything's fine?"

"Reid will pull through," Max said confidently. "And until then we should probably go cover up"—he smiled apologetically—"your entire face with makeup."

"Is it that bad?" Jason asked, turning so we could look at his new shiner.

His eye was beginning to swell shut.

"No." We all shook our heads and laughed nervously.

I added, "I didn't even notice it."

"Me either." Colton coughed. "It's a really faint bruise."

Max rolled his eyes and gripped Jason's shoulders. "Bullshit, you look like hell. But on a happier note, at least you won't have to look at her while she plunges her evil talons into your chest and rips your heart out. Yay you!"

Jason looked around Max's body, directing his attention at me. "Is it normal to want to kill him half the time and then love him the other half, then want to kill him again?"

"Welcome to my world." I sighed.

"Wait." Max looked around. "Am I the *him* to whom you're referring?"

"Jason!" Mom wailed, running into the room. "Come quick! We can't find Jayne!"

"Yeah, because that's going to make him want to run and join the search party," Max grumbled.

# CHAPTER THIRTY-ONE

## MILO

It was the search party from hell. Funny, hell had been the theme of the week, so it seemed almost perfect as we all started combing the grounds for Jayne.

I asked Jason why bother.

His one good eye narrowed in on me with ferocity.

"Chill, Cyclops, we'll find Jean." I laughed. "Hey, it's almost like Jayne, that's pretty funny."

Jason wasn't laughing.

He simply stared creepily with that one eye and stomped off toward the large oak trees in our backyard. What? Did he think she was swinging from the trees?

I laughed again. "Me Tarzan, you Jane."

"You high?" Colton came up behind me. Solo. Thank God.

I turned and gave him the best smile I could—you know the smile, the one you hope is distracting enough to keep a guy from saying the one phrase you don't want him to utter after a drunken night of stupidity.

"Hey, champ." He laughed softly and wrapped his arm around me. "Are you okay?"

Ding, ding, ding! We have a winner!

"Swell," I croaked. "Don't remember a thing."

"You lost at cards."

"You cheated!" I pushed against him.

"You made me take off my pants."

"Only because you cheated."

"I kissed you—hard."

I shivered.

"Oh, and you puked."

"Yeah, I know."

"Yelled at me in the car." He continued talking as if I needed an actual list of the shameful things I'd done. "Oh, and when we got home you tried crawling onto the roof and when I wouldn't let you, you started yelling, 'I'm Iron Man, bitch, suit up!'"

My face froze in horror. "Okay, I remember everything but that."

"Probably for the best." Colton nodded.

I was going to kill Max for not telling me I'd done that!

"Considering it didn't happen." Colton smirked. "Just paying you back for seeing me naked."

"Please, like it was a chore for you to drop your pants," I hissed. "What, did you sprain your pinky finger? Get your little boy caught in your zipper? Hmm?"

"Little?" His eyes narrowed. "You called me a freaking super-hero!"

"Guys!" Max ran up to us, then dropped to the ground and picked up a few pieces of grass in his hand, letting them slowly fall from his fingertips. "Jayne's been here. I'd bet my life on it."

I sighed and gave him an irritated look. "You were kicked out of Boy Scouts."

"I was too advanced for their curriculum." Max stood and held his hand in the air, closing his eyes.

"What's he doing?" Colton asked.

"Shh!" Max whispered. "I'm finding Jayne."

"You look like you're getting sworn into office," I replied. "Put your hand down and go see if she took any cars."

"Oh." Max's eyes blinked open. "Good call. I'll just leave you two alone, unless you need a chaperone or something. Don't want Colton dropping his pants again. And dude, for real, that's not how you get chicks. That's how you get a shiny new seat in prison next to a dude who looks like a lady but has the wrong parts—feel me?" Max walked off toward the front of the house where the cars were parked.

"I, uh—" Words died on my lips as Jenna sauntered toward us. *Yes*, she sauntered. I swear her hips were moving so far outside her body I wanted to scream.

"Colton!" She smiled brightly. I prayed her teeth would fall out within the next few hours. "I checked all the bedrooms and even found—uh-oh."

"What?" Colton asked. "What did you find?"

"Look." She pointed above us; I quickly turned around to find Jason at the bottom of one of the oak trees and Reid shimmying across one of the branches.

"I believe I can fly!" he sang. "I believe I can—shit!" He slipped off one of the branches and nearly fell to his death.

"Reid! Get down here!"

"I think about it every night and day!" He continued singing and then got choked up. "Spread my wings and fly away."

"Guys!" Max ran up to us, all out of breath. "We may have a problem, I checked the cars and then went inside to double-check bedrooms and Reid's room had an empty bottle of—oh, shit."

"Hey, Max!" Reid waved. "Look! I'm a bird!"

"I was thinking more . . . plane." I shrugged.

"No." Colton nodded and then gave a solitary clap. "That, my friends, is Superman."

"Reid! How many happy pills did you take?" Max shouted.

Reid held up three fingers and almost slid off the branch.

"Great. There went that plan!" Max stomped over to the tree. "Reid, shimmy your ass down here before I get a shotgun and shoot you out of the leaves."

"But I want to fly down."

"Then imagine you're flying and drop."

"Dude!" Jason smacked Max. "That's like ten feet."

"Then let's hope he doesn't break his drugged ass, besides, he's high as a kite, he won't feel a damn thing."

Reid nodded and then slowly, actually quite gracefully, fell from the tree, landed on his feet, somersaulted, and jumped back to his feet, lifting his hands in victory above his head.

"Nine," I said.

"Ten." Colton held up his hands. "Perfect ten."

"Eh, he struggled on sticking the landing. I'm going to say seven." Jenna tilted her head to the side. "But he gets an extra point for flair."

Jason groaned and started hitting the tree with his hand. "We have pictures in less than two hours!"

"Found her!" Mom shouted from the house. "She was in the attic!"

"The attic?" My eyes met Colton's. Our attic? Our special place.

"No worries!" Mom waved. "She's getting ready in one of the bathrooms. Pictures in ninety minutes, guys!"

# CHAPTER THIRTY-TWO
## COLTON

"Are you drunk?" I watched as Jason swayed on his feet, then gripped my shoulder with his hand.

"No." He blinked his good eye. "Just having trouble focusing on walking in a straight line due to my inability to perceive depth."

I raised my eyebrows.

"And if you must know I'm slightly"—he held up two fingers as a form of measurement—"in-intoxicated." He let out a burp and winced. "How does it hurt my face to burp? I swear. I blame Milo."

I shrugged. "It's just easier that way."

"Are you still going to do the thing?"

"What thing?" I lied.

"The whole I-love-you thing where you rip off your shirt and show her how much you love *Star Wars* and that you're willing to make a fool of yourself?"

"Nah." I narrowed my eyes. "Change of plans."

"Max said—"

"Screw Max!" I growled.

"Chill." Jason held up his hands. "They're not really together."

"No." I clenched my fists. "And I know he's only trying to help now, but he's kissed her way too many times for me to actually want to pull him in for a hug rather than a swift kick to the balls."

"Everyone ready!" The photographer walked out onto the lawn and looked around. "Where's the wedding party?"

Jason and I raised our hands.

Pathetic.

"Oh, er, I'm sorry, I was under the impression . . . Of course, um, never mind. Why don't we just get a few shots of you two first, hmm?"

"Let's get this over with," Jason growled.

"You could at least be a little excited." I rolled my eyes. "For me, Jason, do it for me."

"You're right, man." Jason hung his head. "Forgive me?"

"Course." I pulled him in for a tight hug.

"Keep it there!" the photographer shouted. "The light's perfect, just keep it there."

"Uh . . ." My arms were wrapped around Jason, his head was resting on my shoulder. Awkward didn't even begin to describe the moment.

"Okay, now Jason, I want you to look toward the camera, remember you're in love, all right? Good, good, now place your hand at the small of his back."

"What the h?" I hissed in Jason's ear.

"Shut it!" he whispered back. "The sooner we get done, the sooner the pictures are done, and I can go find Milo so she can render me blind!"

"Fine." I clenched my teeth together.

"Oh, perfect, yes, that's nice." The camera went off. "Now, the other fella there, I want you to turn your head so that you're almost touching noses."

"I'm murdering you tonight—in your sleep," I said through a tight smile.

Jason winced. "Not if Milo gets to me first."

"*Touché.*"

"Lean in!" the photographer yelled.

I clenched my teeth. "Please tell me that you're packing a gun."

"Cell phone."

"Thank God."

"Now." The photographer was right in front of our faces with the camera. "Just a little kiss on the cheek."

"What?" I yelled and pushed away from Jason.

The photographer shook his head. "These pictures are forever, you know. You're going to look back and wish you would have taken more intimate photos."

"I highly, highly doubt that," I grumbled under my breath, taking a tentative step toward Jason and wishing for alcohol to make me forget that I was about to touch my best friend in a familiar way.

"Just do it," Jason hissed. "Let's get this over with."

"Fine." I leaned in just as Jason leaned in, I turned my cheek but he went the opposite way, and ended up missing my cheek—only to land on my mouth.

The camera flashed.

"What are you guys *doing*?" Milo covered her mouth as her eyes watered with laughter.

"Oh." The photographer turned. "Hello, I'm just taking some pictures of the happy couple."

"Wow." Milo grinned in approval. "That's special. Hey, if I give you my e-mail address can you send me a few copies? And make sure the resolution is really clear, I'm thinking of making a poster."

"Wait." I pulled away from Jason. "I'm the best man."

The photographer flushed, almost dropping his camera. "Ah, that explains it then."

"Explains what?"

"No chemistry." He shrugged. "No romance. I thought something was off—that was the worst wedding kiss I'd ever witnessed."

I pointed at the photographer. "Hey, I'm attracted, it's not like I don't like my boy. It's just not in that way."

Yeah, wrong thing to say.

Milo burst out laughing. "No, Colton, really, keep going, it's a romantic speech."

"To hell with that!" I stalked toward Milo and pulled her in for a scorching kiss. My lips met hers with such force she stumbled backward. When I pulled away I looked at the photographer. "See? I like women."

"No!" a voice wailed.

"You lying, cheating hussy!" Max screamed.

"Oh, dear God," Jason moaned.

In that moment Jayne came around the corner with the bridesmaids, the groomsmen, her family members, and Grandma—escorted by Reid.

He smiled and waved.

Then again, he was probably still high. *Note to self: lock his bedroom door tonight.*

"Name your second!" Max shouted loudly, then winked like he wanted me to go along.

"That's easy." I rolled my eyes.

Jason puffed out his chest.

"Milo."

"What?" He hit me.

"She's more dangerous than you are by a long shot, admit it. Plus I figure if Max is going to shoot me it would be nice to fall into Milo's arms before I die."

Her breath hitched.

That's right. I caused that reaction. Damn it, I was losing control of myself. What the hell had I been thinking? I just wanted to grab and kiss her before I even had a chance to prove to her how I felt.

"Fine, then I choose Jenna." Max grinned.

"I feel left out," Jason grumbled.

"You have one eye, you're no longer welcome on *Survivor* island, and I'm pretty sure if we were in a plane crash—you'd get eaten first. Just sayin'." Max raised his hands.

"Er, the pictures?" The photographer waved his camera.

"I'm ready!" Jayne interrupted our tense moment and latched herself on to Jason. "Let's do this before my groom gets another black eye."

Max leaned over to the photographer and whispered, "She beats him."

"Oh, I see." His cheeks burned red.

"But we don't report her because he likes it—he's one of those." Max made a whipping sound and winked.

So everyone was drunk. Fantastic.

Milo was still staring at me, her face pale.

"Look, I'm sorry for kissing you." I shook my head. "I just reacted and—"

She lifted her right hand, and I flinched, thinking she was going to slap me. Instead I was the happy recipient of a left hook.

"Shit!" My chin throbbed as I fell to my knees.

"Stop apologizing for kissing me!" With a tearful sob she yelled, "I'm not even engaged! It's you! I love you, asshole! But right now I hate you. I hate you for making me feel like I'm convenient, but most of all I hate that it's so easy for you to use me and then just put me back on the shelf. Do you think I'm happy there? Do you think I enjoy knowing what it's like to be kissed by you, only to be rejected?"

"Milo, I—"

"No!" She wiped her eyes. "Sorry, Jason."

With a curse she stomped off across the yard.

Max's eyebrows lifted. "Well?"

"Well what?"

"Are you going to go after her or are you going to be a jackass and choke?"

"Stand in for me?"

Jason cursed.

"I've always wanted to be in a wedding."

"Crap!" Jayne yelled. "I forgot my veil!"

"Oh, I know where it is, here, I'll help." Reid ran after her, looking a little less high.

"Pictures?" Mrs. Caro said in a hopeful voice as people scattered once again across the lawn and into the house.

I didn't hear the rest of their conversation. My sole purpose was to find Milo, kiss the hell out of her, and apologize.

# CHAPTER THIRTY-THREE

## MILO

I ran blindly through the house, my heart pounding against my chest as I tried to catch my breath.

Asshole.

I was sick of it—sick of being the girl he used to prove he was still in full possession of his balls. It felt like a pissing war. Like Colton was only using me to prove that he was the better man. Was I some prize he needed to win in order to prove his manhood? Did he think I was made of steel? That I had no feelings whatsoever? Even if everything I'd said had been true—even if I had really been with Max—the fact that Colton still thought it was okay to kiss me whenever the hell he felt like it?

It felt like he owned me.

And I hated that truth.

Because it meant he had all the power.

And I was just the type of girl to pine over him for the rest of my life—unless I cut him out.

Without a second thought, I went into the guest bedroom at the end of the hall and pulled open the door to the attic.

An old memory surfaced with each step my heels took on the stairs.

*"I got the dragon, Milo!" Colton yelled. "Don't worry, I got him."*

*"Colt." I shivered in my box castle. "I'm afraid."*

*"Don't worry, Princess!" he shouted. "I brought my sword—dragons are terrified of wooden swords, you know."*

*"Really?" I perked up. That was nice to know. "Hey, Colt?"*

*"Yeah, Milo?"*

*"Does the wood sword ward off mean girls too?"*

*He was silent. "It scares off everything bad in the whole world, Milo. I promise."*

*"Colt?"*

*"Yeah?"*

*"Thanks for slaying the dragon."*

*"It's my job." His reply was swift, easy, as if it were real.*

But it hadn't been real, not at all. Because if he'd truly meant it, if my reality was that he would slay all the dragons—then he wouldn't keep hurting me. The hero isn't supposed to hurt the girl, he's supposed to save her. For my entire life Colton had made me believe he was the hero out to save me, not only because it was his job, but because he wanted to, because he felt something.

Clearly he felt nothing.

Emotions clogged my throat as I reached the top of the stairs. The box castle looked exactly the same. The wooden sword was lying across the floor, and the stupid hat I used to wear was lying next to it.

With a curse I grabbed the hat, put it on, then grabbed the sword and started using it to knock the boxes over.

"Stupid, stupid, stupid!" I swung as hard as I could.

"What the hell are you doing?" a calm voice said behind me.

I didn't stop.

"Milo—"

"Leave me alone, Colt!"

"I would." His arms came around me. "But you're doing it all wrong."

"What?" My hands dropped, the wooden sword clattered to the floor. "Doing what wrong?"

"That's not how you storm a castle."

I shook my head. I would not laugh; I refused to smile. That's what Colton did! He got so far underneath my skin that even if I was contemplating jumping out the window or stabbing him in the eye with a toothpick—one word from him and I was suddenly on cloud nine.

"Not this time," I mumbled.

"What was that?"

"Hi-ya!" I karate-elbowed him or whatever the hell it's called, grabbed the sword, and started swinging wildly in his direction.

"Put the sword down, Milo."

"No!" I tapped him in the shoulder with it and took a stance. "Leave me alone! Go back to Jenna!" I was getting no points for maturity. That much was true. I swatted him again. "I'm serious, Colt, leave me alone!"

"*No*, damn it!" He grabbed the sword from my hand, but I refused to let go, meaning I slammed across his chest so hard that I lost my breath.

"I said let go." I stomped on his foot.

He winced, but held me firmly. "I'm not leaving you."

"That's just the thing," I whispered, my eyes searching his. "You always do." I shrugged. "I can't do this anymore, Colt. I can't live in this fantasy. I'm not in the castle, you don't slay dragons for me anymore. This . . ." I looked around. "Isn't real."

"The hell it isn't." His hands went around my face. "Tell me this isn't real—what we have. What we've always had. Tell me it's not real and I'll walk."

"You'd do that?" I choked. "You'd leave me?"

"If I knew you wanted nothing to do with me—I'd leave. And before you go chewing my ass off for being that type of guy—just know. I'd rather leave, and know you were at peace, then stay and be the cause for the constant war."

"I'm not really with Max," I blurted.

"You don't say." He chuckled.

"Son of a bitch, you knew!" I screamed, pushing against his chest.

"How the hell am I the villain in this story? You lied to your entire family, put Jason's health at risk, are most likely going to have to pay for Reid's therapy, and nearly drove me insane!"

"Aw, really?" I sighed.

"God, you're such a basket case." Colton rolled his eyes. "I say all that and the only thing you hear is that you were successful in nearly making me lose my damn mind?"

I nodded.

"I'm done," Colton said softly. "In fact, I'm pretty sure I'll both regret and remember this day for the rest of my life, but—" His mouth touched mine, just barely before he pulled back. "If you ever turn into an evil genius where you see yourself needing a partner in crime, or even just someone to beat up on. Sign me up."

"Huh?"

"I love you." He smiled. "So damn much that I'm pretty sure if I wouldn't have found out you were a lying little brat—you would have found Max's body in the pool."

"You love me?"

"Again, I just admitted to homicidal thoughts and you hear . . . nothing but the love?"

"Say it again?"

"I almost killed Max."

"Not that part!" I smacked him.

"I love you." Colton cupped my face with his hands. "You're crazy as hell—but you're my crazy. I want to live in that head of yours. I want to hear about the crazy things you conjure up in that imagination of yours. I want to slay your dragons again, but this time . . ." His voice lowered. "I'm not leaving the castle. I'm not going back down those stairs. I'm staying."

"You're staying?" I asked, confused and elated at the same time. My heart slammed against my chest.

"Yeah. I'm not just going to save the damsel—I'm going to rescue her, then I'm going to kiss her, then I'm going to marry her, then I'm going to fight with her, then I'm going to love her again. I'm sure there will be more dragons ahead of us—but we've had lots of practice, so I think we'll be safe."

"Maybe bring your sword, just in case," I whispered, handing him the wooden sword.

"Yeah." He took it. "Just in case."

He dropped the sword, which clattered against the ground just as our mouths met in a frenzy—both of us pushing against one another so hard that it was more of an attack than consensual kissing.

"Damn it!" Colton grabbed my arms and pulled me down to the ground, and right into the castle.

"Yeah." I pushed him against the small wall under the arch of boxes. "Never dreamed about this when I waited for you up here."

Colton pulled back, his eyes as dark as smoke. "You dirty little liar."

"What!"

"You thought about this." His hand moved from my face to my chest, and then rested on my hip as he softly unzipped my dress. "And I sure as hell dreamed of this."

Giggling, I captured his mouth with mine as my fingers fumbled awkwardly with his shirt.

"Colton? Milo?" Max's voice sounded from the bottom of the stairs. "You guys up there?"

"Shh!" I covered Colton's mouth and panicked. If I said nothing he'd walk in on us and ruin my special moment! "Um, yeah, kind of busy, though."

Nothing, and then, "Oh, what are you doing?"

Colton gave me a helpless look, then licked my hand.

"Uhh," I giggled as he nibbled each finger. "Playing dragon slayer?"

"Can I play?"

"No!" I shouted, then I laughed. "Um, I mean, it's more of like a two-player game."

Colton's eyes darkened as he tugged my dress farther down.

"Are you the dragon or the slayer?" Max wanted to know.

Holy crap, why wouldn't he just leave?

"Um, I'm the slayer."

"So Colton's the dragon," Max confirmed.

"Yup!" Holy . . . that felt good. His tongue flicked my ear and then moved to my neck. I moaned and then my mouth was covered by Colton's.

"Okay," Max sighed. "But just, uh, remind Colton that he should put a helmet on his dragon, you know since they can be so . . ." Cough, cough. "Dangerous when they, uh, invade." Cough.

My eyes widened in horror.

"You feel me?" Max asked. "Because dragons breathe fire and if you've never experienced . . . er, fire before, then it may be wise to use—"

"Got it, man, thanks!" Colton yelled.

"Good talk!" Max called.

# CHAPTER THIRTY-FOUR
## COLTON

My hand was still braced on the bare skin of her back as I heard Max's footsteps echo across the room and out into the hall.

The door slammed.

"You think he's gone?" Milo whispered. Every inhalation she took wrecked me, I could feel it in my palm, my fingertips. Hell, I felt it in my blood.

That I'd stayed away as long as I had was an absolute miracle.

"Yeah." I tilted her face toward mine and captured her mouth, tugging at her lips before pulling back and sighing. I wanted her so damn bad I would have sold my freaking soul in order to have an hour, minutes, seconds with her.

But the timing—was off.

Story of our lives.

I kissed her again. "We should—"

"—go rescue Jason, tell Max he can stop pretending to be in love with me, and make sure Reid's safely tucked away from the watchful eye of Grandma."

Defeated, I sighed, not wanting to move an inch.

"Hey." Milo turned around, her dress slipping off her shoulders.

*Damn it, just a bit farther.*

"Zip me up?"

"No." I pouted, crossing my arms.

"Colt . . ."

"Jason will be fine."

"He can barely see out of one eye, Colt, and—"

Loud footsteps interrupted what she was about to say. With a curse I pulled her back into the box castle and looked around the corner.

Jayne made her way up the stairs, her wild eyes looking around the room until, with a curse, she finally located something.

*Ah, her phone, she must have left it up here when she was pouting.*

"Damn." She checked messages, then quickly made a call. "No, no, no, I just lost my phone." She snorted. "God, I need a strong drink. Are you kidding me? He doesn't even know there is no baby, and by the time he finds out, it won't matter anyways. Dr. Boomer would do anything for my family. It wasn't hard to get him to back me up." Another snort. "No, he won't get fired because nobody will know. Besides, it's not like sleeping with the good doctor was a chore, right?" Her laugh was so loud I winced. "By the time he even finds out there's no baby it won't matter."

Milo shifted next to me as Jayne gave us her back.

I tried to grab Milo but it was too late. She had that look in her eyes—the crazy one that said, *Don't mess with me or I'm going to make you look like my brother.*

With an evil grin, she popped out from underneath the box castle.

And tackled Jayne to the floor.

The cell phone went flying.

Jayne started screaming.

Milo was koala-ing Jayne's back as she got whipped one way, then the other.

"Get off of me!"

"No!" Milo shouted. "You don't even love him!"

"I do too!"

"Do not!"

"Girls," I interrupted, holding my hands in the air—the universal sign of peace.

But not for women.

For women I may as well have held a sign that said, "You're fat."

"Stay out of this, Colt!" Milo snapped.

"Milo—"

"Aghhhh!" She finally tackled Jayne to the floor and managed to straddle her.

Someone else ran up the stairs.

Max. Of course.

"Sorry, it's just—" He looked down at Jayne and Milo, nodded, then took a seat and patted the spot next to him.

"Care to help out?" I pointed as Milo started pinning Jayne's hands down.

Max tilted his head. "No, no, I'm good. Have a seat."

"But—"

"Do you really want to be known as the guy that breaks up a chick fight?"

The man had a point.

"Wish we had beer." Max pouted. "Oh, and my money's on Milo."

"Yeah." I pointed to the girls. "But Jayne's scrappy."

"Ooo!" We both winced as Jayne used her nails to scratch down Milo's arm.

"What the hell!" Jason appeared at the top of the stairs.

"Have a seat." Max smiled and patted the spot next to him.

"Jayne! Milo!" Jason went over to grab Milo.

"Really, really bad idea," Max said under his breath.

Sure enough, he was able to get Milo unlatched from Jayne's body but the momentum of his pulling her from Jayne's body sent them both flying backward—directly into the box castle.

Boxes went everywhere.

And that's when Jayne started screaming again.

Like something out of *The Shining*.

"Calm down." Max rolled his eyes. "They fell in a pile of boxes, big deal."

"H-holy shit." I ran over to Jason's side.

He shook his head and winced. "Man, that hurt."

"Don't move!" I pulled Milo to her feet, only to have Jayne stumble into her arms.

Max got up and approached the scene of the accident.

"Is that blood?" He pointed to Jason's arm.

"Yup." I quickly assessed the situation.

"I don't like blood."

"Yeah, well—"

Max hit the floor—and took a now-stable Jayne down with him.

"Get him off of me!" Jayne yelped. Max's head had fallen directly between her breasts.

Milo pulled out her phone and snapped a picture.

"Could you not!" I hissed.

"What?" She shrugged. "It's evidence!"

"That your fiancé, who isn't really your fiancé, was sleeping with your brother's fiancée in the attic while your brother was impaled by a ski pole?"

"Holy shit! That's a ski pole!"

"Jason." I gave him a calm smile. "Stay cool, it's totally fine, I just don't want to pull it out and have you bleed all over your nice suit."

"Lies!" he yelled. "I'm dying!"

"You're not dying!" I yelled right back and got down on my knees. "Just let me have a look, okay?"

"What's all the racket up here?" Mrs. Caro appeared at the top of the stairs, followed by Mr. Caro, Reid, Grandma, and Jenna.

"Jayne tried to kill Jason!" Milo shouted.

"Oh, dear Lord," I grumbled. "Nobody tried to kill anybody!"

At that point Max stirred across Jayne's chest, lifting his head, only to get slapped so hard it looked like he passed out again. This time his lips were pressed against her skin.

"Get him off!" she shrieked.

Jason groaned.

Stealing the entire family's attention.

"Son, you're bleeding!" Mr. Caro got down on his knees next to me. "How the hell did you get a ski pole in your arm?"

"Long story," he grumbled. "But it starts with Milo and ends with her too."

All eyes turned to her.

"What?" She threw her hands into the air. "It wasn't my fault! If Jayne would have just agreed to leave Jason alone then it wouldn't have happened!"

"Never!" Jayne shouted from the floor. "I'm gonna be your sister-in-law, bitch! Better get used to it!"

Milo's mouth snapped shut.

Mrs. Caro rose to her full height and stomped over to Jayne. "Listen here, you social-climbing whore! I've sat back calmly while you ruined my son's life. I've said nothing—even when you disrespected me and my family repeatedly. But I draw the line now!"

"Oh, wow, you're drawing lines now. Should I be afraid?"

"I doubt anything scares you—and if it does, you just spread your legs and close your eyes!" Mrs. Caro screamed at the top of her lungs.

"Marcy!" Mr. Caro scolded.

Grandma burst out laughing.

"Oh, don't worry." Jayne's eyes narrowed. "I'll remember to do that. After all your son has been very, very, very accommodating."

Everyone started yelling at once.

And then a gunshot rang out. Causing part of the ceiling to crumble next to Jason's head.

"All right." Grandma held a small pistol in the air. "Everyone cease arguing, I'm putting a stop to this sham."

"Who gave her a gun?" Max said in a groggy voice. "Seriously? Who gave Grandma a gun?"

"Keep it in my purse." Grandma shrugged. "In case those thugs decide to steal me in the parking lot." At that point her wig slid off onto the floor, showing us a few solitary gray tufts. Hey, look at that, she still had a few strings of hair! Go Grandma!

"I don't think you have to worry about being stolen," Milo muttered under her breath.

"There will be no wedding," Grandma sniffed. "You do not have my blessing."

"You can't control me!" Jayne shouted. "And for the love of God, get off of me, Max!"

"No!" He stayed pinned against her. "Not until you admit it!"

"Admit what?"

"You aren't pregnant!"

"Fine!" Jayne's eyes went wide with anger. "I'm not pregnant! It doesn't change a damn thing! I'm the best he's ever going to get and—"

Milo charged toward Jayne, fist flying. I intercepted her just in time . . . for Mrs. Caro to finish what her daughter had started.

# CHAPTER THIRTY-FIVE

## MILO

"I'm fine! I promise!" Mom held her swollen hand in her lap, a satisfied grin flashing across her face. "Got her good, didn't I?"

Wrong thing to say, as Jayne chose that moment to make her way into the kitchen and send Mom a seething glare.

Everything fell silent.

Jason had broken up with her in the attic. Of course, as with all things Caro, that was after Mom punched her in the face, before Max passed out for a third time, and before Reid wrestled Grandma to the floor. Luckily Reid was able to scoot the gun away from her greedy little hands before she made a reach for it again.

"I guess there's nothing left to say." Jayne sniffled, reaching for her purse.

Jason's eye narrowed as he leaned back in the chair. Colton was busy wrapping up the gaping wound the ski pole had left.

"I would have made you happy," she defended, her eyes blinking away tears.

"You would have put him in an early grave," Grandma piped up.

I'd thought she was sleeping.

Her eyes were still closed.

Curious, I stared as she continued to talk without opening them. "You would have stolen that boy's joy and made him miserable every day of his life—and I know misery, that husband of mine was no walk in the park."

I coughed. "He was blind."

"He was weak!" Grandma slammed her hand against the table.

I winced, half expecting her to dig into her purse for her gun. Instead Reid sent me a reassuring look and patted the pocket of his suit.

I wasn't sure if I was relieved he'd stolen Grandma's gun, or concerned, especially considering the effects of his medicine were starting to wear off, and every few seconds he burst out laughing and then just stared at the ceiling.

"Fine," Jayne huffed. "I can tell I'm no longer welcome."

"Sharp as a nail." Max wandered into the room, his face pale. "Oh, why are you still here?"

"You used to want me." Jayne's lips trembled.

"I was eighteen," Max defended. "I also thought buying a monkey and keeping it in my closet was a stellar plan."

"Fred." Reid sighed. "Damn, that monkey was quick, didn't even see him sneak up on me like that."

Max winced. "Sorry, man, I forgot about—"

"It's cool." He nodded. "I'm still a bit out of it, yeah, whatever."

"You had a monkey?" This from Jason. "Badass!"

Max stole a guilty look at his brother. "He had a fascination with Reid."

"And when you say fascination." I paused. "You mean—"

"It wasn't my fault!" Reid shouted.

"Shhh, shh!" Max ran over and pulled Reid in for a hug. "Remember, it's not your fault, okay?"

"Mom, Dad, Max, the monkey has my balls, the monkey has my balls!" Reid started shaking.

"This entire family is insane." Jayne stomped out of the kitchen and slammed the door behind her.

Meanwhile Max and Reid pulled apart and went from looking insane to looking completely normal.

I narrowed my eyes as suspicion struck. "There was no monkey, was there?"

"Nope." Max smirked and gave his brother a high five. "I can't believe you still knew that skit from camp."

"I remember everything," Reid said.

"So what now?" I looked around the room. "I guess we should start calling guests and—"

"No!" Mom shouted, slamming her good hand across the table. "We're not un-inviting anyone!"

"Okay." I held my hands out in front of me. "I was just thinking—"

"Stop thinking, Milo!" Max shouted. "Your mom's clearly over-wrought!"

"I am," Mom whimpered. "But I think now is as good a time as any to tell you kids . . ."

"Oh, no," I whispered.

"We're moving." She looked out the window. "This is our last real event here—and I won't have it ruined by that, that, that—"

"Don't hurt yourself," I interrupted.

"Hussy!" she shouted. "We're having a wedding and that's that!"

I raised my hand. "Unless you plan on marrying Jason off to Reid, we have no bride or groom. The marriage license says—"

Jason laughed. "About that."

"What?" I almost didn't want to hear.

He scratched his head. "I, uh, forgot to get a marriage license, so legally we wouldn't have been married today, but we'd have three days to get the license and make it official."

"So we went through hell for nothing?" I jumped to my feet, ready to charge my brother and mess up his other eye.

"No." Colton's arms wrapped around me from behind as he whispered in my ear, "Not for nothing."

My mom's eyes widened as an excited grin erupted across her face. "Yes, that will do. That will do just fine, Colton."

# CHAPTER THIRTY-SIX
## MILO

"Time out!" I held up my hands and made a T. "What will do?"

"You." Mom grinned, then started clapping her hands.

"Mom, don't clap, it makes you look like a seal."

Colton leaned in and whispered, "Your mom just bitch-slapped Jayne—let the woman clap. Hell, give her a medal. As far as I'm concerned, she can do whatever the hell she wants."

Max watched our exchange and started making a driving motion with his hands. He honked a horn, kept driving, and then motioned to Reid, who then got on all fours and collapsed as Max's imaginary car ran him over.

"Are you high too?" I asked, fighting the urge to feel his forehead.

His answer? "The wheels on the bus go round and round—oh, look! I just ran over Milo."

My eyes narrowed. "Hilarious."

"Champagne for everyone!" Mom yelled. "We celebrate!"

"Getting run over by a bus?" I yelled.

"Marriage!" Mom said, ignoring me.

"I'll drink to anything," Jason grumbled from the table. He had his arm raised high above his head and was leaning to the side. The guy needed an all-inclusive vacation—away from me.

"What are we drinking to?" I took the champagne.

"Guests will be arriving in an hour!" Mom shouted. "So I'm going to need everyone to pitch in."

"Jason can't marry himself," I felt the need to point out, you know, just in case I was the only person left in that room with a working brain.

"Oh, silly." Mom chuckled and did a little dance in place. "He's not getting married."

"Max and I aren't engaged." I shook my head violently. "You know that, right?"

"I'll take care of things." Colton grabbed my shoulders and turned me toward the hall and pushed. "Walk."

"Walk where?"

"Just walk."

"I'm not into it, you know, that whole dominant-submissive thing? I don't get it." But I kept walking. "I don't like being ordered around. It makes me want to punch you in the face. It doesn't make me hot."

"It takes nothing," Colton whispered, his breath blazing across my neck, "to make you hot, especially when it comes to me."

I stopped in my tracks, seething. "You arrogant son of a—"

"In you go!" He pushed me into the bedroom, but didn't follow. The door slammed shut.

"Colton!" I banged on the door. "Let me out!"

"Not yet!" He gave a sinister laugh. "I'll let you out in a bit. Oh, and just let us take care of everything."

"Take care of what?" I pounded harder. "I swear I'm going to run you over with my car!"

"I love you!"

"I hate you!"

"You love me! Oh, and Milo—I have a question for you."

I stopped pounding. "Wh-what?"

"Will you . . ."

My heart started to pound.

"I guess what I'm trying to say is . . ."

Holy crap. I leaned against the door.

"*If* it's not too much to ask . . ."

Was he?

"Can you not call your brother and complain to him that I locked you in the room? I have a plan—but you gotta let me romance you my way."

"NO!" I shouted. "And this isn't romance, it's kidnapping!"

"Aw, sweetie." He chuckled. "You should have said something if you wanted me to tie you up!"

"I loathe you!"

"We'll see . . ." Colton's laughter echoed down the hall, then disappeared.

# CHAPTER THIRTY-SEVEN
## COLTON

"She pissed?" Jason asked, taking a long sip of his champagne.

"I think." I took a seat in the kitchen. "The question should be—when isn't she pissed? That woman's like a tiny ball of rage just waiting to rain on someone's parade."

"Parades terrify me," Max piped up.

Jason nodded in understanding and slid the champagne toward him and Reid.

"Parades?" I couldn't help but ask. "Really?"

Max shot me a look of terror. "The clowns are allowed out of their tiny cars, Colton. Have you ever even been to a parade? They hand candy and balloons to small children and have permanent smiles on their faces. No one"—he shuddered—"should have a permanent smile."

"So if I dressed up as a clown for Halloween—"

"Do it, you son of a bitch. I'll shoot you on sight." Max threw back the contents of his glass and slammed it on the table.

"He's serious," Reid piped up, his language slightly slurred. "When I was ten, I was the clown in the class play. I walked into his bedroom to see if he would help me with my wig and he shot me in the face with his Nerf gun."

"We're thankful he still has his eye." Max nodded. "Truth."

"R-right." I watched the exchange with interest. Reid was the older brother but it seemed Max had done his fair share of bullying when he was younger too.

"All right." Mrs. Caro barreled into the kitchen and took a seat. "We need a plan."

"I'm great with plans," Max said.

"Not this one." I stood.

All eyes were directed to me.

Well, really I should say a few eyeballs looked at me, considering Jason could hardly see and Reid looked like he was seeing three of me instead of one—damn drugs were still doing him in.

So I had Jenna, who seemed to be hanging on Max's every word.

Jason, who, as discussed previously, probably couldn't find his way down the hall, let alone help decorate.

Reid, who by the looks of it probably still thought he could fly.

And Milo's parents.

"So?" Mrs. Caro clapped. "What should we do first?"

I looked at the ragtag team seated around the table. "All right, I'm going to need your help. We're going to build a castle."

Max perked up. "A castle? Where?"

"Glad you asked." I slapped him on the back. "We're going to build a castle right next to the altar so that the princess knows without a shadow of a doubt—"

"That you're insane?" Max shot me a thumbs-up.

"That I'm her prince." I gave a nonchalant shrug even though it was a bigger deal than I let on. "I'm going to storm her castle."

"Back in my day, we just called that sex," Grandma chimed in from her side of the table.

Shit. I'd forgotten about that woman. She was sitting at the end of the table, her hands demurely in front of her.

"Here, man." Max slid something toward my hand. "Take it."

I looked down at the peach-colored pill. "What the hell?"

"It's best if she doesn't interfere." Max nodded.

"So you want me to drug Grandma?"

"Of course not!" Max laughed nervously. "She's not mine! I refuse to claim her. Besides, we'll have Reid do it."

Reid stood and wobbled. "The hell I will."

"Dude, can you even feel your toes?" Max asked.

Reid's eyes widened in horror. "My feet! My feet! Where are my feet?"

"Guys!" Jason snapped. "We have to hurry—we only have an hour to perform a miracle."

"I studied to be a doctor," Grandma whispered under her breath.

"You were a vet." Jason rolled his eye. "Big difference."

"A cow's teats and the teats of a—"

"She needs to stop saying *teats*." Max heaved a sigh. "Look, Reid's shaking again."

I held up my hands in exhaustion. "Fine, Grandma, you stay here and keep the table company, Max, you're with me and Jason, we need to build the castle. Mrs. Caro, you and Jenna can go to Milo, make sure she looks like a bride, and for the love of God don't let her run past you. Tackle her if need be!"

"You can tackle cows too." Grandma sighed. "Like I said, same thing."

Max whistled and then winked with a firm nod toward the pill. "She'll go to happy land, dude, it's worth it."

# CHAPTER THIRTY-EIGHT

## MILO

It had been a half hour.

I'd stopped pounding on the door and was now rummaging through the different drawers of the guest room for a protein bar . . . those things never went bad, right?

Starved, I walked into the adjoining bathroom and was half tempted to start eating cough drops when a soft knock on the door interrupted my search.

"Yes?" I said in an exasperated voice. "Have you come to set me free?"

"No." The voice was Jenna's. "Actually, I'm here to help you, but you have to promise not to run past me or punch me in the face."

"Jason's black eyes were total accidents." I crossed my arms defensively. "Swear."

"Honey, you don't need to defend yourself to us."

"What do you guys want?"

After a moment of silence Jenna said, "We have food."

I chewed my lower lip and looked down at the bag of cherry cough drops in my hand. "What kind of food?"

"Chocolate-covered almonds, fruit snacks, three different types of cheeses, and some crackers."

I scowled and looked down at the floor. "Do the crackers have sea salt?"

"Yup!" Dang, I could practically see Jenna's beaming smile through the door.

"Fine. I won't run."

The lock turned and Jenna and my mom both entered, then slammed the door behind them, barricading it with their bodies.

"Guys, chill." I rolled my eyes. "I'm not an escaped convict."

Mom's eyebrows rose as if to say, *Sure you aren't, honey. Sure you aren't.*

Geez, you hit one person with a ping pong ball and accidently impale him and suddenly you're a felon!

"The food?" I sniffled, sitting on the bed.

"Here." Jenna unloaded a giant basketful of goodies onto the bed. It was like staring at heaven. No, seriously. I wasn't one of those girls who got tiny hunger pangs when it was time to eat, then took a few sips of water, burped, wiped my mouth, and announced I was full.

Hell, no.

Carbs. Give. Me. Carbs. Give me protein. Give me chocolate and I'll be your best friend.

My mom was actually so concerned with my chocolate addiction when I was little that she had to repeatedly tell me that if a nice young man or woman offered me candy I had to scream at the top of my lungs.

Unfortunately for her, she never told me that Santa was supposed to offer candy to kids. Thus my being blacklisted during the Christmas of '04 from the mall.

I swear that damn Santa still gives me the stink-eye.

"So!" Mom clapped her hands. "We don't have a long time, so there's really nothing to be done with that hair of yours."

I touched my hair self-consciously with one hand while I gnawed on a Snickers bar with the other. "What do you mean? Time?"

"Yeah." Jenna tapped her chin with her pointer finger. "But I think if we keep it down and just wrap it into a low bun it will look really classic."

"Great idea!" My mom reached for my hair and pulled. There was no escaping. She was like a girl who had just discovered her first Barbie and didn't realize that plastic hair didn't grow back.

"Ouch!" I snapped as my roots begged for relief. "Mom! This is why I never let you do my hair when I was little!"

"You're fine." She pulled again. I sighed.

She tugged again. My head followed the direction of the tug, it had no choice unless it wanted to get ripped off.

*Not fine, not fine, not fine.* "What's going on?"

Jenna walked out of the room and returned with something in a garment bag.

"Just in time!" Mom announced, forgetting to let go of my hair as she walked over to Jenna and pulled me onto the floor. "Oh, sorry, honey."

"I'm good." I pushed to my feet and approached the shiny black bag. "What's this?"

"Your dress." Jenna giggled. "Duh."

"I already have my dress for the wedding." I pointed down. "I'm wearing it."

"Right, but Jason's wedding isn't happening," Mom explained. "So you need a new dress."

"For the new pretend wedding?"

"For . . ." Mom looked at Jenna, then thrust her hand into the air. "For your father's and my vow renewal."

A tear started rolling down her cheek.

"He's been such a good, *good* man, and all this time, he's stood by me. Through . . . thick and thin, through war and peace."

Weird speech, but I hugged her anyway.

"And we can't get the money back—it's too late—so we thought it might be nice, with friends and family around us, to make that commitment, especially in front of our children."

And suddenly I was feeling emotional because I'd done nothing except lie to her, lie to Colton, cause harm to Jason, and allow Grandma to sink her claws into an innocent young man who might not make it through the night without getting taken advantage of.

"Mom." I sighed and fell into her arms. "I'm so sorry! You guys deserve this, you deserve a chance to renew your vows. I feel selfish, and stupid. I was throwing a fit and—"

"Oh, sweetie." Mom laughed. "We're used to that."

"I'm sorry for that too."

"Honey, the heart wants what it wants." She peeled my arms away from her body and held my hands out in front of me. "Never apologize for fighting until your last breath for what you want in life. That's how things happen, you know."

"What do you mean?"

Mom's eyes twinkled. "You have to want love more than your next breath. Love shouldn't be something you jump into because it's the right time in your life or because your friends are all married. It should be something that happens naturally, and in the end it turns into the supernatural because suddenly you can't imagine waking up every day without that other half. You no longer want to be an individual but a team. There is no coexisting in marriage—it's a partnership—and you have to want it, you have to sometimes make yourself want it, but the need has to be before the want. Do you get what I mean?"

"Kind of." I nodded.

She slapped her hand over my mouth and pushed me against the bed, both plugging my nose and making it so I couldn't breathe out of my mouth. Holy crap, my mom was killing me. She'd officially snapped. I knew I was the bad kid, knew it!

I thrashed about for what felt like minutes when really it was like ten seconds.

Jenna watched in absolute horror.

Then Mom pulled away her hand. As I gasped for air and stared at Mom like the lunatic she was, she leaned over and whispered, "You have to want it as much as you want your next breath—you have to want Colton as much as you need air to survive—love is survival." With that she pulled back, stood, and offered a bright smile. "So why don't we get you dressed?"

And my parents wondered why their kids hadn't turned out normal.

What's worse?

She made absolute perfect sense.

# CHAPTER THIRTY-NINE
## COLTON

I was nervous as hell.

It wasn't like the wedding was going to be real in the sense that we had actual licenses to sign or anything—but for me it was real. If she wanted to do it over again, I wouldn't blame her. Didn't all girls want a chance to plan their own wedding?

But to pass this up?

An opportunity to tell her how I felt, in front of her friends, her family, my family, everyone she'd ever grown up with, including some of Jayne's angry friends, whom someone had clearly given alcohol to, if their loudness was any indication?

Somehow it just seemed right.

It also seemed right that we'd alter the ceremony a bit. I mean, it wasn't like I was going to go all crazy and make Max dress up as a dragon I had to slay or something . . . First off, we wouldn't have been able to find a costume in time, and second, the wooden sword wasn't big enough to look impressive—according to Max.

"Colton," Reid yelled. "How many lights you want up here?"

Reid was the only one who wasn't afraid of heights; then again, his depth perception was suffering severely. I had no idea what was in those small pills but it was enough to keep Reid in flight mode while he hung lights in the tree.

"Don't go too high," I yelled up at him.

"No worries!" He climbed to another branch. "If I fall I probably won't feel it anyway."

"Truth," Max said, suddenly by my side, handing me a glass of wine.

I took the wine and sipped. "Aren't you supposed to be working?"

"Finished." He shrugged.

"No way."

"Way. Though Jason was more of a hindrance, so I told him to go sit in the corner."

I looked in the direction in which Max was pointing. Sure enough, Jason was in the corner, a bag of peas held to his head with his good arm, and a bottle of wine next to his feet.

A wave of sympathy washed over me, and I nodded. "Rough day for him."

"Ha." Max rolled his eyes. "Living with Milo, I'm surprised he made it through adolescence."

"Hey." I nudged him. "You're her best friend, how do you make it?"

"My parents own a liquor franchise on top of the hotel chains, meaning I get free booze," he said. "And I have these handy-dandy little earplugs I put in when she starts singing off-key or quoting *Star Wars*—they work wonders—and I've learned she has at least five different facial cues for when she's asking me a question or merely filling the atmosphere with the sound of her own voice."

I stared at him for a minute. "The things you say both terrify and enlighten me in so many ways."

"Truth." He clinked his wineglass with mine. "So guests should be pulling in. Should we get Reid down from his perch?"

"Yeah."

"Reid!" Max yelled up at the tree. "You need to come down now."

"It's nice up here."

"You're not a bird," Max said gently. "And you actually hate heights, so the minute those drugs wear off, which should be in about—"

"Holy shit!" Reid shouted. "Max, I'm in a tree."

Jason came up behind me and looked up. "Someone should get him down."

"I'm not going." Max held up his hands. "I fell from a tree when I was five."

"Well, I'm not going!" I shouted. "I have to get married!"

"Send Grandma," Jason offered.

"Great." I sneered. "Yes, let's send your mentally unhinged grandmother up the tree. Surely that will get Reid to want to come down? If anything he's going to keep going up until there's nothing but air, say a prayer, and project his body from the highest branch in hopes of making it into the swimming pool without dying."

Max looked at the tree, then at the pool. "To be fair, he'd probably make it."

"Guys!" I yelled.

Mrs. Caro came running out of the house. "It's almost time! Guests are arriving!"

"Aw, shit." I looked at Reid as he clung to the tree branch. "Buddy, you think you can just slowly climb down?"

"Dude." Reid shook his head. "I literally see five of you right now. I don't even know where to put my hand, so even if you do climb up here to rescue me, I'm most likely going to grab ahold of something that doesn't have fingers and we all know how uncomfortable that would be."

Max choked on his laugh.

"You're his brother." I elbowed him.

"There are some things," Max said in a sad voice, "that even brothers cannot help brothers with."

"I take back what I said about you," I grumbled, walking toward the ladder that led up to the tree.

"About me being smart?"

"You're an ass."

"I just love a good donkey ride," Grandma's voice said to my right. I swear to all that is holy the woman appeared out of freaking thin air.

"Grandma," I sputtered. "Didn't see you."

"Shall I fetch the ass for you?" She leaned in and whispered, "I can get him out of that tree in a jiffy."

"There will be no jiffying of any kind!" Reid shouted from the branch.

"What the hell kind of life have you lived, squirt?" Grandma yelled right back. "*Jiffy* don't mean that!"

"She called me squirt," Reid whimpered. "She kissed me and wants to take advantage of me and she called me squirt. I think . . . I think I'm scared again."

"No more drugs!" Max scolded.

"Course not!" Grandma agreed. "That man's as virile as a cactus! He doesn't need drugs to perform!"

"A squirty cactus!" Reid repeated. "Forget it, Colt, I'm just going to fall, maybe a concussion will give me amnesia!"

"No!" I gently pushed Grandma away and started climbing the ladder. "I'm coming to get you!"

"Fine." Reid peered around the branch. "But hurry up, I think I see ants."

"Ants suck," Max said in a helpful voice.

"I'm allergic," Jason joined in. "I wanted an ant farm so bad when I was little."

"I had one," Max said in a dreamy voice. "When I was ten, I named the farm Max's Ant Oasis. Good times. Good times."

"Glad you two would have been friends!" I snapped as I reached the top of the ladder. "Okay, Reid, you have to grab ahold of my hand and get on the ladder with me. It will hold us both but you can't make any sudden movements, okay?"

He nodded and reached for my hands.

"Almost there," I said encouragingly, when I felt a jolt from the bottom of the ladder. Holy shit, Grandma was climbing up behind me. "Jason, Max, do something!"

Max and Jason ran toward the ladder as Grandma started to gain speed. Great, not the best time for her to suddenly develop a second wind.

"Reid, hurry!" I stretched my arm farther just as Reid grabbed hold of it. He slammed against my body, causing the ladder to bang against the tree and the branch to shake all over the place. But hey, he was safe, so what were a few bruises?

"That was close!" Reid looked down and laughed nervously.

"Shit!" Jason screamed from the bottom of the ladder. "Shit! Shit!"

"Look!" Max pointed at Jason's neck. "Now you have your own ant farm!"

"They're biting me!" Jason started scratching his neck and arms, then went running, arms flailing, straight for the pool. He jumped in, still screaming.

"Allergic to ants," Max called up, reminding us. "He'll be fine, we'll get him some cream. All right, come on down, I've got the ladder. You too, Grandma."

"Ah phooey." Grandma climbed down. "I wanted to rescue Reid."

"Reid's dead," Reid mumbled, then hung his head against me.

"Well drat," Grandma sighed as she reached the ground. "That's another one with a weak heart. Can't have a weak heart in the bedroom. Just causes problems when you want to Kama Sutra."

"That sentence is going to haunt me for the rest of my life," Reid whispered, his eyes still closed. "Freaking haunt me."

"I had so many good ideas. I earmarked the pages." Grandma continued to talk as Max led her away from Reid, who was very much alive, but I'm sure he was second-guessing that decision.

Once we reached the bottom of the tree, more guests had piled into the front yard a good distance from where we were.

"Go get ready, man." Reid shrugged away from me. "I'll turn on the twinkle lights so the effect is perfect."

"I feel like if I leave you, she'll find you," I said, hesitating between wanting to get ready and wanting to protect the poor guy's virtue.

"I'll be fine." Reid nodded, his eyes watery. "I'm doing this for you, you know."

I reached for his arm. "And if she finds you . . ."

"If I perish . . ." he whispered, closing his eyes, "I perish."

"Good man."

With a firm nod, he pulled me in for a hug and walked off toward the outlet.

# CHAPTER FORTY

## MILO

"This is a really pretty dress." I turned around in front of the mirror and couldn't help but smile as the sweetheart neckline seemed to make my boobs look bigger. The entire bodice was see-through white lace except for a few strips of material around the front where my very perky boobs were pushed together, creating more cleavage than I'd ever seen in my entire life. The bottom of the dress billowed down to my feet, with a small section drawn up over my leg like a slit. It was the dress I would have chosen had I been given an unlimited amount of money. It was also the type of dress a girl wore for a wedding—not a vow renewal. Mom had said it was just something she'd picked up for the wedding "just in case." The receipt had today's date on it, which made me wonder, but I wasn't going to say no to something so pretty.

I was going to enjoy it.

"You look beautiful." Jenna fastened more bobby pins into the back of my low bun and pulled some pieces of hair forward, laying them softly against my face. "Perfect." She sniffled.

"Are you crying?"

"No." She sniffled again and looked away. "Just have mascara in my eye."

"Look, Jenna." I put my hand on her shoulder. "I'm sorry about . . ." Wait, I'd never actually done anything to her, I'd just thought those nasty things. "I'm sorry for having a bad attitude, it's just I saw you with Colt and I assumed—"

Okay, she was full-on crying now. Her shoulders shook as she cried into her hands.

"Um, Jenna?"

"He doesn't even recognize me!"

"Colton?"

"Jason!" she wailed. "He doesn't even remember!"

"Remember . . . your face?" I offered, patting her on the back. "Or did something happen?"

She flushed and looked down at the floor.

"Jenna?"

"He slept with me."

Well, crap. I opened my mouth, but really, I couldn't think of anything to say that would make her tears stop flowing or get her to forgive my jackass of a brother. On second thought . . . "I can give him another black eye if you want?"

Jenna laughed. "Yeah, well, he deserves it."

"Are you sure he doesn't remember? I mean, I know we're talking about the same Jason who had a Spiderman lunch box throughout eighth grade, but . . ."

"Don't you think he would have said something?" Jenna looked up at me, her green eyes blurred with tears. "I mean, it's not like we kissed and that was it."

"Were you drunk?" I blurted.

"No!" She bit down on her lip. "Well, okay, I wasn't, but he may have been slightly . . . inebriated."

"Jenna, he's a man. He's also an ass. He's an ass and a man." I sighed. "You can't really expect him to remember things if he's drunk. That's like letting a dog loose in a park, hiding a piece of meat, and expecting him to come back to you rather than eating the meat. He's gonna find the meat, he's gonna eat it, then he's going to get tired, go to the bathroom, and take a nap."

She shook her head. "What?"

"Never mind." Clearly my analogies only worked on Max and Colt. Either that or I was hanging out with Max too much.

Ah, yes. It was the Max effect. Suddenly explaining serious life situations by way of *Finding Nemo* and crapping dogs seemed like an intelligent idea. Damn Max.

"Look." I held her hands. "Would it help if I talked to him?"

"No!" Jenna's eyes widened with terror. "Don't you dare say a word! Swear to me—"

"It may help."

Her eyes narrowed. "No offense, Milo, but I would never use your name and the word *help* in the same story, let alone the same paragraph or sentence, you get the picture?"

"Harsh."

"Sometimes the truth is." She smiled through her tears.

"You girls ready?" Mom busted through the doorway, hands on hips and a few red marks on her arms.

"Mom, what happened?"

"Ants." She said it like a curse word. "Everywhere. Apparently our tree is infested."

"Right," I said slowly. "But how did they get on you?"

"Jason," she said in that same irritated voice. "He has them in his pants."

I leaned in and whispered to Jenna, "How's that for karma?" Then I cleared my throat. "His balls are probably the size of watermelons, you must be so proud."

"That child is a walking disaster. Oh, and I gave him Benadryl. Though I wasn't aware he'd consumed so much alcohol. Max is absolutely certain Jason's still breathing, so there's that."

I raised my hand. "Max isn't a doctor."

"No?" Mom asked. "Oh, well, he seemed so informed on the topic of allergic reactions."

"One time Max shaved his head, took a vow of silence, and told people he was a Tibetan monk. Believe me, he can make anyone believe anything."

Mom looked behind her, then back at me. "Should I be worried?"

"Did you get Colt? He's a paramedic, you know."

"Well, he was helping Reid out of the tree!" Mom threw her hands into the air. "What was I supposed to do?"

"The tree?" I repeated. "Why was Reid in the tree again?" Hadn't that already happened?

"And that woman," Mom spit, "will be the death of me!"

"Wait." I shook my head. "I thought Jayne was gone!"

"Your grandmother," Mom said crisply, "is either high on blood pressure pills or smoking hallucinogenic materials."

"Mom." I exhaled. "Calm down. It's not like Grandma's growing pot or something." I laughed nervously, then made a mental note to check my grandma's basement—the same basement she spent all her time in because, she claimed, it was temperature-controlled. Well, crap.

"I don't have time to worry about this." Mom smiled as she walked around me. "You look beautiful, and we can't wait any longer. Let's go."

She grabbed my arm and pulled me down the hall. My dress swished as I moved with her. Where was Dad anyway? Maybe at the end of the aisle? I wasn't really sure how a vow renewal ceremony went but—

My thoughts froze.

Lights. There were hundreds of lights in the giant oak trees; they looked like fireflies.

And the aisle? It had lanterns lining the white cloth runner as it led all the way up to Max and Colt.

*Wait! Max and Colt?*

Colt was beaming. Next to him were pillars with lights wrapped around them and then tulle wrapped above that, causing a canopy effect under the tree—it looked like a fairy book castle.

The music started.

I looked to my left.

With a wink my dad took my arm in his and whispered, "You look beautiful. I'm so proud to be giving you away."

I opened my mouth—but the wedding march started. For the first time in my life, I didn't want answers.

I wanted to walk down the aisle.

Toward Colton.

Because if this was a dream—I never wanted to wake up.

And if it was real—I was going to enjoy it. Because the little boy who had slain all my dragons when I was little—had grown into a man.

And I loved him.

# CHAPTER FORTY-ONE
## COLTON

In all the years I'd played dragon slayer with her, in all those stolen moments when I'd pretended to be injured as I threw myself down onto the ground and my wooden sword clattered down the stairs— I'd always secretly wondered what it would be like to be kissed by the fair maiden.

To be rescued by her.

It's funny: as a little boy I'd always had it in my mind that my job—my responsibility—was to run toward danger, show I was tough enough to withstand it, and then earn my reward.

But now, as I watched Milo emerge from the house and start walking toward me with her father, everything became so ridiculously clear that I couldn't help but chuckle a bit and then smile at my bride.

Just because we'd stopped playing together when we were kids, didn't mean I gave up my job of protecting her, of fighting danger.

There was the time her date abandoned her at her first dance and I stayed with her the entire night.

The moment she accidently crashed the car and I helped her fix everything before her parents found out.

The summer she almost drowned and I gave her mouth-to-mouth—only to find out later—when I was done freaking out—that I loved the feel of her lips against mine.

All her life—I'd been there. Sure, I'd hung up my sword and cape. She'd put her princess hat away.

But our relationship had never changed. The dynamics of who we were as friends had slowly been molded into what we would become as a couple.

A partnership where I imagined I was rescuing her—when in the end, she rescued me.

Just by smiling.

By breathing.

By trusting me.

By kissing me back.

She was mine as much as I was hers.

The music faded as Milo stopped in front of me, tears blurring her eyes, making them look that much more beautiful.

"You did this?" she whispered.

I nodded and took her hands. "I had help."

"But—" She stepped into my arms and leaned up to whisper in my ear, the fabric of her dress sliding against my suit. "Are you sure?"

Chuckling, I pulled back and tilted her chin up, the way I'd done her whole life when I was about to give her a very important speech where she had to listen carefully.

"You're brother's face is covered in ant bites, Reid nearly fell out of a tree, Max was going to drug Grandma, and we finally did have to slip something into her drink to sedate her. I wouldn't go through all of those things, if I wasn't sure I wanted to be attached to this family for the rest of my life—if I wasn't sure I wanted to be your husband for an eternity."

Her sharp intake of breath nearly brought me to my knees as the tears, once held in, poured down her face.

With a squeal, both of her arms flew around my neck. "You."

"Me what?" I was too happy to care that everyone was watching us—gaping like idiots.

"It's always been you."

I set her on her feet. "Does that mean you can take down those posters in your old bedroom and replace them with pictures of me?"

"Silly." She rolled her eyes. "Your name is written in invisible ink behind the posters. I had to do something just in case you came into my room and discovered my secret."

"Hmph, secret." Max coughed next to Colt.

As if realizing she had an audience, Milo quickly tucked her arm within mine and cleared her throat. "We're ready."

"Dearly beloved—"

"I have a few words." Grandma stood.

Jason quickly tugged her down and gave me a thumbs-up. Funny, because his thumb was the only working body part currently in his possession.

"Who's that?" Milo whispered.

"Your grandma."

"No, the guy next to her—holy hell!"

The pastor cleared his throat.

"Is that Jason?"

"Dearly beloved!" the pastor said, a bit louder this time.

"Should he go to the hospital?" Milo whispered.

"After." I grinned and kissed her hand. "We'll take him after."

"If he lives that long," Max said helpfully.

I shot him daggers. He merely shrugged and motioned to the pastor. "Do go on, I believe you were saying, 'Dearly beloved.'"

The pastor smiled tightly. "Dearly—"

"You sick son of a bitch!" a woman wailed from behind us.

"Oh, dear Lord," I snapped.

The pastor blanched.

I turned slowly as Jayne made her way up the aisle.

"Jason, you—"

She paused and looked at me, then Milo, then around the audience. Her confused eyes suddenly turning embarrassed as she realized she wasn't interrupting her ex-fiancé's wedding, but mine.

"Jayne!" Max shouted. "There you are. We've been so worried!"

*Uh-oh.*

"You have?" she asked in a doubtful voice.

"Yes!" Why was Max yelling? "When you didn't come back after your walk we thought you were done for! But here you are!" He put his hand over his heart. "I was afraid I'd scared you with my forthrightness . . ."

"Does he even know what that word means?" Milo whispered.

". . . in asking for your hand in matrimony, dear, lovely woman of my heart!"

I snorted. "It's like a bad play."

"My hand?"

Max walked slowly down the aisle. "Your lovely, lovely, small, feminine hands. The same hands that caressed me last evening when I was distraught."

"Is it me or did he suddenly develop a British accent?" Milo whispered.

"Sounds Australian."

"No," Milo hissed. "He sounds drunk."

"You love my hands?" Jayne beamed.

"Both of them." Max nodded. "All ten fingers. All ten toes."

Milo nudged me. "Where did the toes come from?"

Max grabbed Jayne and sighed as he jerked her head toward his chest and started patting it. "Even your elbows."

Jayne sniffled. "I've always been insecure about those."

"Shh!" Max pressed his finger to her lips and shouted, "Those elbows made me feel for the first time! They made me love!" Raising his voice even louder, he addressed the crowd. "I'd marry her for those damn elbows! I'd marry her and I'd give her children! And I'd—"

"Max!" I hissed.

"Right." He turned to Jayne. "Shall we sit while they perform the ceremony?"

She gave a watery nod and put her head on Max's shoulder as they sat toward the back. I didn't miss, however, the little bus motion Max made with his hands before he made a cutting motion across his neck and then stuck his tongue out as if he'd died.

Yeah, he'd taken another one for the team.

"Dearly beloved!" The pastor was nearly screaming now. He paused, sighed, then continued, "We are gathered here . . ."

# CHAPTER FORTY-TWO
## MILO

The pastor's lips were moving, sounds were coming out of his mouth, but my focus was completely on Colton.

This couldn't be real, right?

But I felt his hands in mine, I could practically taste him we were standing so close, and every once in a while he'd release my hands to touch my face.

"Milo?" the pastor asked.

Breathless, I shook my head and asked, "Yes?"

"Do you take this man?"

Colton squeezed my hands tighter.

My gaze narrowed in on his face as his smile fell, his eyes starting to widen with a bit of fear. Ha! Served him right. I went through hell. HELL, I tell you!

"Well," I cleared my throat.

Colton leaned forward and whispered into my ear, "Skinny-dipping, wine, moonlight, swordplay."

Those four words sealed my fate.

"Yes," I all but shouted.

The pastor nodded. "And Colton, do you—"

"Yes," he said loudly, then leaned down. "I'll take her in the pool, against the wall, in bed, outside . . ." His lips grazed my ear as he pulled back. "It will be my absolute pleasure."

Was it hot outside?

I looked away from Colton—had to look away.

My eyes naturally fell to the front row, and my deformed brother who was at that precise moment waving a hand in the air and swatting away invisible flies. Poor kid, he was going to need a heck of a lot of meds to get through that allergic reaction. Was a person's nose supposed to swell that much? Was it even safe?

"I now pronounce you"—the pastor muttered "finally" under his breath—"husband and wife! You may kiss the bride!"

I grinned.

I couldn't help it.

Great, so our kiss in front of everyone was going to be one of those awkward toothy kisses where no lips were involved—only clanging.

Except when Colton's hand came around my head, when he pulled me close, I stopped smiling.

*Not* because I wasn't happy.

But because my only focus was on his lips, and then at the tender way he looked at me—the way I'd wanted him to look at me my entire life.

Our mouths met.

They fused.

I didn't want to let go.

But Max started coughing. I knew it was Max because he was the only one brave enough to ruin the moment. Damn him.

Note to self: kill Max later.

Colton ran his tongue along the seam of my lips. Dear Lord it was going to be a fun night.

"Cough, whore, cough," Max sputtered.

We pulled back. I glared at him from the front of the altar.

He mouthed one word. "Bus."

And yeah, all was forgiven. I owed him—big time.

Colton lifted me into the air just as the music came on.

And that's when I burst into tears—again.

"*Star Wars*?" I blurted through my watery mess. "You used *Star Wars*–themed music?"

Colton smirked. "Just wait until you see what I have under this suit."

"Uh." I laughed nervously. "That's, uh . . ."

"Hell." Colton bolted down the aisle like there was a fire lit behind him. "If that's the way you react to nakedness we have a long road ahead of us."

"As long as the road is straight." I felt my cheeks heat. "Not narrow or, er, sideways."

"Aw, you made a sex joke." Colt kissed my forehead, my very hot-feeling forehead. "I'm so proud."

"I'm growing up!" I beamed.

"Yeah." His eyes greedily scanned the front of my dress. "You have. Now, let's get everyone out of here so we can celebrate, the right way."

"Oh." I nodded. "In the bedroom?"

"Hell, no." He set me on my feet and kissed my cheek. "In the pool."

"The pool?" I repeated.

"Naked." He winked.

# CHAPTER FORTY-THREE
## COLTON

"Dude, I know you want cake, but you have to go to the hospital." I tried to steer Jason toward the door, but he'd somehow developed superhuman strength and was in the process of bracing himself against the frame as I attempted to push him through. Don't ask me how he was doing it one-armed. It was a medical marvel. Actually, I take that back, he was a medical marvel. I mean, how could he even see?

"No!" Jason shouted. "I've gone through hell and all I want is a piece of damn cake! Then you can take me to the hospital where they'll poke and prod me and—"

"Dude." Max walked up with a large piece of cake hanging out of his mouth. "You aren't E.T., they aren't going to poke and prod you like you're some new species."

"Aghhhh!" Jason surged away from me and charged toward the cake.

"Hmm." Max put another piece in his mouth. "On second thought, he should be dead, so maybe they will poke."

"Don't say *Jason* and *poke* in the same sentence."

"Or prod." Max nodded. "Lots of prodding, and the doctor saying things like 'Okay, bend over and cough.'"

"Uh." I scratched my head. "Highly doubt his examination's going to be that extensive."

"Ants"—Max nodded—"are like sand. They get everywhere."

"And that mental picture I could have totally done without, thanks." I slapped him on the back.

He demolished the rest of his cake and handed me a plate. Just as I was taking a big bite he said, "So, you ready for sex?"

I choked.

Frosting went everywhere.

I also earned a few stares from family members and a totally inappropriate wink from Milo's grandmother.

"It's cool," Max continued. "I mean, I'd be nervous too."

"I'm not nervous." My damn fork shook as I dove into the cake and took another bite—to keep myself from passing out.

"Sure you are." Max shrugged. "I mean, why wouldn't you be? You're her first, what if you totally blow it? And I don't mean that in the literal sense."

I choked again.

"Think of it this way—"

"I'd rather not think of this at all."

"That's not a good sign, you have to have a game plan!" Max nudged me and then motioned for me to follow him over to the kitchen.

He grabbed a pen and paper and leaned over.

"Now." He drew two stick figures.

"Uh." I laughed nervously and looked around. "If you're going to show me how babies are made, just don't. Please, don't. I'm not a virgin."

"Aha!" Max lifted the pen into the air. "But she is, therefore, diagram. Observe." He started scribbling X's and then O's and then arrows pointing to different parts. To be honest it looked a hell of a lot like a football play.

"So, you start here." He circled her head.

"I decapitate her? Good plan, Max. Solid."

"Um, no." Max rolled his eyes like I was the one losing my sanity. "You kiss her, you have to start slow as to not scare her off, then you slowly, and I do mean slowly, move south." He drew an arrow down.

"Max—"

"Once you reach this region." He circled one stick figure's, well, um, stick body. "You need to be sure not to pressure her, I think the—"

"Whatcha guys doing?" Milo asked from behind me.

Freaked out, I did the only thing I could think of doing. I threw my cake into Max's face and laughed. "You lose!"

"What game were you playing?" Milo asked, laughing.

"Yes," Max said, as bits of red velvet crumbled off his face, leaving a smear of bright white icing clinging to his cheek. "I'm dying to know."

"Tic-tac-toe. I won."

"So you threw cake in his face?" Milo started wiping it off of Max while he glared.

"Yeah, well." I sniffled. "He kept saying I didn't know the rules to the game, and I do. Like the back of my freaking hand. I know exactly where those X's go, where the O's need to be. Hell, call me Mr. Tic. Tac. Toe."

"Lies," Max spit. "Your O's are going to be all over the place! And all because you didn't pay attention to the X's!"

"Damn you and your X's!" I thrust my finger into his face. "I'll prove it once and for all!"

"Oh, yeah, HOW?" Max shouted.

"Game! Right here! Right now!"

It was then that I realized exactly what I'd said.

Max blushed. "Dude, I don't play . . . that way."

Milo, probably wanting to help, said, "Guys, it's okay. I mean, if you need a judge, I can sit here and watch."

"No!" we shouted in unison.

Max blushed. "It's not for . . . viewing pleasure."

"Because that would be . . ." I looked heavenward. "Against the, uh . . . wrong."

Milo looked between us. "You guys take games way too seriously."

Max gave Milo a smug grin. "Only the best ones do, my love."

"Hands off," I growled, pushing him out of the way. "Come on, Milo, it's time to play."

"Oooh!" She jumped up and down. "Are we going to arm-wrestle or play a board game or something?"

"Sure." I snickered. "Or something. See ya later, Max."

"At least remember the diagram!" he yelled.

# CHAPTER FORTY-FOUR
## MILO

I fought to keep up with Colton's ridiculous pace. "Um, hey, psychopath, where are we going? There are guests who—"

His lips crushed against mine. Guests, what guests? Tongue . . . was that his? I moaned as he pulled me into his arms, his mouth hot and urgent.

"Screw the guests, you're coming with me."

Had he not been holding me up I would have swayed on my feet. "And we're going where, exactly? To hide in Max's car?"

He paused as if the idea had merit, then shook his head. "Stupid diagram."

"For tic-tac-toe?" I gripped his hand. "Colt, if you suck that bad I can help you."

He groaned.

"No, really!"

More groaning and cursing.

"I totally went on Google last time I played and found out all the tricks!"

"Please don't say *tricks*." He bit down hard on his lip and nearly made me pass out from the heat of his lustful glare. "Let's go."

And we were back to running through the neighbors' backyards.

Until we got to his house.

"Colt." The pool cover was off. Memories of that night plagued me, made me want to turn and run in the other direction. *Jason's sister, Jason's sister.* "What are we doing?" Was he going to reject me again? Was he regretting the fact that we went through that entire ceremony in front of everyone? Holy crap! I was going to have been married for less than three hours!

I needed to sit.

"Milo." Colton started pulling at his tie, then his jacket. Clothes fluttered to the ground in a flurry. "We're going swimming."

"Now?" I hissed. "Colt, we have like a hundred people back at the house, Jason may die if he closes his eye, Reid asked how tall our roof was just in case he needed to jump, and Max told my mom he used to be a gigolo. I think we have enough stress in our lives without—"

Oh, dear Lord.

His boxers fell all the way to the ground.

All the way.

To.

The.

Ground.

God bless the USA.

Would standing up and doing the Pledge of Allegiance throw the mood off? Because I was suddenly so very thankful for that New York–born man.

And he was all man.

I kid you not, if his name were in the dictionary, right next to it would be "Hot body."

That's it.

No more words. Words in a situation like this totally killed the moment. For example, I could wax poetic about the way the moonlight seemed to shimmer across his very bare, tan chest. Shoot, I could even say his abs were so ripped I was afraid if he took a deep breath he was going to pull one of them. Then again, if he pulled a muscle I was the only person close enough to be of aid.

We'd play nurse and soldier.

I'd ask him to tell me where it hurt.

He'd point to ab number two, or maybe three. I do like the lower abdominals . . . Then I'd gently caress the rippled skin and whisper words of encouragement like "Don't worry, you'll make it. I know CPR."

Because um . . . you could never be too careful when a person . . . er, strained his body, and I learned in first aid that you should always, always be sure the person was breathing.

By sticking your tongue down their throat.

Swear it was totally in that textbook.

Probably because I wrote it there, but—

"Milo." Colton's smooth voice interrupted the mental image I'd created of our nurse/soldier story. No idea where the whole soldier thing came from. Probably because I was ready to say the Pledge of Allegiance. Something was seriously wrong with me.

He was a firefighter.

Which was kind of like being a soldier.

Because he risked his life every day.

Colton took a step toward me. Damn it, give the man a Purple Heart! I hope he wasn't second-guessing being married to me.

Because I would be second-guessing it if I were him. I mean, I'm clumsy, the childhood friend, and apparently extremely violent.

"Milo." He said my name like a caress. "Take your clothes off."

"Um." I tugged at my very pretty, very expensive dress and shrugged. "It's kind of . . . nippy." Holy crap. Shoot me now. I'd just said *nippy*. Why couldn't I have said *cold* like a normal person? No, I had to say *nippy*.

Colton smirked and looked down the front of my dress. "I can see that."

"Stop staring." I laughed nervously.

"Why?" He pulled me into his arms. "I can stare all I want. You're mine, remember?"

"Sure." I nodded. "I also remember telling you I wasn't into the whole alpha thing."

"Too bad." He shrugged, tossed me over his shoulder, and jumped into the pool.

I wish I were one of those girls.

The ones who cry really pretty tears, and whose screams don't sound like a hyena giving birth. But I'm not that girl. I'll never be her.

The scream that erupted from my mouth probably called pigeons home. Dogs started barking in the distance.

I'm sure I looked like a raccoon.

But Colton wasn't distracted by my scream or by the fact that I had mascara running down my face.

Nope. His eyes were glued to my body.

"Colt—"

Ignoring me, he dove under water.

And that's when I felt his hands on my bare legs, higher, and then higher. I would have happily drowned if this had been the precursor to my death. No joke. His fingers slid against my thighs and then, with the damned slowness of a tortoise, he pulled my lacy thong all the way down.

With.

His.

Teeth.

*I pledge allegiance to the flag of—*

Colt emerged from the water, a smug grin on his face as my underwear dangled from his teeth.

"Cute."

He threw them to the side of the pool and held up three fingers. "One, two—"

"Why are you counting?"

"If you don't take your own dress off in three seconds I'm doing to do it for you." He smirked. "That little show I just put on is going to get a hell of a lot hotter. So, either you shimmy that tight little body out of that dress or I'm going to do it for you. And I really have trouble with zippers. Who knows how long it will take me to pull it all way the way down, not to mention the fact that I have a crazy obsession with the curve of a woman's back and—"

"Stop!" I laughed. "Man, you're bossy."

Colt's eyes darkened. "You haven't seen anything yet."

The dress had to go. Like yesterday.

His eyes drank me in, I couldn't remember how I'd even gotten the damn thing on! Zipper? Buttons? Did it go over my head? Crap!

Colton grabbed my shoulders and turned me around. "You're sexy when you're turned on."

"I'm not," I lied.

"Sexy?" His hands found my zipper *HA! I knew it was a zipper!* Score one for Milo!

"A-aroused." Right. I couldn't even say the word.

"No?" The zipper went down very, very slowly, but what was worse, his hands followed, touching, lightly grazing my back. It was stupid, really—that a simple touch could make me melt.

But there it was.

Apparently there was magic in his fingertips.

The zipper stopped.

His hands moved.

And then he tugged a bit harder.

Um . . .

And harder still.

"Colt—"

"It's stuck."

"Not the two words I would have chosen to use," I said. "But okay, what's wrong?"

"The damn dress!" Colton shouted. "It won't go any further. Knife. I need a knife."

"You are not knifing me in the pool!" I tried to get free from him but he grabbed me with those magic fingertips and superhuman strength and held me against him.

"I'll make it fast!" He laughed.

"Colt!"

"Really," he promised. "Like a Band-Aid."

I slumped into his arms. "I hate you right now."

"No you don't." His hands moved to my dress again. "I'm going to try one more thing."

A large rip sounded.

And my dress floated up next to me. I was too shocked to do anything except gape when Colton pulled the dress off me and threw it to the side of the pool, a look of pure satisfaction on his face.

"Did you tear my dress in half?"

"I feel like cutting down a tree right now."

"Huh?" Shivering, I swam over to him.

"Or shooting a duck."

"You're killing the mood."

"Burping." He nodded and winked. "That, Milo, was pure masculine awesomeness. Seriously, if we were stuck in the Stone Age—I would have been the guy inventing wheels and shit."

"COLTON!"

"Yes, baby?" His grin was huge.

"You think we can, um . . ." I shrugged as my face heated, probably to a nice shade of scarlet, and pressed my lips together.

"What?"

"You know?"

"No."

"Colt—"

"Milo, say the words. Marriage is all about communication and being open with one another, how can I see to my wife's needs if she doesn't—"

"Oh, my gosh, just have sex with me already!" I shouted.

My voice literally echoed in the night sky.

Great. So some five-year-old camping outside with his friends was probably going to have some questions for his parents in the morning.

"Get over here." Colt reached for me but I swam away.

"No." I kept swimming toward the deep end. "You ruined the moment and then made me ask my own husband for sex!"

"Before last year you were still spelling out *sex* in the air rather than saying it out loud. Progress, it seems, is being made if you can actually say it . . . I mean come on, sweetheart, if you can't say it you shouldn't be participating in it."

"This is not helping my mood!" I kept swimming away.

I was living Nemo's life.

*Just keep swimming, just keep swimming, swim, swim, swim, what do you do you—*"Shit!" His hands moved to my waist.

"Caught." Colton's lips moved against my ear. "And I won't have sex with you . . . I'll make love to you, I'll tease you, taunt you, make you scream, taste, caress, I'll do all those things." His hands braced my hips as he pulled me back against his body. "And nothing is going to keep me from you."

I relaxed in his embrace as his hands ran from my shoulders all the way down until he gripped my hips, flipped me around, and kissed me hard on the mouth.

"I love you." Colt's lips found mine again. He tasted like mint. "I'd freaking go to a *Star Wars* convention for you." His tongue pushed against mine, then retreated. "I'd name our first child Luke." His hands lifted me against him, then slowly grabbed each leg and wrapped it around his waist as he pulled our bodies together.

With a gasp I pulled back, but his mouth wouldn't let me retreat, I didn't have time to do the normal Milo thing. Where I compartmentalized every sensation and made diagrams about my feelings and obsessed like a lunatic. All I could focus on were the sparks—the things he made me feel that I'd never felt before.

"Milo." Colton's voice was gentle as he kissed me, said my name again, kissed me, then sighed against my mouth. "Focus on me, all right, sweetheart?"

I nodded.

Words were failing me.

"Of course I saw them!" Max shouted. "I'm not an idiot—and I can still see out of both eyes, thank you very much."

Colt and I froze. I mean froze in each other's arms. Maybe if we were really quiet they would just walk right by.

Right, they wouldn't see two naked people in the pool.

Or the ripped dress on the concrete.

Or the underwear.

"Well, tic-tac-ho." Max laughed. "You guys having a midnight swim? Why didn't you say something! I would have totally joined!"

"Arousal gone," Colt ground out, and then he swore. "Totally gone."

"Not that kind of swim, Max," I said in a nervous voice. Jason was standing right next to Max, meaning he could see me naked in the arms of his best friend, whom I'd just married. To be fair it wasn't like we'd been caught doing something wrong, but still, it was my brother. I think he'd be happy if I drank chocolate milk my entire life and never even uttered the word *sex*.

"Hey, Jason," Colt said nervously. "Can we, uh, help you guys?"

"It's okay." Max sat in one of the pool chairs. "You guys finish your swimming, we'll wait."

"Pervert," Colt said.

Max winked and snapped his fingers. "Oh, right, now I remember. Your mom and dad are pissed because guests were asking about you guys and I didn't have the heart to explain the whole tic-tac-toe thing to your mom in front of Grandma. That woman's hearing's just fine. Besides, it would have given her ideas about Reid."

I moved to stand behind Colt so nobody would see my nakedness and asked in a shy voice, "Is Reid okay?"

"Sure." Max nodded. "We left him with Grandma."

"What?" Jason roared. "You said you took care of him!"

"I did!" Max lifted his hands into the air. "It's not like I left him defenseless. He has Milo's pink Taser."

"Oh." Jason nodded. "Good idea."

"Guys!" Colt cursed. "Just give us a minute, okay? We're naked, turn around or something and we'll get out of the pool and sneak back into the house."

Max turned around. "Not my fault you're still naked, had you paid attention to my diagrams you would have already been in—"

"Max!" I yelled.

"Just saying. He would have been a lot further. Feel me?" He put his hand over Jason's one eye. "All right, guys, do your thing, get some clothes on, you can screw all you want later."

"I'm not deaf," Jason grumbled. "A person can't un-hear things."

"Screw, screw, screw, screw, screw," Max said in a singsong voice. "If you say it over and over again it's not as traumatizing. You try it."

"Hell, hell, hell, hell, hell . . ." Jason shook his head. "Nope, I still don't feel better."

With a grunt Max fell over.

"What just happened?" Colt asked while he grabbed his shirt and put it over my naked body.

"Jason punched me," Max groaned.

# CHAPTER FORTY-FIVE

## COLTON

I was seriously contemplating homicide.

I could practically feel my hands around Max's neck. Rat cock-blocking bastard! Jason was legally blind by this point so he couldn't have found his way down the street, let alone through the neighbors' backyards in search of us.

Poor kid.

But Max?

Yeah. We'd have words later.

"Colt, I look terrible! My mom's going to freak out!" Milo fastened the last button of the white shirt and put her hands on her hips, making the shirt ride up. Yeah, that was a vision I could live with for a while.

Until Max ruined it by coming up behind her and whistling.

The dude wanted to die.

"Stop staring," I snapped.

"Whoa." Max lifted his hands into the air. "Grouch much? You need to get laid."

I lunged for him, but Milo blocked my way.

Max grinned and blew me a kiss.

"Son of a bitch!" I fought against my wife. "Let me at him!"

"For shame!" Max scolded. "You need to save your energy for later. Don't you think?"

"I wouldn't have to save my energy if you wouldn't have peeping-Tommed us!"

"That's not actually the right way to use that phrase," Max said in a haughty tone. "Geez, it's not like I brought binoculars and put a tracking device on Milo."

"Can we have this discussion elsewhere?" Jason piped up. "You guys need to get back to the house, we need to save Reid, and it's totally possible I forgot about Jenna."

"Technically, Jenna's Colton's responsibility." Max gave me another smug grin. "So many women, so little time, am I right, my man? High five." He held up his hand. I briefly contemplated snapping it in half, then rolled my eyes.

"Oh. My. Hell." Jason shook his head. "Is that—" He swallowed and started backing away.

"What?" I looked where he was pointing as a giant-ass raccoon started lumbering its way across the concrete.

"How did you even see that, Cyclops?" Max whispered.

"I think I've finally finished my mutation." Jason backed away. "Pretty soon Professor X is going to come searching for me and I'm going to go to a better place, away from evil people like my sister who like to inflict pain on mankind."

"Take a hit like a man." Milo gripped my hand. "Be the man, Jason."

"Shh." Max put his hands up for silence. "No sudden movements. Raccoons can smell fear."

"No they can't," I argued.

"They can!" Max's voice sounded desperate. "I saw it on the Discovery Channel."

"You watched a show on raccoons?" I asked. "By choice?"

"I like animals, okay!" Max said. "Sue me."

"Guys!" Milo gripped my hand tighter. "We can go out right here, come on."

We moved slowly toward the other side of the yard and opened the gate. The hinges creaked.

"No fear!" Max shouted just as the raccoon started charging us. "Every man for himself!" Max ran past me and Milo.

Jason followed, but because his depth perception was off he hit the actual fence instead of the gate. I grabbed him right before he fell into the raccoon's clutches.

"Git!" I yelled at the furry creature. It backed away and sauntered off.

"Holy shit, you're the One!" Max started clapping. "We've been searching for you for decades! Finally, the One! The raccoon whisperer." He bowed. "I'm not worthy."

"Shut up." I pushed Jason into Max and grabbed Milo.

"Are you wearing a *Star Wars* shirt?" she asked once we were safely out of earshot of Jason and Max, who were arguing over *The Matrix* movie facts.

"It's a figment of your imagination." I cleared my throat and looked away.

"You love me."

"I do."

"You're wearing a *Star Wars* shirt."

I paused and pulled her into my arms. "So you're saying I'm badass now."

"You have an R2-D2 on your shirt." Max came up behind me and slapped my back. "*Badass* probably isn't the phrase I'd use . . . just sayin'."

I lunged again.

Milo shook her head and kissed me softly across the mouth. "Leave it . . ." With a shy smile she stood up on her tiptoes and whispered in my ear, "That way I can rip it off later. You know, return the favor."

"Hell, yes."

"If you're done taking advantage of my sister—you guys have a party to return to."

"Oh, look!" Max pointed toward the sky. "See, I told you Reid would be fine."

I looked up. "Well, shit."

"He's not fine." Milo groaned and covered her face with her hands. "He's on the roof!"

"I knew I should have locked him in the bathroom." Max tapped his chin. "Oh, look, Grandma's with him too!"

"He's going to jump." Jason shivered and wrapped his good arm around his core. "I can't even blame him."

"Reid!" Max yelled. "Are you okay?"

Reid just stared.

I couldn't see his eyes but I imagined they were full of fear, terror, horror. "Reid! Sweetie! It's so high up here!" Grandma started moving toward him. Reid turned and walked closer to the edge.

"Walk away from the light, Reid!" Jason shouted up at him. "It's not worth it, just, just let her—you know—and then it will all be over with."

"Truth!" Max said. "She'll probably fall asleep afterwards and then we can all get drunk and this will be like a very, very, very bad dream."

Reid's shoulders slumped as Grandma wrapped her arms around him and placed her head on his back. "Oh, you're so very big and strong, you naughty boy, playing a game of cat and mouse! Well, this kitty's all riled up and ready to play!"

"I think"—I shuddered and tried to blot out the images of Grandma—"I've lost all ability to perform sexually just now."

Max sighed and elbowed me. "Should have used my diagram."

"Not now, Max!" It was Milo's turn to lunge.

"Oh, Reid, turn that little face around so I can give you a proper kiss."

I swear—I just saw tears rolling down the poor kid's face. I was willing to break into a pharmacy just so I could get him drugs.

But they didn't sell those kinds of drugs.

The ones that made you forget.

Unless he was lucky enough to get a roofie.

One could only hope, or in Reid's case—pray.

# CHAPTER FORTY-SIX
## COLTON

It took us a good fifteen minutes to convince Reid not to jump—and even then, I'm pretty sure he would have taken the plunge off the roof had we not intervened.

He and Grandma went back into the house, while Milo and I went in search of clothes.

Things were going smoothly, until Max opened his mouth.

"I'm glad we're friends," he whispered as we all crept down the hallway. Max and Jason were shielding us just in case someone saw Milo or me in our current state of disarray.

All we had to do was make it to her bedroom so she could change.

A few feet.

*A few feet.*

"What?" Jason looked up at Max through his good eye. "What do you mean?" They stopped walking.

Max shrugged. "I've always wanted a guy friend. I don't have many on account of my devastatingly good looks and all-around winning personality. I tend to intimidate those of the same sex—it's not like I can help the fact that women want me to impregnate them. It's probably my strong chin or spicy musk."

"Please don't say *musk*." Milo cringed.

"Can we keep walking?" Seriously. A. Few. Feet.

Jason nodded, but I couldn't tell if he was smiling because his face was still a bit puffy from the ants. At this point it looked like he'd been stuffing marshmallows in his cheeks and had forgotten to take them out. "I get you, man." He licked his lips. "I get you."

Max nodded his head. "I know, dude, I know you do."

"You're all right." Jason held out his hand.

"Brothers don't shake hands—"

"—they hug," Jason finished.

"Dear God, save me from more movie references." I sighed as the guys embraced.

And then panicked as Milo's aunt slowly turned toward the hall.

"Guys, hurry—"

"Milo! Colton?" She placed a hand to her chest and coughed. "What are you guys doing?"

I can only imagine what it looked like.

A one-eyed, swollen Jason embracing Max. Milo and me watching, one of us without many clothes.

And then Reid and Grandma made it worse by emerging from the room opposite the guest room—holding hands.

"Oh, my." The aunt fanned herself and looked behind her and then a certain gleam lit her eyes.

"Oh, no, no, no, no." I held out my hands in front of me. "It's not like that."

Grandma slapped my ass and whispered, "I beg to differ, champ. Who's next?"

Max raised his hand.

Jason smacked him.

"Fire!" Milo shouted.

Grandma screamed.

The aunt with the thick glasses fainted.

And I grabbed Milo and pushed her into the bedroom, slamming the door behind us.

"We left Reid!" She opened the door again.

"Leave him, besides, he was only holding Grandma's hand."

"*No* man gets left behind!"

"There's nothing we can do for him now!" I pushed against the door. "He's already been taken . . ."

"No." Milo shook her head. "I won't believe it. I can't believe it."

"Milo." I exhaled. "Reid's gone."

A loud knocking sounded at the door.

"I know you're in there!" Mrs. Caro shouted. "Now stop screwing around and get out here to greet your guests or so help me God I'm breaking down this door and I don't think any one of us is mentally stable enough for that encounter!"

"We'll be right out!" I said in a hurry.

"We will?" Milo put her hands on her hips. "But I thought—"

"We have to get rid of them—all of them, and then it's just you and me." I tilted her chin. "Promise."

Her smile made my knees go weak. "Me, you, and Chewbacca?"

Max's voice sounded at the door. "I named my penis once too."

"Why can't you be the one getting punched?" I shouted back, vaguely remembering that he had in fact been punched numerous times.

"Maximus. That was the name, then I realized I was putting undue pressure on my nether parts to perform and it wasn't emotionally fair to do that to my person."

"Go away!" I groaned.

"Now it's just Max Jr." He sighed. "Or if you're picky, Big M."

"Max!" Milo banged on the door. "Go find Reid."

"He's right here."

"Is he okay?"

"Reid, tell them you're okay."

A throat cleared, and then Reid said in a very quiet voice, "I've been—compromised."

"See?" Max's voice was muffled. "Totally fine."

"Give us five minutes?" I asked nicely, hoping it would make a difference if I used my inside voice rather than yelling again.

Max laughed. "Amateur, it should at least take fifteen, and that's being generous."

I opened my mouth but Milo elbowed me. "'K, thanks, Max, 'bye."

We waited in silence, then Milo sighed. "You're still there, aren't you, Max?"

We heard a shuffling of feet and then, "Yeah."

# CHAPTER FORTY-SEVEN
## COLTON

It took us a good five minutes to get presentable, and even then Milo still looked like she had taken a midnight swim. Her skin was flushed, and the little black dress she was wearing did nothing to hide her body from me.

A body I desperately wanted.

Part of me was thankful that Max had interrupted—a thought I would take to my grave lest he decide to move in with us and make a career out of keeping me from sex.

It was Milo's first time.

In a pool? Not the most romantic move I could have made. Wincing, I took a slow sip of wine and watched her across the room. She was talking to her aunt, the same one who had accused us not a few minutes ago of having an orgy in the hall.

Milo waved in my direction. I waved back and just watched her. I watched her laugh, I watched her drink, I watched her drum her fingers against her cup.

I wanted those hands on me.

Not the damn cup.

"Frustrated sexually?" Max said next to me in a low voice.

"Tell me, do you ever quit, Max? Or is your goal in life for no one to have sex if you aren't getting any?"

He snorted. "I get plenty."

"Where's Jenna?"

"With Jason. I told her to take care of him on account that he can't see how many fingers I'm holding up and was asking me why the ants were on him still."

"He's hallucinating? That can't be good."

"I may have slipped him a mild sedative." Max shrugged. "At any rate, they're on the way to the hospital—finally. And they'll most likely be making out by the end of the night—that is, if Jason can actually find her mouth. Jury's still out."

"Wow, Cupid, nice work." I patted him on the back.

"Shhh," Max whispered. "No sudden movements. Baby powder."

"What?"

"Baby powder." Max closed his eyes and inhaled. "Grandma's near."

"How do you even—"

"Aha!" Grandma shouted, appearing in front of us. "Max, where's that brother of yours? I've been looking everywhere!"

"I think you tuckered him out." Max's smile was tight. "Either that or he went and ran in front of oncoming traffic in hope someone would run him over."

"What's that?" She cupped her ear.

"You killed him!" Max shouted.

Grandma grinned and tapped Max's chest with her pink fingernail. "Are you saying you're going to stand in for him?" Her eyebrows arched.

I think I puked a bit in my mouth as Max's eyes widened in horror.

"No, but thank you, ma'am." Max backed away. "I'm gay."

"You're what?"

"Gay." Max nodded. "So, very, very"—his eyes pleaded with mine—"gay."

"Shit." I put my arm around him and smiled at Grandma.

"But didn't you just get married?" she asked me.

"Twin." Max coughed. "That was his twin, er, Carlton."

"Oh." Her eyes narrowed. Good thing she was old and senile.

Max nodded and then kissed me on the cheek. "See? Totally not into elderly women with enough strength to hold me down for twelve hours straight while they feed off my beating heart." He slapped my chest. "I'm all for men!"

Conversations around us stilled.

Max coughed. "To the bride and groom?"

"Please let everyone be too drunk to care," I mumbled.

"Drat." Grandma snapped her fingers. "Guess I'll go take a nap then. Ta-ta."

I sighed in relief when she rounded the corner and walked down the hall to the bedrooms.

"You can let go of my hand now." I bit down on my lip. "I mean, unless you're digging holding it and then hell, who cares? I'm still having sex tonight and now everyone really thinks you're gay."

Max's eyes narrowed as he released my hand and scowled. "Damn Reid. If he was capable of pleasing a woman, she wouldn't be coming back for seconds!"

"Please don't ever repeat that sentence again."

"Damn baby powder." Max continued talking. "I swear it's like her tell."

"Huh?"

"She smells like baby powder." He sniffled. "I have a theory that she powdered Reid up before she—"

"Please! No more stories." I held up my hand like a shield, knowing I'd need years of therapy if he finished that sentence. "I may never be able to sleep with my wife because of you. I'll never look at baby powder the same again."

"Look." Max pointed at the couch. "Reid's back."

"Reid's drunk off his ass." I laughed as Reid held a bottle of tequila to his lips and started dancing in his seat, eyes closed. The champ was probably living the dream. Pain-free. Grandma-free. That was the life.

"All in all"—Max looked around the room—"I think the weekend went pretty good." He slapped my back. "We should do this again sometime."

"Right." I rolled my eyes.

"Colt?" Milo walked up to us and smiled shyly. "Um, Mom says we don't have to stay any longer, so . . ." She looked down at the ground, blushing to the roots of her hair.

Max puffed out his chest. "I got this."

"Max—"

"Let me." He thrust his chin high into the air. "It's the least I can do for interrupting you guys in the pool. But dude, for the love, just look at the damn diagram, seriously, one glance won't kill you."

"Max—"

"What I do, I do for my friends. Milo, I love you. Now go make babies." He saluted us, then walked into the middle of the crowd of people and started taking his clothes off.

"Aw, how cute." Milo laughed. "He's creating a diversion."

I smirked as Grandma made her way down the hall; a look of pure evil crossed her features. "Right, and he's about to get taken advantage of, poor chap." Inspiration struck, and I gripped Milo's hand in mine and whispered in her ear, "I have an idea, let's go."

# CHAPTER FORTY-EIGHT
## MILO

Last time Colton said the words "I have an idea," I ended up getting frostbite on my ass.

I'd had to sit in a tub of hot water for what felt like days while I thawed out. I was only six so I don't remember much—what I do remember? The fact that he called me "icicle cheeks" for three years straight after it happened. Never mind that he was the one who dared me to—well, never mind. Water under the bridge.

I gripped his hand and followed him out of the house. "What's your bright idea? Set Max on fire and make a run for it?"

"No."

"Too bad."

Colton's eyes narrowed. "You're a bad friend."

"Well," I huffed, "you're a bad husband!"

He stopped walking. "Pardon?"

I looked down at my feet. "You heard me. I'm tired, I'm hungry, it's possible Reid's going to sue Grandma for improper touching, my brother hates me, and, and, I'm sexually—"

Crap. I stopped talking. I really, really needed a censor for that mouth of mine.

"Sexually?" Colton chuckled. "What?"

"Nothing." I tried to walk past him but he grabbed me by the shoulders, holding me in place.

"Sexually."

"Stop saying *sexually*." I hissed. The fact that that word was coming out of his mouth while he was touching me, while I wanted to pounce on him, was not doing me any favors—physically, that is.

I felt trapped in my body.

Like a caged animal just waiting to get set free.

See! That's probably why I inflicted pain on others—it really wasn't my fault! It was Colton's! "Aha!" I shouted.

"Aha, what?" Colt asked in a mocking tone. "My hands are on you for three seconds, and suddenly all traces of sexual frustration leave? Damn, I'm good."

"It's your fault!" I snapped, staggering away from him. "I've had a crush on you for how long? And suddenly we're married and, oh, my gosh, why didn't I think of this before?" Panic set in. I was attracted to him. I wanted to be the ice on his Popsicle, the charm on his bracelet, the milk on his mustache—you get the point. And he didn't care! Nothing about him screamed sexual frustration. My mind whirled, my breathing quickened.

He didn't want me.

Not the way I wanted him.

In that moment I kind of wanted to cry, because what guy, what man actually lets a guy like Max, a guy who—let's be honest—cries during Cheerio commercials, interrupt what could have been the best pool sex to ever take place in the history of the universe? So I have high hopes. That's not a crime!

"Milo?" Colt reached for my hand. I let him take it, mainly because I was still thinking about the pool, and what could have happened, and the fact that I had been naked and Colt hadn't told them all to go to hell and leave us alone.

"Do you think I'm pretty?" I asked in a low voice, not willing to look him in the face because I was that embarrassed.

"Not really. No." He shrugged.

My heart dropped into my stomach as I tried to pull away from him, but his hand tightened around mine as he jerked me across his body.

"Girls like you, sorry, women like you aren't merely pretty. Pretty is the definition of something you put on a nice shelf for people to stare at. Pretty is a Christmas tree."

"But—" I sniffed. "I really like Christmas trees!"

Colt groaned. "Milo, I'm not saying you're a Christmas tree."

"I can be a damn tree, Colton! Just give me a chance! I'll even put those tiny silver balls on and—" Yeah, I needed to stop talking.

"Sweetheart," Colton whispered. "You would be a very pretty tree, but what I'm trying to say is pretty . . . Pretty is something you can't touch. Pretty is what moms warn little boys about. Hell, I can't even count how many times my mom said, 'Colt, that's a pretty, don't touch it.'"

"So I'm not a tree," I croaked. "And now you can't touch me?"

Colton shook his head, showing some frustration. "Women are such pretzels! Geez, let me finish!"

"You know I hate pretzels, Colt!"

"Holy shit, where's Max when I need someone to say something stupider so I look like the good guy?" Colt groaned and leaned his forehead against mine. His whisper came out hoarse, almost raw. "You're the sunset."

"Oh."

"Because I can't describe your beauty—and every day I see you, it's like seeing a new sunset, you're never the same. I always notice something different about the way the light reflects off your eyes. Or the way your hair feels when I run my fingers through it. You're not just pretty. You're indescribable. You're terrifying in your beauty—and I. Love. You."

So maybe we didn't have pool sex, but that speech was pretty epic. I was having a hard time breathing while trying not to swallow my tongue, so I nodded before saying, "So you're attracted to me?"

"Do bears shit in the woods?" a male voice interrupted.

"A little late, man." Colton shook his head and chuckled. "But thanks, Max, for totally ruining what could have been a really special moment. No really, I appreciate it."

"Blue Christmas balls." Max nodded. "Not such a merry Christmas or happy New Year? Feel me?"

"What?" I looked between the two of them as Colton flushed bright red. "What do you mean?"

"Oh, look." Max thrust his fist into the air and sang, "And a happy New Year!"

Colt and I said nothing. Merely waited. It was Max. There had to be a point to his insanity, otherwise he was just that—insane.

"Fine." He sighed. "Don't sing, but at least thank me for being the *best* best man ever."

"You weren't my best man."

"We never established it." Max shrugged.

"I established it," Colt argued. "And it was Jason."

"Jason couldn't see, nor was he even aware he was alive for at least half the day—dead people don't count."

"Nor do drunk ones, yet here we are," Colton said in a singsong voice.

"Remember this moment." Max nodded and took two steps toward us. "As the day Max saved Christmas."

"It's not Christmas."

Max rolled his eyes. "It's more badass-sounding than 'the day Max saved the marital bed.'"

It was my turn to blush.

"Boutique hotel down the street, the one with the flowers in front and the bar with five-dollar mimosas." Max grinned. "Honeymoon suite." With a bow he finished, "Paid for in full."

"Aw, you did that with your paper route money!" Colton teased.

"Ass." Max rolled his eyes. "And if I did have a paper route I'd skip your house every damn time." His gaze met mine. "But for Milo." He shrugged. "You guys deserve some time uninterrupted. And I wanted to give you that, so take any one of the cars except for Reid's since he's probably going to have to sleep in it tonight on account that Grandma keeps copping a feel, and enjoy yourselves."

With a watery grin, I went up to Max and wrapped my arms around him. He truly was one of the best people I knew. Had I not crushed on Colton all my life, I would probably love Max.

But his story . . .

I had a feeling it was just beginning. So I stepped back while Colt shook his hand and then silently went to Colt's truck and climbed in.

"So," I asked once it roared to life. "What was your plan going to be?"

"I was going to find a hotel but that sounded so cheap, so honestly? I was just going to sit in the car with you and try really hard not to peel your clothes off while we talked and drank wine straight out of the bottle."

I gasped. "Be still my heart!"

Colt's eyes narrowed. "Yeah, well, when you aren't thinking with your head, all you can focus on is just getting that one person alone, no matter how you do it or what it takes to get that person away from others."

"Because I'm not a Christmas tree," I said confidently.

Colton laughed. "Right, because you aren't a Christmas tree."

"A sunset." I sighed.

Colt's eyes met mine. "The most beautiful sunset I've ever laid eyes on or ever will."

# CHAPTER FORTY-NINE
## MILO

You know that feeling you get when a really good song comes on the radio? Or when Justin Timberlake is on SNL with Jimmy Fallon and you laugh so hard you have tears streaming down your face and you're just excited to be alive? Okay, so maybe I'm taking it to a bit of an extreme.

But I had that type of nervous excitement coursing through my veins. The drive to the hotel wasn't very long.

Had it taken longer I might have calmed down.

Instead I was picking all the nail polish off my nails and had the stupid Madonna/Justin Timberlake end-of-the-world song going in circles around my head.

*We've only got four minutes to save the world.*

Holy crap, what if I'm terrible at sex?

It happens to people.

I mean, there has to be a learning curve, right?

Colt turned the car off.

*Three minutes to save the world.*

*Two.*

*One.*

"Colt!" I gripped the seat belt with my hands and breathed in and out through my nose. "We could just stay here if you want."

"In the truck?" He looked around. "I love you too much to stay in a truck all night. Come on, let's go."

"Uh . . ."

"Milo," Colt sighed. "Sweetheart, how am I ever going to look at the sunset when it's so damn dark?"

"What?" I blinked.

"It's dark outside," he said slowly.

I nodded and gulped at the same time.

"And I really," he whispered in a low voice, "really want to see you."

"You want to see me?"

"Without the cover of darkness . . ." He leaned over and kissed my cheek. "Or clothes."

Air wheezed out of my mouth.

And I started choking.

On him.

Not like away from him, which would have been okay—you know like when you swallow a bug and cough to the side, then smile and say something like "Those darn bugs."

No.

That would have been forgivable.

I coughed in his face.

Like an elderly person from a home who was on oxygen.

"Sorry." I covered my mouth.

"Are you going to make it?" Colt laughed. "Or do you need more alcohol?"

"A drink." I nodded. "A drink would probably be wise considering the circumstances."

"Circumstances?" His finger traced my jaw. I shivered and nearly lost control of my body. I had a terrifying vision of just ripping his clothes off but getting so aggressive that I accidently squashed him with my enthusiasm.

"Just . . . I . . . It's you. And you, like this, make me nervous."

"I understand."

"No." I laughed. "That would be impossible."

"Try me."

I gave him a doubtful look as he unbuckled my seat belt and then very carefully threaded his fingers through my hair. "Kissing you is terrifying, breathing your same air makes my knees weak, when I'm around you it's a tie between wanting to chase you down—or just kiss you until you can't breathe."

"People need to breathe, Colt—to live."

"I don't know about that." He sighed. "Sometimes I think I just need you—to live."

Cue tears.

"You still nervous?"

"A bit." I shrugged.

"It's me." Colt's smile melted my insides, his light eyes and full grin were something I'd counted on my entire life. He was my finish line.

"When you won your first swim meet . . . I helped you get the green out of your hair. When you had your first drink—I held your hair while you puked. When your first boyfriend—the jackass—dumped you . . . I held your hand. It's me, Milo. Just you and me. Forever . . . us."

I kissed him.

My mouth collided with his.

And it wasn't fear that was driving my behavior anymore.

But love.

And a total sense of being at peace—finally finding my home— in the boy who used to live next door.

# CHAPTER FIFTY

## COLTON

H-h-e-e-l-l-l. I was going to die.

I was already burning from the inside out—sexual frustration isn't a laughing matter. No, seriously. You know how in sex ed the teacher tells you that not having sex won't kill you?

God, I could still hear Mrs. Thompson's shrill voice in my head. "It's not going to fall off if you don't touch it!" Then she'd smack the desk with her giant-ass ruler and start talking about the pitfalls of herpes.

Mrs. Thompson was wrong.

She was probably going to burn in hell too.

For lying.

To teenagers.

That was a sin somewhere, right? You shouldn't lie to people under the age of eighteen. They're minors! You're forming the minds of children, for shit's sake!

I was past panic.

Sweat started to seep out of every pore on my body—I was try-ing that hard not to go all vampire on her and bite Milo's neck, then tear every last shred of clothing off her body in an attempt to alleviate the ache that had started over twenty-four hours ago.

Men are supposed to go to the ER if they have an erection that lasts longer than four hours, so honestly—I had every freaking right to be panicking.

"Colt?" Milo touched my arm. *Damn it! Stop groping me.* For real, if she didn't stop I couldn't be held responsible for my actions. I was going to screw her in front of the receptionist and go to prison.

Prison. Hell, I'd be a sitting duck. I was too pretty for prison, unless Max came with me; then I'd just switch spots and let him get dominated.

*Dominate.*

Poor word choice.

"You look flushed." Milo felt my forehead.

I smacked her hand away and swore.

"Colt?" Her eyebrows pinched together. "Are you sick?"

She traced her lips with the tip of her tongue.

How had I never noticed how damn sexual her mouth was until now? How her lips were the perfect size, bottom and top, damn she'd feel good on me. "S-sick." I coughed. "Yeah, I, uh . . . stomach."

Okay, so it was a little lower . . . same thing.

"Just sign here." The receptionist grinned and handed over a pen and paper. I signed as fast as I could, mentally cursing all pens and paper everywhere. And forced a smile.

"Is that it?"

"Of course!" The lady pulled out a pair of old-fashioned keys and handed them over. "You're in room number two." She sniffed and held out a small map, circling the lobby. "We're here, if you just walk down this hall to your right." She drew an arrow.

Okay, either she thought I was stupid or she was doing it on purpose. I wasn't blind! I could see the room numbers! I could follow arrows!

"And take another right." She circled the room number.

Holy shit. I was actually contemplating stabbing her with the pen. I mean it would be a flesh wound and all—I wasn't *that* crazy. Or was I?

"Now if there's anything else I can do for you—"

"Nope!" I interrupted and grabbed the map. "But thanks, we appreciate it."

Milo gasped as I dragged her down the hall, right, and another right.

"Aha!" I shouted once we found room two. I was like freaking Lewis and Clark; I would have blazed my own Oregon Trail.

Screw maps!

"Colt?" Milo cleared her throat. "Are you sure you're okay? You've been acting funny ever since we were kissing in the car and—"

"Say 'kissing' again." I slid the key into the lock just as she laughed and said, "Kiss," only the *ss* of *kiss* sounded more like a hiss and no worries I'm a dude so it wasn't lost on me that I was putting the key in the lock. In the lock, people!

"Shit." I pushed the door open and almost collapsed on the floor.

"Aw, is it your stomach?" Milo came up behind me, wrapping her arms around my middle and laying her head on my back. The door shut quietly behind us, blanketing the room in darkness.

"Yeah. I may need help." I sighed heavily as I took a few calming breaths. "You know, getting out of my clothes and all."

"Oh!" She released me. "Sure, Colt, I mean, anything."

Damn, her innocence was incredible.

I kind of loved her more for it.

She truly thought I needed that kind of help.

Surprise.

"Turn around," Milo whispered.

I did as she said, and tried desperately to make out the lines of her face. Where were the damn lights? I was torn between wanting to see her—all of her—and wanting to reach out and touch her. *Patience* was officially my least favorite word in the dictionary—right next to anything with the word *Max* in it.

"We don't have to . . ." I felt Milo's shrug under the edges of my fingertips, and I know it sounds crazy but just feeling her, just touching her, knowing the door was locked, knowing that it was just me and her, took away my panic as well as my urgency.

I had Milo.

And we had our entire future.

And yeah, I might have been slowly dying.

But I had Milo.

Under my fingertips.

I could feel each breath she took like it was my own . . . It was finally how I'd always dreamed it would be. So instead of panicking and slamming her against the nearest wall or dipping her body over a chair like I was some sort of sex-crazed maniac, I touched my forehead to hers and kissed her mouth.

Her arms snaked around my neck as her body arched into mine.

Amazing how when you kiss the right person everything seems to suddenly fit together. I think that's how life works—we're all missing pieces of a giant puzzle, and then when you find your match, it hurts like hell not being able to join with them.

And then the moment you do—you can't imagine a life without being right next to them—without being on the same team. Did I even exist before Milo? I was breathing—but I wasn't alive. I was functioning—but I wasn't truly living.

"I promise." I kissed her soft lips again. "I promise to go slow, Milo. You deserve the perfect night."

"I do," she agreed, making me laugh, "deserve the perfect night."

I nodded as her fingers started playing with the hair at the back of my head. Damn those nails felt hot.

"But"—she pressed her body harder against me. No doubt she knew it wasn't my stomach that was hurting anymore—"if you don't get me naked within the next five minutes I'm going to attack you and it won't be pretty. I mean look at Jason, I was trying to be helpful and he's in the hospital." She bit down gently on my lower lip, then whispered, "No telling what's going to happen when I start attacking the man I love." She bit again.

"God, I want to be wrecked by you." I shuddered.

With a laugh she pinched my ass and pressed an open-mouthed kiss across my lips. Her tongue snuck out, licking the seam, making me want to weep a bit. "So what are you waiting for?"

"Nothing." I swore. "No more waiting."

"Colt?"

"Hmm?"

"You're hesitating."

"No, I'm not." I slowly traced the outline of her face with my fingertips. "I'm just thinking."

"What about?"

"You."

"And?"

"How damn beautiful you'll look in a few hours—and knowing that I'm going to be the one to put that look on your face. Yeah, I guess I'm thinking about that face and how I'm luckier than hell that I get to wake up to it every morning and fall asleep to it every night."

"Colt—"

Without letting her get one more word in, I captured her lips with mine. They were so warm—already swollen—and tasted so good I wanted to hang out there for a while, just holding those lips captive, then slowly moving down to the rest of her body. If kissing her made me want to explode, my mind couldn't even comprehend what would happen once she was mine.

Once our bodies were joined.

I moved my hands to the back of her dress and slowly unzipped it, letting it fall to the floor, careful not to remove my mouth from hers lest I really actually die.

Milo stepped out of the dress, heels still on. Hell, yeah, she was going to have to keep those. I couldn't see them, but sometimes an imagination is a scary thing.

She surprised the hell out of me when she reached out and lifted my shirt over my head, then slowly grazed the front of my chest with her nails.

Holy shit, I was going to pass out before we even started.

Her hands moved to the front of my pants. She hesitated, so I covered them with mine and urged her on. "Aw, Milo, getting shy?"

She jerked the pants down so hard I was almost castrated—okay, so maybe her innocence wasn't such a good thing in that type of situation.

"Careful," I hissed.

"Oh, sorry," she said in an innocent voice. "Did I hurt you?"

"You did that on purpose."

"You were getting cocky."

"Kind of the point," I fired back and then stopped when her hands reached my boxers and slid them off.

Heels, heels, heels, she was still in high heels. I kind of felt like singing—in fact singing would be a good idea because then hopefully I would last longer than five seconds when our bodies were pressed together.

Milo's breath was hot on my stomach as she leaned down in front of me and then stood.

"Tease."

"I have no idea what you're talking about," she said hoarsely and then tried stepping away from me.

"Not so fast." I grabbed her by the waist and lifted her into the air, wrapping her legs around my waist as I walked her toward the bed. "You think you can just tease and retreat, is that it?"

"That's kind of been the definition of our relationship, Colt," she whispered and then let out a little moan when I dipped my hands into her bra and cupped her breasts, pulling the lacy torture device away from her soft body.

"Tease and retreat." I massaged.

"Uh-huh." She whimpered. "I mean, what?"

"Is that what you want?"

"Is—oh, that feels, really, really—"

"Milo?"

"Yes?"

"All right, if you say so." I pulled my hands away from her body, feeling the loss like a punch to the gut, and sat up.

"Where are you going?"

"Just giving you a little taste." I reached for the rest of her clothing—which thank God was only her underwear—and very slowly pulled it off, throwing it onto the floor.

"Taste?" she whimpered.

"Tease and retreat." I licked her foot.

She tried to jerk away; I pressed her legs against the bed and licked the inside of her calf, then kissed her knee. "Damn, you have beautiful knees, you know that?"

"Colton!" She clenched the comforter in her hands.

"Yes?"

"Just—"

I kissed the inside of her thigh.

"I'm going to kill you."

"You"—I kissed the other thigh—"love me."

"Not right now!"

My hand slid up from her thigh to her hipbone, then pulled back as she sighed again and then said, "Bastard."

"Tsk, tsk, Milo." I spanked the side of her ass and chuckled. "Insults will get you nowhere."

"You're. Killing. Me."

"Welcome to the club." I spent a good amount of time kissing her stomach, lingering on her belly button as my hands explored every inch they could find, which of course earned more curses and insults, but I kind of liked it.

Passionate. She was passionate.

"Colton!" Milo all but screamed. "I swear if you don't—"

"Don't?"

She was panting, silent, but panting.

"I need—"

"What?"

"Stop interrupting and put me out of my misery already!"

My lips found hers in a flurry of need as I finally allowed my body to rest against hers, careful not to let all of my weight crush her. Milo wrapped her legs around my waist again and bit my neck as I slowly, painfully, pushed into her. My vision blurred as I tried to tell my body to go slow, when really? I was done around twenty-four hours ago.

"More."

"Milo—"

She jerked me forward, rocking her hips up.

And I was lost.

# CHAPTER FIFTY-ONE
## MILO

*I'm having sex.*

With Colton.

When he moved inside me I seriously almost passed out—from pain at first—and then from something completely and utterly incredible.

My entire body shook with both desire and fear. It was a tie. His skin was so smooth as it slid against mine, but him being inside me? I was unable to explain what it felt like, to be filled, to be so complete with my soul mate. It shouldn't have worked, it should have been hell. Instead? Pure heaven. I gripped at his back, pulling him closer, needing more of him.

I squeezed my eyes shut as Colt's mouth found mine again, his tongue joining in almost perfect cadence with our bodies as if matching every stroke with every push, every tug. Too many feelings were exploding out of me—so many that I almost couldn't keep up. I was with Colt, finally. My heart was beating so out of control that I knew he had to hear it. His eyes met mine as he continued to kiss my neck.

His hands moved to my hips as he slightly withdrew, making me feel such loss I whimpered. With a smirk he pulled me up and angled our bodies differently so that I was almost in his lap. It was intimate, so personal I almost jerked away, even though it felt better—amazing. It was the most intimate thing I'd ever experienced. Looking at the love of my life, face-to-face, feeling him inside me and knowing that this was it. Me and him, forever. What I'd lived for—was in that moment.

"Milo," he whispered against my mouth. "I. Love. You."

He reached between our bodies.

And I blacked out.

Okay, I didn't black out.

But it felt like I blacked out.

Covered in sweat, I lay there like an idiot, with a total idiot-like smile on my face as Colton started swearing all over the place and then finally, as if he had no energy left in his body, managed to fall to the side and swear again.

"You okay?" I asked.

"Nope." He swore again, then started laughing.

"Why are you laughing?"

"Because," he chuckled. "I want you again."

"But we just—"

"What can I say? I've waited a long time and my body, it seems, isn't quite satisfied with just one moment. Good thing we have all night. And just in case you didn't catch it before, Milo . . ." He kissed my temple. "I love you more than life. More than my life, more than Max and Jason's put together." I laughed and lazily pushed at his shoulder. "The love I have for you isn't going to fade—even if I do end up like Jason."

"In the hospital?"

"Yeah. Or Max."

"Thrown under buses?"

"Or Reid."

"Drugged?"

"Hey." His mouth tickled my ear. "You can drug me anytime you want."

"Aw," I sighed, my body buzzing with happiness. "Our pillow talk is so sexy—drugs, my best friend, my brother—really, you're so good at this."

"Is that a challenge?" As if he'd suddenly drunk an entire bottle of Red Bull he got up on his hands and knees and glared.

My body was already starting to respond as I flushed with heat from head to toe, already buzzing with excitement. "Yes."

He pounced.

I laughed.

And an hour later I knew exactly why he was so good—at everything.

# CHAPTER FIFTY-TWO

## MAX

*Meanwhile, back at the house . . .*

"I should be an opera singer."

Jason squinted at me through his good-ish eye and rolled it; at least I think he rolled it. It kind of bounced up, then to the side, so he could have been seizing for all I knew, but whatever. Point is, I could feel his doubt at my ability to sing a middle freaking C.

"I'll prove it." I stood shakily. You'd think that after all that bread at dinner I'd be able to kill a bottle of champagne on my own. Not. I staggered over to the piano and hit the key.

"Please don't." Jason covered his ears. "They're all I have left."

"Dude!" I snorted. "You have your balls, right? Most important thing, *amigo.* Now watch."

His beady eye narrowed. "Funny."

"Okay," I sighed. "Listen—don't watch."

"Listening. Only because I'm drugged and Jenna's fallen asleep across my body and moving means I'm a complete idiot."

I nodded in understanding. "Because she's hot."

"No, you ass, because she'd fall."

"Lies."

"Just play your damn song!"

"So now you *want* me to play it," I muttered, falling onto the bench and swaying backward a bit.

"Baby when the lights go out . . ." I pounded the keys and looked up, and crooned slower, "Every single word cannot express . . ."

"Please stop making eye contact," Jason seethed, his eyes narrowing as he put a pillow in front of him like I had been singing to his parts.

I stopped playing. "Scared you'll dig it too much? I feel you. So much man is . . . a rarity."

"Do you ever stop talking?" Jason asked. "Or is this normal for you?"

"I'm sorry, you're going to need to repeat the question. I don't understand." I totally understood, I just really found joy in pissing Jason off, there was also the whole "My best friend is currently getting screwed by Colt" and I really, really didn't want to have to kill him and bury the body if he didn't get things right.

Jason closed his eye and winced. "Why is this weekend not ending?"

"Because the universe hates you, and you agreed to marry a bloodsucking wannabe Real Housewife of New York, who would have used her nails as a way to kill you so we'd all end up on *Dateline*—crying."

Jason flinched. "That entire speech made no sense at all and I'm pretty sure it wasn't grammatically correct."

"You're not grammatically correct," I fired back, pounding on the piano keys. "And I don't care, that shit with Jayne was crazy. I basically saved your life."

Jason threw his hands in the air. "How do you figure? Did you marry me instead? Did you get rid of Jayne?"

Just then Jayne walked round the corner, a bottle of champagne in her hand. "Max, I'm ready for our playtime."

My balls actually quivered with fear.

No, really.

It's medically possible.

It's been proven that balls can actually shake from fear and trepidation—and I'd just experienced it.

Plus, she had claws.

Like superhuman claws that—once she dug into my tender flesh—would most likely end up rendering me paralyzed from the waist down.

I turned to Jason. "You were saying?"

He immediately closed his eyes and acted like he was sleeping.

"Someone's not getting a Christmas present this year," I muttered, then stood. "Ah, Jayne, you look . . ." I shook my head. I had nothing. Nothing. She looked like hell. Her lipstick was smeared halfway across her face, her mascara was meeting said lipstick down her cheek, making little cross signs on her almost-concave face.

I shuddered and spit out, "Lovely, just, lovely."

"Aw, Max!" She reached for me. I flinched again.

Reid chose that moment to stumble into the living room, a look of pure horror on his face.

"Dude." He pushed Jayne out of the way. "We have to go."

"But I was having so much fun," I said dryly, thanking my freaking lucky stars that my brother wasn't stuck in a bedroom with Grandma, or worse, dead because he couldn't live with the memories of what it was like to be smothered by her.

"She's insatiable," he whimpered. "And a man can only do so much, you know? And I mean, she's—look, we just have to go."

"Fine." I pretended to be heartbroken when I took Jayne's hand in mine and forced my eyes to fill with tears. "Parting is such sweet,

sweet sorrow, my Jayne, I mean Juliet—damn, the names are just so easily interchangeable."

"Oh, Max!" Her lower lip quivered.

Ha, funny, her mouth and my balls had something in common. Fear.

"Can I have your number?" I said smoothly, effortlessly. Damn, I should have seriously been an actor. I could say shit like that all day and pretend like I didn't want to stab her with the nearest utensil no matter how rusty it might be.

"Of course!" She fumbled a bit while pulling her phone out of her purse. I had half a mind to feel sorry for her. Then I saw her teeth and razor-sharp nails again and did a little jump backward. I even lifted the pants a bit—just to make sure the boys were still secure and hadn't totally abandoned me by going back inside my body—rendering me sexless.

"What's your number?" she asked, her fingers hovering in anticipation.

Well, damn, she just made it way too easy. With a happy sigh I fired off a cell number—my ex-girlfriend's.

And honestly? Jayne had nothing on that bitch. The ex would chew her up, spit her out, and ask for more in the morning. Pity.

"Let's go." Reid tugged my arm.

"'Bye, guys." Jayne pouted.

"'Bye." I patted her head and shouted our departure to Jason. "Dude, slow down."

Reid was full-on sprinting toward my Jeep. "She can smell fear!"

"Who?"

"Grandma. I swear that nose of hers is like a tracking device, she can smell me. Find me anywhere!"

"Gross, dude." I shook my head. "Nobody needs to hear that."

We both got into the car and pulled out of the driveway.

"So." Reid hit the steering wheel. "Know any hotels we can go to?"

I smirked and looked at my watch. *Ah, they should be done by now.*

"Sure, there's this great little boutique hotel just down the road . . ."

# CHAPTER FIFTY-THREE
## COLTON

"Did you hear that?" I tried to lift my arm but lacked the energy to do so; my superhuman strength had been completely spent. I seriously wasn't sure I could even get up to get a drink of water if I wanted to.

Milo was an animal.

I'd be proudly sporting bruises come morning. I couldn't wait to point at my arm and smirk at Jason. Ah yes, his good eye was going to get its fill.

"I'll make love to you," a male voice crooned, "like you want me to."

Milo sat up, causing the sheet to fall to her waist. My body, tired as it was, suddenly felt like it had gotten a shot of adrenaline. "Did you hear that?"

"No," I lied, as the sound of music trickled into our room. "Nothing."

"I'll make love!" the voice started screaming and the music was turned up louder.

"Someone's singing."

"You're dreaming." I laughed nervously so I wouldn't cry. I reached out to pull her back down into the bed, but she got up and walked over to the door.

"Milo, it's probably some drunken guest hanging out in the hall."

She looked through the peephole in the door and laughed. "Close."

*Please don't say Max, please don't say Max.*

She turned around. "It's Reid."

"Thank God."

"With Max."

"Damn it!" I smacked my hand against the pillows and pouted.

"Aw, they look tired." She giggled.

"Step away from the door!" I shouted. "They'll hear you!"

"Our boy band rocked," said a muffled Reid.

"Dude!" Max chuckled. "We had all the girls rockin' to our swaying hips. What, what?"

I groaned into my hands.

Milo turned and put her hands on her hips. "We can't just leave them out there!"

"We can." I nodded emphatically. "We will. We can and we will."

She smirked and stretched seductively next to me. "You have those crazy eyes, the same ones you had when Jason told you his pee-pee was bigger."

"Damn it, woman! I was seven! And can we not talk about your brother's"—I waved into the air—"when we're both naked?"

"Aw." She sauntered toward me. My eyes glazed over as they took their fill of her gloriously naked body. "I love you."

Irritation forgotten, I pulled her into my arms and kissed her swiftly across the mouth.

The singing got louder.

My kisses turned into a string of curses against her lips.

"Colt," she whispered. "Let's put on some clothes and let them in."

"No," I pouted and crossed my arms. The last thing I wanted was Max and Reid on my honeymoon! "I won't do it."

"I bet I could make you." Her one eyebrow arched. I looked at it, then at her lips, then back at that damn eyebrow.

"How?"

She shrugged. "If you don't let them in, you'll find out."

"Damn unfair life." I reached for a bathrobe and pulled it on. Then pointed at Milo. "Put on your dress and a bathrobe and like a towel or something."

"So I sweat to death?"

Yeah, I was losing it.

"Er, um, just put on lots of clothes."

She winked and stepped into her dress, having it zipped and looking presentable within seconds.

At least now I'd get to take it off again, right?

Someone pounded on the door.

Muttering a curse, I opened it up and came face-to-face with hotel security. "These boys belong to you?"

I painted what I hoped was a mystified look on my face and shook my head. "No." Behind me, Milo's scream of delight rang through the room, damn near shaking the walls.

"Yes!"

"Betrayer," Reid seethed from his drunken spot on the floor while Max kept singing Boyz II Men.

Milo stepped under my arm and greeted the security guard. "Thanks for finding our friends."

"Sure thing," he grumbled. "Just make sure they sober up and sleep it off. We don't want them driving in their condition."

I wanted to say that Max was always like that, but bit my tongue.

Milo nodded, thanked him again, and helped Reid off the floor while Max and I had a stare-down in the hall.

"So," Max asked smoothly. "How'd things go?"

"You bastard."

"Ah." He put his hand over his heart. "Harsh words for the man who got you laid."

"Don't ever"—my voice shook—"repeat that sentence . . . ever again."

Max opened his mouth.

"Ever," I interrupted.

He shrugged. "Can I come in now?"

"Sure, cock-blocker, have at it."

"Whoa!" He started laughing, uncontrollably swaying a bit on his feet.

Oh, good, I'd get to clean up puke in the morning. So much to look forward to. No more naked Milo. Nope, most likely it would be me and a naked Max in the bathroom. The joys of adulthood.

He leaned forward and squinted at me. "So you didn't get any."

I smacked him on the back of the head and sent him stumbling forward a couple of steps. "Oh, I had plenty. Tell me, how's Jayne?"

Max muttered something under his breath while Milo helped Reid to the chair.

"How's Jason?" Milo asked. "And Grandma?"

Reid started screaming and scrambled for the door. I literally had to hold his shaking body in the chair. It took him a few seconds to calm himself before he nodded and closed his eyes.

Max cleared his throat. "We, uh, we don't use her name anymore on account that Reid nearly ran in front of two cars while crossing the parking lot to get to the hotel. He was spurred on by my utterance of her name and ran around the hotel screaming for a good ten minutes before I knocked him out."

"Hmm." Milo laughed. "I thought I heard a dying dog or something. So that was Reid?"

Reid opened his eyes and glared. "I panicked, okay? I mean, what if she had followed me?"

"In her walker?" I asked. "Plus she doesn't have a driver's license."

Reid shook his head. "She'd find a way. Believe me."

"So . . . this is cozy." Max sniffled and looked around. "Damn, I'm a good friend."

"Yes, I was saying those exact words until I heard singing in the hallway."

Max rolled his eyes. "That wasn't singing—it was crooning. Half my cousins were conceived by Boyz II Men."

"And when you say conceived, you mean to the song."

Max laughed. "Or do I?"

I closed my eyes and prayed for patience. "You guys can't stay here."

"Colton!" they all said in unison, including my blushing bride.

She punched my arm. "Where else would they go? Reid's terrified and it's not like they can go back to the house. They aren't even fit to walk, let alone drive!"

I glared at Max—in fact I had an entire conversation with him in my head. It went something like this.

I narrowed my eyes, meaning, *I hate you.*

He narrowed his right back, meaning, *I know, but deal with it, bitch.*

I bit down on my lip and made a cutting motion across my neck with my hand, saying, *Look, you touch her, I'll kill you.* Yeah, we were married and she was mine, but still, the vision of him being with her was still fresh in my mind. His hands had been on her, my woman.

He lifted his hands in the air and waved a bit as if saying, *It's cool, dude. I don't like her in that way.*

I nodded once in understanding.

He nodded twice.
We exchanged a fist pump.
And suddenly all was well in the world again.
Men—we're easy.

# CHAPTER FIFTY-FOUR

## MILO

I yawned and had settled happily against Colt's chest when the thought hit me. *Tomorrow.* Holy crap! I was supposed to be driving home tomorrow!

"Oh, no!" I jerked away from him and tumbled to the floor, taking Max with me. Reid was over in the corner—he'd given us strict instructions that we weren't to touch him when he was sleeping.

We listened, mainly because Max swore Reid carried a Swiss Army knife and none of us wanted to be caught on the other end of it.

"I was sleeping!" Max pouted from underneath me.

Colt scrambled off the bed and pulled me to my feet. "What? Are you hurt? What's wrong? I swear if Max touched you—"

"How could I be guilty? All I did was breathe!" he argued.

"If Max breathed wrong on you . . ." Colt continued, his eyes fierce.

"No, it's not Max." I pressed my fingers against my temples. "It's just . . . I was planning on going back to town tomorrow. I have a month left of school!"

"We know," Max and Colt said in unison.

"But I just got married." I said it slow . . . because they were men.

"Right." Colt nodded.

Helplessly I turned to look at Max, but he wore the same blank expression Colt did. "Guys! This is a really big deal. I'm married and I'm leaving and . . ." *Oh, no, here come the tears . . .*

"Milo." Colt put his hands on my shoulders. "How many days are in a month?"

"Don't ask her things she doesn't know!" Max snapped.

I rolled my eyes. "Thirty or thirty-one unless it's February."

"Or a leap year," Max offered helpfully.

"Right." Colt grinned. "A month is nothing compared to a lifetime. Besides, I work for seventy-two hours straight and then I get three days off. I'll come see you."

"Really?" I perked up. "You would do that?"

"Yeah." Colt pulled me into his arms and kissed my cheek. "I mean, shouldn't your husband help you pack? Besides, I figure you'll want to shop a bit in the city to furnish your new house."

"We have a house!" I shouted, jumping into his arms.

"Duh," Max said, sounding bored. "What? You thought you were moving into a cave?"

"A house." Colt kissed my mouth. "A nice house where we'll have privacy . . . away from the watchful eyes of—"

"—Jason," Max offered. "—Reid, Grandma, parents."

"Max," I sang sweetly.

"What?"

"No, I meant—" I shook my head. "Never mind, I'm so happy." I laughed as Colt swung me around.

"Hey, you guys want me to sing again?" Max asked.

"No," we said in unison.

"Can you feel the love tonight . . ." he started.

Reid jolted to a sitting position, his eyes bloodshot. "Guys, I just had the craziest dream that I was at this wedding in a tree and the grandma took advantage of me and—" He looked around. "Aw, shit."

"Hey!" Max held up his hand for a high five. "The drugs wore off! Yay you!"

Reid scowled. "Don't touch me."

Max put his hand down. "Fine, welcome back, Reid. We missed you, and we aren't the only ones, hint hint." He started laughing and then bent over and mimed a limping gait with an invisible walker.

Reid paled.

"Aw . . ." Max winced. "Too soon?"

Reid didn't speak; he just nodded.

"So," Colt whispered in my ear. "Any regrets?"

I laughed. "What? Lying to everyone I love, then ruining my brother's wedding and taking the best man?" I tilted my head as if I had to think about it. "Nope, none."

"I have regrets," Reid piped up.

"Shh," Max silenced him. "They were having a moment." And then he sang. "The peace the evening brings. The world's for once in perfect harmony . . ."

"Oh, what the hell?" Colton rolled his eyes as we all joined in.

"With all its living things!"

# EPILOGUE
## JASON

My best friend and my sister.

My sister and my best friend.

Together.

I flinched a bit as Colton laid a giant-ass kiss on her face, and then I told myself to calm down. I mean, they were married. Hell, they'd been married for two months now. It shouldn't bother me that he was touching her, but I swear it was still a gut instinct to want to grab something sharp and toss it at Colton's face.

Violence was apparently becoming my new thing. Especially considering the hell I'd been put through during their wedding weekend, which should have been my wedding weekend . . . but whatever.

"I don't know why you watch this crap," Max said from the opposite couch.

"Shh!" Milo hushed everyone. "It's getting ready to start!"

Poor Colt. Milo was sitting on his lap so he was as trapped as they come. I, however, could leave any time I wanted. Except . . . I was bored out of my skull and every time I left Max alone, bad things happened.

He really needed to find a job—soon. I was getting tired of him hanging around. Not that he was lazy by any means. He just had way too much free time on his hands, and the free time always ended up meaning that I had to hang out with him because, oh, right, I had no girlfriend.

Jenna didn't count, as I'd only taken her out four times and it hadn't progressed past coffee.

Max said he was going to move in.

The hell he was.

"This evening on *Love Quest*." The announcer spoke in the background as a series of catfights broke out across the screen. Women pulling hair, the poor bastard who was supposed to find true love looking like he wanted to kill himself. Yeah, somehow surrounding myself with twenty beautiful women didn't sound appealing, not when I watched this show.

It sounded like death.

It looked like torture.

You'd have to be insane to want to try out for a show like that.

"Do you know a contestant who's looking for love? Go to www. lovequestcasting.com to nominate them!"

"Holy shit, that would suck." Max ate a mouthful of popcorn and shook his head.

"Yeah." A small grin twitched my lips. "It really, really, really would."

And suddenly I knew exactly how I was going to get my revenge.

# ACKNOWLEDGMENTS

I hate this part because I always seem to forget people who are really important. I'm going to start off and say that I'm just so incredibly thankful that God has allowed me to write . . . I thank him every single day that I'm able to get up and follow my passion. I'm not gonna lie, sometimes I get emotional just thinking about it. I can't imagine doing anything else and I'm so blessed to be able to say I'm an author.

Erica, agent extraordinaire, you are amazing. Seriously. I call you, I panic, I freak out, I give you ideas, and you simply organize me and make it happen like real MAGIC! Thank you so much for going to bat for me and for being one of the best agents a girl could ask for!

Bloggers . . . I hate just saying *bloggers*. I hate that I'm grouping you guys together, but there are just so many of you who change my life daily. I feel like if I start naming you, then, well . . . this page is going to get really long. Just know, I really do read every review, every post, every tweet, and even if I don't respond I so appreciate your support! I know I wouldn't be where I am today without the constant support from the blogging community. You guys have a thankless job, I just wish I could give you all a high five and free books for life. Maybe free books and free Starbucks for life . . . right, I'll get on that!

To my husband and two dogs who are often ignored because I'm stuck in the writing cave, thanks for putting up with me! And to all my publishers who make the magic happen—thank you for believing in me . . . and, um, thanks for telling me when something sucks and helping me fix it when it needs fixing.

Melody, it was such a joy working with you. Thank you for helping me make sense.

Skyscape, thank you for believing in this story!

# ABOUT THE AUTHOR

*Photo © 2014 Lauren Murray*

Rachel Van Dyken is a *New York Times*, *Wall Street Journal*, and *USA Today* bestselling author of Regency and contemporary romances. When she's not writing, you can find her drinking coffee at Starbucks or plotting her next book while watching *The Bachelor*.

She keeps her home in Idaho with her husband and their two snoring boxers. She loves to hear from readers! You can follow her writing journey at www.rachelvandykenauthor.com.